## Gus ge's cheek

"This business gets right inside you, doesn't it?" she said. "It makes your blood sing."

"Your blood sings. Exactly." Then Gus was bending closer, both his hands framing her face, and she was leaning toward him, raising her lips to his. But he didn't kiss her. At the last minute, he drew back, but his fingers lingered on her face. "Look," he said, regret in his voice, "I can't do this. I gotta take you back to that damn office. Watch yourself there. Fish is into more money laundering. Maybe even murder." Gus stepped away from her.

Susannah cast him a glance that was half grateful, half resentful. He didn't seem to notice and hardly spoke as he drove back to the office. When he pulled up before it, he leaned toward her and gave her a short, hard, intense kiss.

"Take care of yourself," he said against her lips. "Because you're mine."

"Is this part real?" she asked, trembling. "Or are you just pretending? Because you're supposed to be my lover? And because it seems right—at this moment?"

"We both can't answer that now," he rasped. "Now we can only play it as it lays."

He kissed her again.

Award-winning author **Lisa Harris** met her
husband when he was hosting the local
television late show, "Fly By Night Movies."
He was dressed as a giant housefly. Lisa was
one of the show's writers and its props
mistress. Her husband shed his fly suit to
found his own film and video production
company. Lisa now writes full-time and has
published almost thirty novels—humor,
romance and mystery. Despite her success,
she still feels nostalgic for the days when "I
had two hours to scrounge up a Mexican
sombrero, a set of antique Colt revolvers and
a horse that wouldn't spook when ridden by a
giant fly!"

## Books by Lisa Harris

HARLEQUIN ROMANCE
3304—I WILL FIND YOU!

# UNDERCURRENT
## LISA HARRIS

## Harlequin Books

TORONTO • NEW YORK • LONDON
AMSTERDAM • PARIS • SYDNEY • HAMBURG
STOCKHOLM • ATHENS • TOKYO • MILAN
MADRID • WARSAW • BUDAPEST • AUCKLAND

ISBN 0-373-25585-3

UNDERCURRENT

**Printed in U.S.A.**

## 1

SUSANNAH KNELT before the fishbowl in the living room, making faces at Oswald, the Siamese fighting fish. She was wearing an oversize green T-shirt, cut-off jeans and a bridesmaid's veiled cap, which she had jammed on her head, back to front. The veil was iridescent blue, precisely the same color as Oswald. So much netting sprang from the headpiece that Susannah felt she resembled the fish with his profusion of fins.

"Either this atrocity has to go," Susannah told him, "or we've got to mate."

Oswald rippled his fins and turned his gaudy tail to her, as if bored.

"Be that way," Susannah said and stood. Glumly she regarded herself in the mirror. The cap and veil *did* make her look like Oswald—there was no denying it. It also made her glasses sit crookedly.

She was going to have to talk to the bride—her sister, Laura. Laura was letting Aunt Mimi make the gowns and veils for her wedding. Aunt Mimi was taking a lot of artistic licence, and Laura was too crazy in love to notice.

She glanced up at a cluster of family pictures on one oak-paneled wall of the living room. Soon a wedding portrait would join the collection—Laura and Jay Jarrod.

Susannah had always loved this little house set atop Spellbound Mountain, overlooking the forest. But soon, after the wedding, it would be empty except for her. Laura would be gone, and so would their younger brother, Tim.

Susannah would be alone on Spellbound Mountain, slowly turning into another Aunt Mimi. A spinster schoolteacher, spending nights with her computer books and business texts. She already had glasses and wore her auburn hair pulled severely back. Soon, she thought with wry resignation, she would be hankering to get a cat, and who knows, she'd probably end up peering under the bed at nights.

Ah, well, somebody had to keep the clichés alive. Why not her?

She looked into the mirror again. Her sister, not she, was the family beauty. Laura was petite and shapely, with a pretty face and striking red-gold hair. Susannah considered herself odd looking, at best. She was tall and far too skinny, in her own estimation. People said she had beautiful hazel eyes, but she never took such compliments to heart.

She crossed her allegedly "beautiful" eyes and made another fish face. Then she adjusted her swooping veils and began to sing "Under the Sea" from *The Little Mermaid*. She did an impromptu calypso dance, waving her arms like fins. She was getting quite caught up in it when the phone rang.

"Hello," she said, trying not to sound breathless.

"Hello, Suzy-Q," said a deep voice with the teasing hint of a Hispanic accent.

Susannah recognized the voice immediately. She couldn't speak. He hadn't phoned in so long—not since Laura had fallen in love with someone else. But it was *his* voice.

"Susannah?" he said, and her heart seemed to stop beating.

Without further preamble, he said, "I want you. I need you. I have to have you."

Her heart beat again—so hard that her chest hurt. Her hand tensed on the receiver.

"What?" she asked warily. "What did you say?"

It was Gus Raphael on the other end of the wire, and he was up to something typically outrageous. She knew he was, because Gus was *always* up to something. That was why Laura had rejected him.

Instead, Laura had chosen Gus's friend Jarod, a quiet, direct, man. When Laura and Susannah's disabled brother, Tim, had been lost in the forest wilderness, it had been Jarod, a professional tracker, who'd found and rescued him.

Gus hadn't phoned since Laura had gotten engaged. What did he want now? Did he think, folly of follies, he could win Laura back? Would he never get over her?

"I want you," Gus repeated in his lazy voice. "I need you. I have to have you."

"Excuse me," she said as calmly as she could, "you have the wrong sister. Laura isn't here. In fact, she's out being fitted—for her wedding dress." To make certain he got her point, she repeated it: "Her wedding dress, Gus."

Gus was silent for a full five seconds. Susannah held her breath.

"Her wedding dress," he pronounced sarcastically. "Something nice in buckskin, I assume. What's she doing for a veil? Mosquito netting?"

Susannah clenched her teeth. Her emotions confused her, and she struggled to keep them hidden.

She loved her sister deeply, but she did not, frankly, understand Laura's taste in men. How could she throw Gus over for anyone—even Jarod? And here Gus was, as deeply in love with Laura as ever. Susannah could tell.

She chose her words carefully. "She's wearing lace. It's going to be a very traditional wedding."

Gus gave a derisive snort. "Jarod in a monkey suit? I want a picture of *that*. Where's he taking her for the honeymoon? The Dismal Swamp for two weeks of eating nuts and berries?"

"His cabin," she replied defensively. "He's got his wilderness lodge almost done. It opens next spring."

"I shouldn't have introduced her to him. I should have remembered that women always go for that 'Last of the Mohicans' type. If she wanted somebody from a real jungle, why didn't she pick me? I grew up in New York."

Susannah smiled because he could always make her smile, but she wished fervently that his voice didn't affect her so madly.

She understood too well why Laura had once fallen in love with Gus. He was dashing and a little dangerous, plus he had an appealing self-deprecating humor. But, for Laura's taste, he was also too glib for his own good.

"I, the fearless FBI man," Gus grumbled. "I was supposed to come into town like the Lone Ranger. My faithful sidekick in the fringe and feathers was supposed to make *me* look good. I bring him down there to save your brother and impress my girl. Instead he takes off with her. He'll never wear a tuxedo. Never."

"Bite the silver bullet, *kemo sabe*," she said as flippantly as she could. "You'll be getting an invitation—soon." She wondered if he'd accept it. Laura blithely said she didn't care a bit if Gus showed up. Susannah wondered if she herself would be the one bothered.

"Save the stamp," Gus muttered. "Why would I come?"

"Because Jarod's your friend, for one thing. And Laura's willing to let bygones be bygones, for another."

"I've already nobly renounced her. I don't need my nose rubbed in it. A wedding—*Santa Maria!* I'm a sensitive man. What is this torture—an invitation? Forget it."

Susannah picked up the phone and paced to the afghan-draped sofa but was too restless to sit. "Gus, what's this about? They're still getting married, if that's what you want to know. They're not going to call it off. She's in love with this man. I'm sorry, but that's the way it is."

"Maybe a bear'll eat him," Gus suggested darkly. "Maybe he'll fall on a porcupine and be stabbed to death."

"Gus!"

"All right, all right. I wish them every happiness, etcetera, etcetera. I'll send them a toaster oven. May Jarod electrocute himself broiling beef jerky."

"Gus!"

"All right, all right. I don't want to talk about her, anyway. It's you I want. What are you doing this summer?"

Susannah gripped the phone even more tightly. Her oversize horn-rimmed glasses were forever sliding down her nose, and determinedly she pushed them back into place.

For some reason, she was breathless. "Doing? This summer? Now that school's out? I thought I'd take a graduate course at the university."

"Why?" Gus asked sardonically. "Like you're not smart enough already? You're going to learn so much about computers, you'll turn into one someday."

*Maybe I already have,* she thought with a twinge of uncharacteristic bitterness. *Robo-Susannah, the computer-driven android. It thinks, thinks, thinks, but never feels. And nobody expects it to.*

"Cancel the class," Gus said. "I need you. I've got a job for you. I told you I'd call in my markers someday. That day's today, little sister."

He really needed her? What, in the name of all that was holy, could he want?

"You *owe* me," Gus persisted, apparently taking her silence for reluctance. "Who brought Jarod there to save your brother? Me. I told you—your family *owes* me."

Susannah willed her voice to be steady. "I know we owe you."

"I wanted Laura to take Jarod as a peace offering—not as a husband."

"I know." She resisted rubbing her ear, which tickled from his voice. For some reason, Gus's slight Puerto Rican accent pleased her. She could see him, with painful clarity, in her mind's eye. He was a tall, slim man—and not conventionally handsome. His face was too gaunt, for one thing. For another, his dark hair receded slightly.

But when Laura had brought him home the first time, an odd bolt of awareness had struck Susannah. "Why," she'd thought, "he's sexy."

And he was.

In addition, he was the most elegant-looking man Susannah had ever seen. He wore clothes with the élan of Cary Grant.

Her response to Gus Raphael had startled her. Besides, she shouldn't have harbored such thoughts about him. He was, after all, her sister's boyfriend. Until, of course, Laura had her spectacular breakup with him. After that set-to, Laura wouldn't forgive him. Whatever she had once felt for Gus, she claimed, was dead.

Susannah, on the other hand, had found herself increasingly attracted to him. But he'd been too besotted with Laura to even notice her. So now, after all this time, he was interested in *her* help? Was this just a last desperate attempt to get close to Laura one more time?

"What, exactly, do you want, Gus?" Susannah asked as coolly and carefully as she could. She then sat down on the couch and tensely wiggled her bare toes.

"I need a woman—young, good with computers," Gus replied, suddenly all business. "A woman of a certain type. There's going to be an operation down your way—Branson, Missouri."

Susannah stopped wiggling her toes and frowned. "Branson? Where they have all the country-and-western shows? What are you up to now? What's the FBI got to do with country music?"

"I can't tell you. Not yet. I need to see you."

"Why me?" Susannah asked. She crossed her legs. "There are plenty of women good with computers."

"I can explain better in person. Listen: I'm flying down to see you. Tomorrow night. You haven't cut your hair, have you?"

"Tomorrow? That's no notice at all. What's my hair got to do with it?" Susannah demanded, growing more suspicious by the second.

"I'll explain then. I'll be there by nine or so—your time. Don't bother to pick me up. I'll rent a car."

"Gus, you can't just invite yourself like that. Laura won't—"

"I'm not coming to see Laura. It's you, little sister."

"Gus!"

"*Hasta mañana.*"

He hung up. Susannah stared at the phone as if had performed some sort of perverse magical trick. Slowly she set the receiver back in the phone cradle.

"Don't tell me," a teasing male voice said from behind her. "Gus Raphael? What's up?"

She whirled and saw Tim, in the doorway. He was wearing jeans, an ancient T-shirt with a picture of Bullwinkle Moose, and a taunting smile. Susannah blushed, something she seldom did.

"I don't know what's up," she said, avoiding her brother's eyes. "He says he's coming here tomorrow night. I don't know what Laura's going to think."

Tim whistled softly. He moved to the window that overlooked the Spellbound River. He leaned against it, crossing his arms. "Coming here? Why?"

"He says to see me," Susannah said, busying herself with straightening the magazines on the coffee table. "But it's to see Laura. I know."

"Maybe. Maybe n-not."

She shot him a distrustful look. A year and a half ago, when he had turned twenty, Tim had suffered a serious head injury, but lately he seemed much improved. Though at

times, he still stammered and had trouble reading and writing, gradually he was returning to his old, mischievous self.

He gave her a knowing smile. "Maybe he r-r-really is coming to see you."

"Ha," said Susannah without humor.

"Well, I thought sometimes when you looked at him, you
had a gl-gleam in your eye."

Susannah glowered at him, hoping she didn't look as guilty
as she felt. "I most certainly never had a gleam in my eye for
Gus Raphael, of all people," she lied.

Tim shrugged. "There wouldn't be—be—be anything
wrong with it. Laura doesn't want him. I always liked
G-Gus—smart guy. Fast thinking. He's . . . unusual."

Susannah assured an air of indifference. "'Unusual' is
putting it mildly. Go change that T-shirt. It looks a hundred
years old. I've got to drive you to the therapist."

Tim grimaced. "Can't I skip it? I get so s-s-sick of it—" He
nodded toward the window. The May sunshine shone
brightly on the mountains. "It's a great day."

"No," Susannah stated firmly. "You can't skip it. Don't
even think of it."

"Have a heart."

"I do. It's ruled by my head."

"Yeah," Tim said, a rueful slant to his mouth. "Your whole
life is ruled by your head. That's your problem. You kn-know
what I think? I think you're excited that Gus's coming back.
You just won't adm-m—admit it."

"*Timothy,*" Susannah said with warning in her voice. She
stood and put her hands on her hips.

"I'm going, I'm going." He stared pointedly at her veil.
"You know what you look like in that hat? Oswald. I think
you'd better send Mimi back to the drawing board."

"*Get,*" Susannah ordered, taking a step closer to him. He
grinned and headed for his bedroom, limping slightly.

Susannah looked after him, her emotions in disarray. She
was taken aback by his unexpected insight about her feelings

for Gus. She had always thought of herself as calm, level-headed, dispassionate, and self-contained. Was she instead so silly and so transparent that even Tim saw through her?

To be attracted to a man so blatantly in love with someone else showed no pride, no logic, and no grasp of reality. Besides, she told herself, she was a small-town high-school teacher, a bookworm, and a minister's daughter.

What could she possibly have in common with a Hispanic FBI agent with a fast mouth and a talent for trouble? Nothing, she told herself firmly. Nothing at all. Frustrated with herself, she whipped the veil off her head and threw it onto the couch.

LAURA WAS NOT AS nonchalant about Gus Raphael as she'd pretended. She was going to flee—exactly as Susannah had expected. Laura had called Aunt Mimi and asked to stay with her for the night, possibly longer, and Aunt Mimi was delighted at the prospect.

So now Laura stood in her tiny bedroom, packing. The lamplight gleamed on her red-gold hair. "It's *not* that I *dislike* him," she said, packing the open suitcase on her bed. "I know we have every reason to be grateful."

Susannah rested against the wall with its flowered paper, watching. Laura was two years older than she, and outwardly, at least, far more high-spirited. In high school, Laura had always been elected head cheerleader and to the student council. Her bulletin board was full of snapshots and dried corsages and other souvenirs.

Laura quickly folded her lingerie and thrust it into the old suitcase. "I like Gus—I just don't *trust* him," she said. "I hope he's really coming to see you, because *I* don't need to see him."

"Aren't you curious?" Susannah asked with a casual air. "Don't you want to know what he's got up his sleeve?"

"No." Laura said, emphatically snapping the suitcase shut. "He's too unpredictable. I like people you can count on. Dependable people. *Honest* people."

A framed picture of Laura as homecoming princess stood on her dressing table; in the photograph she was radiant and laughing. Susannah stared at it thoughtfully. She herself had only once been elected to something—vice president of the math club.

"Gus is dependable," she said. "And honest—in his way."

"He schemes," Laura challenged. "He can talk a person into nearly anything. I'm grateful to him, but I don't want to see him. I've got other things on my mind."

"He *has* to scheme," Susannah reasoned. "It's part of his job. He has to be convincing—he's always working under-cover."

Laura would have none of it. "Watch out for him," she warned, her eyes flashing. "I *mean* it."

And then, in a whirl, she was off to Aunt Mimi's, without a backward glance. Along with her suitcase she carried an armload of bridal magazines and camping journals.

Tim left to spend the evening with a high-school friend, Roddy McCutcheon. Many of Tim's friends had drifted away after his accident since his behavior had so drastically changed. But Roddy McCutcheon had stayed more faithful, and now that Tim was better, they were doing things to-gether again. Susannah was profoundly grateful for Roddy.

With both Tim and Laura gone, Susannah would have to face Gus Raphael alone. The prospect daunted her, but she vowed to stay levelheaded.

He'd said he needed a young woman who knew about computers—someone of a "certain type," whatever that meant. She supposed he meant a boring, gawky, plain sort—the type no one would notice. Not like Laura.

Susannah had long been used to being overshadowed by Laura's looks and popularity. She had seldom minded since her own values and agenda were very different from her sis-ter's.

However, since the time she'd spent with Gus waiting for Tim to be found, she'd sometimes been . . . jealous of Laura.

Not for the man Laura had gotten—Jarod—but, perversely, for the man she didn't want—Gus.

Gus could only have two reasons for coming. Number one, he was trying one last time to get Laura back. Or number two, he really was hatching some plot—into which he intended to drag her.

Susannah knew that if he asked her to get involved in some wild scheme, she must say no and say it unequivocally. Her family might owe Gus a favor, but she was a schoolteacher, not an espionage agent.

She would tell him anything he needed to know about computers, but she would not, absolutely would *not*, get more involved than that. To do so would be foolish and self-punishing. He was, after all, in love with her sister. Hadn't he told her so himself, often enough?

AS THE HOUR OF GUS'S arrival approached, Susannah began to have desperate hopes: *Maybe he won't come. Maybe his plane's delayed. Maybe he was kidding. Maybe an emergency's come up—like maybe he has to catch an ax murderer or something.*

Her hopes were in vain. He knocked on the door at precisely thirteen minutes after nine. Susannah leaped nervously from the couch, her heart beating crazily.

She hadn't dressed up for him. On the contrary, she was decked out as plainly as possible. She wore black slacks, a plain black shirt, and gray running shoes. Her auburn hair was pulled back in its usual French twist. Her oversize glasses were sliding, as usual, down her nose.

She had not put on eye makeup because she didn't want to seem vain. Her only concession to vanity had been to put on a dash of russet lipstick and powder her nose, which she considered too long. And that was that.

As a result when she moved to answer the door, she felt like a drab, long-legged crane. Gus, of course, would be impeccably dressed.

She squared her shoulders and opened the door. He stood on the porch, smiling down at her with his cynical, one-cornered smile. The golden glow of the porch light spilled down, making the hollows under his cheeks appear deeper.

He wasn't handsome in the ordinary sense at all. Nevertheless, he still evoked that unwarranted, totally atypical response, *Why—he's sexy.*

And he was. But if he knew it, he seldom acted it. He was a wry, self-mocking man. Even though he had no qualms about displaying his mercurial temperament Susannah suspected there were deeper and darker emotions he kept carefully submerged.

He was wearing a casually elegant gray linen suit and his silk tie was vivid with geometric shapes of olive, gray and russet.

He stood a good eight inches over her own five-foot-seven and was too lean, some might say, although his shoulders were surprisingly broad.

His face was a study in contrasts. His cheekbones were pronounced, his chin and the angles of his jaw were sharp, his nose aquiline. It was a very Spanish face, reminding Susannah of the paintings of El Greco—especially his portraits of ascetic, gaunt-looking saints.

Except there was nothing ascetic or saintly in the curves of Gus's mouth or in his derisive eyes. There was laughter in him, but also a hint of explosiveness, a highly controlled potential for danger.

His one-sided smile grew more ironic. "We meet again. You knew it had to happen—didn't you?"

Susannah had the peculiar sensation that her heart fell over dead. But she stayed and standing up, her gaze held his.

"Yes," she said, staring up at him as if spellbound. "I suppose I did."

# 2

HE NODDED IN THE direction of the driveway. "Your sister's car is gone. So, I take it, is she?"

Susannah took a deep breath and forced her expression to be impassive. "She left because you were coming. I'm sorry, but I'd better make it clear that if you're here in hopes that Laura's going to change her mind, you're sadly mista—"

He shrugged, and his smile died. "She's not going to change her mind. I saw the look on her face when she was with Jarod."

"Just so long as you understand," she said, watching him closely.

"I understand all too perfectly," he replied. "Are you going to ask me in, or keep me out here playing Twenty Questions all night?"

Susannah sighed and opened the screen door. He walked inside with the lazy grace of a cat. He cast his eyes around the living room.

It was a small room, full of books and pictures. It resonated with a sense of family, and although nothing about it was fancy, everything was comfortable. Susannah wondered what Gus felt, seeing it again.

"Nothing's changed," he said without emotion.

"It hasn't been that long since you were here." But she knew exactly how long: three months, two weeks, one day.

"Right," he said. "Three months, two weeks, one day." He was looking at the family pictures on the wall.

"Oh," she said, startled. But he was staring, as if transfixed, at Laura's high-school portrait. *Laura's the reason he's kept count of the days,* she told herself. *You have to remember that.*

"Is she still happy?" he asked, nodding toward the picture.

"Very."

He seemed lost in thought. As she studied him, an odd, hopeless pain wrapped around her heart and tightened.

"Good," he said at last, turning toward her. "But you're the one I want to see. You want to go sit at the kitchen table? The way we used to?"

"Sure," said Susannah with a shrug she hoped was nonchalant. They'd spent many an hour at that table, waiting for Laura and Jarod to return with Tim from the wilderness. The memory came back with too much poignance.

She led him into the kitchen, which, like the living room was small, quaint, and paneled in rich oak. Gus had once joked that their house looked as if the Seven Dwarfs should live in it.

"I'll even make you some of my coffee—so you can complain about it," she said lightly.

"Oh, joy," Gus said without an iota of enthusiasm or sincerity. "Just like old times."

He sat at the kitchen table. "How's Tim?" he asked.

She restrained herself from glancing at him, as she went through the familiar motions of making coffee. "Tim? Good," she said, struggling to keep her voice sounding normal. "He's starting to bounce back. He's even out with a friend tonight. And his attitude's improved a lot."

"That's good."

"When he was lost—when he ran away, I mean, out in the wilderness area—he seemed to come to terms with things. He'd been so frustrated after the car wreck. But he accepts now that it's going to take time to recover."

"That's good," he repeated.

*What does he want to know?* she wondered a bit desperately. *All about Laura? I might as well tell the truth.*

She measured the ground coffee, spooning it in. "Tim's going to live with Laura and Jarod—did you know? After the honeymoon, of course."

His answer was toneless. "No. I didn't know."

"Tim's—quite fond of Jarod. They've got a lot in common—love of the outdoors, all that. Tim's still having trouble reading and writing. We all assumed—well, it'd be better if he had more time before he tried to cope with college again. And he'd love learning from Jarod in the meantime. He's excited about it."

She stole a glimpse at Gus, curious if he'd be hurt at the news. He sat straight, his expression unreadable.

"Good," he said again, not sounding happy.

"Jarod's place isn't far from Bangor. Tim can get good doctors there. The odds are getting better that he'll recover almost fully."

"Good."

She switched on the coffee maker, then turned to the table. "Enough about us," she said, sitting across from him. "What about you? Are you all healed? From shooting yourself in the foot?"

Gus's expression changed to one of intense irritation. "I did not shoot myself in the foot."

"Well, you got shot in the foot, and it was your gun—"

"I did *not*," he said again from between his teeth, "shoot myself in the foot. There was a struggle. The guy was trying to wrestle the gun away. It went off. Jarod had to turn it into a crummy joke. I did not shoot myself."

"You don't have to be so defensive," Susannah said, taken back by his resentment.

"I don't like anybody perpetuating the idea that I shot myself in the foot," he grumbled. "It lacks dignity."

"Excuse me. The foot you were shot in—is it better?"

"Yes. The foot I was shot in is better. Thank you."

He paused, then muttered, "If it hadn't been for my lousy foot, I'd have been out there with them, hunting for the kid. None of this would have happened."

"Maybe," Susannah said. She wasn't convinced. Laura not only loved Jarod, she seemed born to love him.

They sat in an uncomfortable silence. Gus began to drum the tabletop with his fingertips. He stared out the window at the night sky.

"God," he said moodily, "we spent a lot of time here."

"I remember." She did, all too well.

"I'd get up at the crack of dawn, worried about them out there, looking for the kid in the cold and the snow."

She nodded. "He just couldn't take what the accident did to him. When he ran away, we were frantic. Frantic."

He turned to her, gave her his half smile. "You'd get up and keep me company. You had this old green robe—"

She stared down at the tabletop. "It was pink."

"Whatever," he said, shrugging off the importance. "And you wore those goofy big slippers shaped like rabbits or something."

"Bear paws," she said, lacing her hands together and not looking up. "They were shaped like bear paws. Tim gave them to me the Christmas before the accident."

"Yeah. Right. Bear paws. I teased you about them."

"Yes. You did."

His voice grew gentler, almost seductive. "And you wore your hair down. I told you I liked it down. But you still have it up. I guess my opinion doesn't count for much, eh?"

Susannah gave him a furtive glance, growing more frustrated by the moment. He was staring at her with something like amused tenderness.

*Why? What's he up to?* she wondered in exasperation.

"All right, Gus." She straightened her glasses and looking him in the eye. "What do you want? Spit it out, will you?"

Any hint of tenderness vanished. He looked her up and down dispassionately. "Do you have contact lenses?"

"Yes. But *why?*" she demanded.

It was his turn to look exasperated, "Then why in God's name don't you wear them? Why is it always those—glasses?"

Her chin shot up combatively.

"I don't like contacts. They make me all squinty."

"Have you tried any of the soft ones?"

"No." What *was* he getting at? gritting her teeth. Laura was right. He was too unpredictable.

"I'll buy you new contacts." He said it as if it were an order she must obey.

"Buy me some?" She found she was clenching her fists. "What *is* this? What is this all about?"

He made a dismissive gesture. "I want you to go to Branson. Work in an office. For a man named Fish."

"Fish?" Susannah echoed in disbelief. "Why would I work for a man named Fish? Why would anybody work for a man named Fish?"

His dark eyes took on a mysterious, teasing glint. "This Fish is a big fish. In certain circles."

"What circles?"

"Money-laundering circles."

Susannah sat back and gave Gus a long, scrutinizing look. He seemed coolly ironic, but serious. "Money laundering—in Branson?" she said doubtfully.

"We think he's sudsing away."

Susannah shook her head. She rose to pour the coffee. "Explain," she said.

"You know how money laundering works?" he asked, giving her that same emotionless, measuring stare.

"I think so," she said. "Somebody gets money illegally. To keep people from being suspicious, the money has to be made to look legal. Information about it is falsified. It could be passed off as restaurant profits or something. Accounts are faked, taxes are paid on it—and bingo!—it looks clean."

"Why, Susannah," Gus said with a satiric lift of his eyebrow, "I didn't know you had such a firm grasp of crime. You surprise me."

*I could surprise you in a lot of ways,* she thought.

"I read a lot," she said.

She poured two mugs of coffee, set one down for Gus, took the other for herself and sat across from him again.

"Fish has a string of properties in Branson," Gus said. "Six theaters, a show called 'The Famous Waltzing Fountains,' and a cave. People pay to see this cave. I can't imagine anybody paying good money to see a *cave.*"

Susannah thought a moment. The situation was interesting. "Eight businesses. All charging admission. He could be cooking the books. Saying he's selling a lot more tickets than he is."

Gus gave her his laziest smile. If cats could smile, Susannah thought, they would smile the way Gus did.

"You're smart, Susannah. I knew you'd get it."

He was trying to flatter her. She didn't allow herself to smile in return. If it was business he'd come to discuss, she'd be businesslike. "How many people can he seat a day? How many tours a day does he give of the cave? How many people per tour?"

"Ah, the mathematical brain at work," Gus purred. "The theaters—6,752. The fountains—four shows a day, 350 seats each. The cave, 32 tours a day. Limit of 20 people a tour. Six days a week. The seventh day he keeps holy. Wholly for golf."

Susannah found the possibilities intriguing, even exhilarating. "And you suspect he's faking the number of tickets he sells. By how much?"

"By at least a third—we think."

She did the math quickly in her head. "That would let him count 17,584 extra tickets a week. How much is the average ticket?"

"Average? The cave and the fountains take down the average. Call it $14."

Susannah's eyes widened. *Wow,* she thought. "That's $246,176 a week," she said immediately.

"Susannah," Gus said, "that's spooky. That's what I don't get about you. You're like a human calculator."

She shrugged irritably. She was what she was, couldn't he accept that? "I can't help it. It's how I am. How many weeks a year is he open?"

"Fifty weeks. Even though he can't be filling things in the winter months. The town relies too much on tourism."

Susannah was fascinated. The numbers went *clickety-click* in her mind. "You're talking over $12 million a year," she said. "Or, to be precise, $12,308,800. No wonder you're interested."

Gus leaned closer. "It's only the tip of the iceberg. We hear Fish is buying into the restaurant business now. In a big way. Next year he may be able to double what he launders."

Gus was going intense on her, and when he was intense, he was hardest to resist. He was trying to suck her into this, somehow, and she steeled herself. "What's this have to do with *me?*" she asked.

"Everybody's got a weakness. For some men, it's money. For some, it's women. Some, power. For Fish, it's all of those—and one more: computers."

Her hands tightened around her coffee mug. His eyes held hers. He nodded.

"Computers," he repeated with satisfaction. "He's computer dependent. He's got his whole office so computerized, it's probably giving off gamma rays."

"Computers don't give off gamma rays," Susannah corrected, trying to fend him off a bit.

"Whatever," Gus said with a sour look. "At any rate, the person he lets run his office has got to be a real hawker."

"Hacker," she said. "An expert in computer science is a hacker, not a hawker."

"What*ever.* Fish has a secretary. Her name is Nora Geddes. She also keeps his accounts. The phony ones. She may not know they're phony. She never sees the real ones. We know that much."

"How do you know?"

"I'm not at liberty to say." His expression was stern, and she knew he meant what he said.

She narrowed her eyes, determined to be as crafty as he. "If Fish has a secretary, why would he want me?"

"He won't have her long. She's going to be busted. As soon as I give the word."

"Busted," Susannah said, startled. "Arrested?"

"She's developed an unfortunate weakness: kleptomania. She steals things from stores. When they bust her, Fish isn't going to like it. The height of tourist season—and he's short-handed. He'll need a replacement, fast. That's where you come in."

Susannah shook her head. "No. Why me? There's no rea-son. Don't tell me the FBI doesn't have a woman who under-stands computers. Get one of your own people. I don't play these kinds of games."

Gus became intense again. "Look—I need *you*. He's a pushover for your type. He won't be able to resist you."

She regarded him dubiously. "I'm not any type."

"Yes, you are. A young Audrey Hepburn."

She felt a small rush of pleasure, but distrusted it.

"Are you trying to say tall and flat-chested?"

Gus looked slightly uncomfortable. "Well...you've got the eyes for it, too. Without those damn glasses."

"I do *not* look like Audrey Hepburn."

"Yes, you do. You just look like her if she—had no style."

Susannah stiffened with resentment. She couldn't imag-ine Audrey Hepburn without style. It was not possible.

Gus dug into the inside pocket of his suitcoat and drew out a small leather folder like a wallet. From it, he took a number of snapshots. "I'll prove it. These are some of the women in Fish's life."

He set down the first photo. It showed a tall young woman with an upswept hairdo and a positively swanlike throat. She was slender and had an elfin face. Her eyes were enormous and beautifully made-up, her nose long, her mouth generous. She did, indeed, resemble the star.

"The ex-Mrs. Fish," Gus said, watching Susannah's reaction. "The present Mrs. Lawrence Rosenblatt of Las Vegas, Nevada. This is her during her Fish phase."

Susannah studied the photo, uncertain. Like the ex-Mrs. Fish, she was tall, slender, wide-eyed. She had the same long neck and wide mouth. She'd always considered her nose too long, but on Mrs. Fish, the nose seemed aristocratic.

"The ex-Fish mistress," Gus said, laying down another snapshot. In it, an extraordinarily slim young woman with a gamin's face stared back at Susannah. Like the first woman, this one had the upswept hairdo of Hepburn in the 1960s. She wore a black dress of exquisitely simple cut.

"The former Fish secretaries—of the last ten years," Gus said, displaying three more photos as if he were laying down a winning poker hand. "Are you starting to see a pattern here?"

Susannah stared down at three more young women with identical builds and elfin faces, pretty despite the slightly too-long noses, the too-wide mouths. Each wore the same hairdo—upswept, with smooth bangs. Each was carefully made-up. Each was dressed in a simple, yet chic style. Beneath the sophisticated veneer, each bore resemblance to Susannah.

"This is *weird*," she breathed. "Does he have a fixation or something?"

"He's quirky."

"You want me to dress up and make myself into a sex object for somebody who's a gangster *and* quirky? No way."

"He's not *dangerously* quirky," Gus argued. "I have it on the best authority that he's a looker, not a toucher. He *couldn't* make a real advance. That's why the ex-Mrs. Fish is the ex-Mrs. Fish, and the ex-mistress is the ex-mistress. Let's just say he's got a flagpole that doesn't rise."

"I see," she said dryly. "You want me to go work for a quirky, impotent gangster with a movie-star fetish."

He shrugged and smiled disarmingly. "You make it sound so squalid."

"It *is* squalid. And if he's laundering money, where's it getting dirty?"

Gus acted as if it hardly mattered. "Colombia. Ecuador. Places like that."

"That means it's drug money, doesn't it?" she accused. "*You* may be crazy enough to enjoy this kind of thing, Gus, but I'm not. No. Certainly not. It could be dangerous."

He shook his head. "It wouldn't be dangerous. First, Fish is harmless. He's not a rough customer. He's the dull, business end of all this. Second, I'll be there with you."

"You? With me? What do you mean, *with* me?"

"One of Fish's peculiarities is that he respects other people's relationships. He probably wouldn't come on to you. But he most certainly won't if you've got a boyfriend. That's me."

"What do I need a boyfriend for?" she asked in dismay.

"Hey," he mocked, "try it. Maybe you'll like it. Why do you need a boyfriend? To make sure nothing dangerous *can* happen to you, that's why. I wouldn't let you into this operation if I wasn't sure you were a hundred-percent safe. With me, little sister, you're safe."

Susannah gave him a superior stare. "Think you can protect me from anything, do you?"

He wasn't fazed. He smiled his cat smile. "That's about the size of it. Besides, I've got a little electronic eavesdropping to do on Fish. Now—are you in? Or out?"

Susannah hesitated. His proposition was insane, of course, and Laura had frequently insisted that Gus himself was more than a little insane, or he wouldn't work undercover.

And yet, he was offering her an *adventure*. Never in her life had Susannah had an adventure. The idea of one caused a strange excitement to ferment in her blood.

Gus leaned across the table toward her. His eyes were languorous, his smile knowing, and when he spoke, his voice was soft. "You're thinking it over. I knew you would. Know how I knew? Because you're *bored*, Susannah. Smart people like you get bored easily. All your life you've lived out here in the country, in the middle of nowhere. You were a preacher's daughter, so you had to be good. Now you're a small-town schoolteacher—and you still have to be good. Good and safe. Safe and good. That's the kind of life you've always lived. Why not—just once—take a chance? Why not—just once—have an adventure?"

Her glasses had slid down her nose again. Gently, with his manicured forefinger, he pushed them back into place, then slowly drew his hand away.

"All your life you've stayed in the background," he said in the same low voice. "You let Laura have the limelight. Or Tim. You stay in the shadow. You hide behind your computer and your multiplication tables and your big glasses. What *is* it you're hiding? *Who* is it? Once, just once, wouldn't you like to let her out?"

He leaned back in his chair and gave her a long look of appraisal. "Sometimes, during those dark mornings, when you and I were sitting in this kitchen, I'd look into your eyes. And I'd think, 'She wants more. What is it she wants?' And I'd look around this place—"

His eyes scanned the small kitchen, half in amusement, half in derision. Then his gaze returned to her. His voice became even more beguiling. "And then I'd think— She wants out. She wants beyond here."

He smiled, slowly, seductively. "So I'd wonder, 'Why does she stay here?' And the answer was: 'Maybe she's just a little—afraid. Maybe she won't go alone, on her own. Maybe she's waiting to be asked.' So I'm here again. And I'm asking. Yes? Or no?"

*Oh, good heavens*, she thought, feeling half hypnotized. *Can he read my mind?* Her heart hammered insanely. She wanted to protest that he was wrong and that she wasn't afraid. Yet she was. How did he know so much about her? No, she corrected, he knew nothing about her. Not really. Not even the true reason her heart beat as hard as it did.

All her life she'd been praised for her coolness, her good sense. All her life, she'd been proud of that coolness and good sense. She marshaled it now, to tell him, politely but firmly, *no*.

"You're still thinking, Susannah," he said in the same seductive tone. "Thinking gets to be a complicated process when a woman's as bright as you. But you're bright enough to know one thing—and it's simple. Never, in your life, are you going to get another chance like this. Never. I know you have the brains for it. Do you have the courage? The hunger? Are you in or are you out?"

She took a deep breath and prepared to tell him utterly and unequivocally *no*. She was not running off to Missouri to become entangled with laundered drug money and a kinky computer nut. "I'm out," she would say with finality.

But instead she found herself saying, "I'm—in."

She looked into his triumphant eyes and felt as if she had just stepped off the edge of a cliff and was falling a long, long way.

# 3

THIS TIME IT WAS Laura who watched Susannah pack. She stood in her sister's small, neat bedroom, radiating disapproval. "You're crazy," she said.

Susannah kept packing. "I've been sane so long it's driven me crazy." This room, with its white walls and plain bluegray spread and curtains, symbolized her life to her: orderly, compartmentalized, sensible, controlled, boring.

"I don't like this," Laura went on, resentment trembling in her voice. "He swoops down here and talks you into some—some insane *caper* in Missouri? Is he dragging you into something dangerous? What's he up to now? Why does he have to involve you in it? Why won't you give me any details?"

Laura, as the oldest, had always mothered the two other children. Susannah, in turn, had always tried to be perfect and predictable, not given to springing surprises. She'd obviously surprised Laura a good deal, and Laura seemed annoyed.

Susannah straightened from her packing and eyed her sister calmly. "I can't give you any details," she said. "The information is classified."

*The information is classified.* The words gave her a rush of excited satisfaction. They were certainly more fun to say than what she usually had to say while teaching: "Your assignment is . . ." or, "I'm very disappointed with your tests," or, "Put down that spitball, Joe-Bob."

"Classified," Laura repeated with disdain. "Gus Raphael should be classified—as hazardous. You're usually so sensible, Susannah. And what, for God's sake, is all *this?*"

Laura picked up a lacy bra and dangled it before Susannah's nose. Susannah coolly took it and packed it with her other new lacy lingerie. "It's part of my equipment."

"Equipment? Gus took you shopping in Hot Springs and *bought* you all this stuff? And charged it to the *FBI?*" Laura glanced scornfully at the new clothes hanging on the closet door waiting to be packed.

Susannah shrugged as if such a thing were an ordinary occurrence. But she had to suppress a smile at the memory.

Gus Raphael was one of those rare men who could not only shop with a woman, but for her. He'd bought her several dresses and a Ralph Lauren summer suit. When she'd tried them on, she'd felt new and different. It wasn't as if Gus were creating a new woman, but discovering the one that she'd always kept so well hidden.

The clothes he'd chosen for her were simple but classic. He had insisted on the frothy lingerie, as well.

"A woman feels better, more confident, when she's got on beautiful underwear," he'd said. "You want to feel chic down to your bare skin."

Susannah had thought of Gus and her bare skin, and had stared at the lingerie in embarassment. She'd never felt so vulnerable—or so alive. "You're spending so much money," had been all she could say.

He'd plucked up a bra, admired it, and said, "The Bureau picks up the tab. Ah—my tax dollars at work. Gives a man faith in his government."

Laura broke into Susannah's reverie. She had her hand on her hip. "And he even bought you new contacts," she accused, pointing to the bureau where the new lenses sat in their plastic case.

"What *is* this?" Laura demanded. "Is he having some corny fantasy? We'll take the mild-mannered schoolteacher, whip off her glasses, let down her hair, put her in a new dress, and whammo! She's a knockout? Susannah, what are you letting this man *do* to you?"

Susannah didn't like the image Laura conjured up. She set her jaw stubbornly. "I don't intend," she said, "to let my hair down. In any way."

"I should hope not," Laura said emphatically. "Susannah, I don't like you going off like this. It's not like you. He can be like—like a Pied Piper, if you let him. He gets involved in dangerous things. He *manipulates* people. He's the prince of dirty tricks."

"He uses dirty tricks to catch dirty guys," Susannah answered flatly. "It's his job, and he's good at it."

"Make sure he doesn't play any on *you*," Laura warned.

"He won't. Our family owes him a favor. I'm paying it, that's all. He says I should be home in two weeks. Maybe less. In the meantime, you're not to tell anybody where I'm at, what I'm doing, or who I'm with. It could put the operation in jeopardy."

*It could put the operation in jeopardy*, Susannah thought with relish. *It sounds so dramatic—I love it.*

Laura made an impatient gesture. "This is so adolescent," she fumed. "I've never seen you like this—you, of all people. You're always the one everybody counts on to be calm and sensible."

Suddenly Laura went quiet, as if a terrible thought had struck her. She stared at Susannah while Susannah packed her dresses into the suit bag. At last she said, "Susannah— you don't have a—well—a thing for Gus, do you?"

Susannah didn't meet her sister's eyes. "Of course not. And what good would it do me if I did? He's in love with you."

Laura went silent again. When Susannah stole a glance at her, Laura's face no longer showed annoyance. It was grave to the point of sadness.

"He hurt me badly once," Laura said simply. "He'd lied about everything—who he was, why he'd come here, everything. He put my best friend's father in jail—it was awful. I thought I'd never get over it. I couldn't stand it if he hurt you, too."

Susannah let her gaze meet Laura's. She saw the fearful look on her sister's face, and she understood. *She's afraid he's using me; that he's going to get back at her—for choosing Jarod instead of him.*

The thought was so horrible, Susannah thrust it away. Another thought, almost as bad, rose up to take its place. What if Gus actually did show interest in her? Would it simply be because he couldn't get her sister and would settle for any way to stay near her?

Her sense of excitement died. She wondered if she were making an utter fool of herself.

Laura seemed to search for the right words. "It's just—that I worry about you. That's all. I love you."

She stepped up to Susannah and hugged her ferociously. "Tell him if he doesn't bring you home safe and sound—I'll *kill* him. I really will."

"I'll tell him," Susannah said, hugging her back. She tried to smile, but couldn't.

"And watch out for him," Laura said, hugging her again. "He's so *tricky*."

"Don't worry," Susannah replied with false bravado. "I'm prepared. He won't take me by surprise."

BUT HE HAD TAKEN HER BY surprise. She hadn't been prepared for what he sprang on her when she met him in Missouri.

"Live together?" she said in horror. "What do you mean, *live* together?"

She stood in the middle of the dingy motel room, her suitcase clutched in her hand as if she was prepared to turn and flee.

Gus took the suitcase from her and set it next to the lumpy-looking bed.

"It's not exactly living together," he said persuasively. "Look—these rooms are a suite. You can shut my part off from yours. You won't even know I'm here."

Skeptical, Susannah glanced around the room. The walls were a mottled gray and looked as if they hadn't been painted in years. The single window was cracked and patched with yellowing cellophane tape. The dresser had a leg missing and was propped up lopsidedly on a pile of old telephone books.

"These rooms are a roach ranch," she declared. "What happened—did the FBI suddenly go broke?"

"Give me a break," he said. "This place is only about fifty yards behind Fish's office. I've got all my electronic gear here. No need to use a van. A van gets conspicuous."

"Well, you stay here with your equipment and the cockroaches. I want a real apartment—by myself."

"How can I protect you if you're by yourself?" he asked. He tried, unsuccessfully, to smooth the faded bedspread. "Here. Sit down. Relax."

"You told me there was nothing to protect me from," she protested. She refused to sit.

Gus's mouth took on a digusted twist. He stretched out on the bed himself, staring up at the cracked ceiling. "Trust me. You're much safer if Fish thinks you've got a boyfriend. I'm the boyfriend. It's like I love you, you love me—all that crap. People in love *live* together. This isn't Victorian England."

"But—"

He cut her off, still not looking at her. "Susannah—here's the scenario. And it's got to seem natural—get it? I showed up in this town three days ago. You're here today. We're a *couple*. We're a young couple, struggling to make it in a new place. Temporarily we're in this kind of . . . low-class establishment. We can get in touch, stay in touch, nothing looks suspicious. And I keep my eye on you."

She put her fist on her hip. "But you *said* Fish is harmless."

He threw her a lazy glance. "I'm ninety-nine-percent sure he's harmless. It's that other one percent that has me worried. My business is taking chances. I know how to take them. Trust me. I know how to stay safe."

She glowered down at him. She hadn't been in the room three minutes and already he was pulling tricks. Rattled, she yearned to rattle him back. "You know how to stay safe?" she demanded. "Is that how you shot yourself in the foot?"

His dark eyes flashed. "I did *not* shoot myself in the foot. You want to take a chance on being alone? Having Fish turn up on your doorstep some night? Asking you to tie him to the bed and dance around him in your garter belt? Is that what you want?"

Susannah was horrified. "You never said *that* could happen."

"You never asked."

"Well," she said in frustration, "how am I even supposed to imagine such a thing? I'm just the minister's daughter from Arkansas, remember?"

He put his hands behind his head and stretched languidly on her bed. "I remember. That's why I'm keeping you close. We'll be adults about this. I'm a relatively safe person. Much of the time."

Susannah shuddered and said nothing. She had received three shocks in a row. First, the motel was little better than a flea trap. Two sagging stories high, it stood a block off the busy main street of Branson. Its brick facade was grimy and pitted, the paint had long ago worn from the frames of its windows and doors, its outside stairways were rickety.

The arrangement that Gus euphemistically called a "suite" was composed of, first, a room with a kitchenette and a small, squalid bathroom. A warped door joined it to another room without a kitchenette, but with an equally dank, cell-like bathroom.

Susannah had flown from Hot Springs to Springfield, Missouri. She'd worn dark slacks, a plain white blouse, and her glasses because Gus had said he wanted her to remain as inconspicuous as possible until she saw Fish.

At the airport, she had been met by a man she knew only as "Fritz." He'd given her the keys to a dented blue Ford Escort sedan. She'd also been given the address of the motel in Branson and a key to her room, number 9.

The second surprise was that the room also happened to be Gus's room. He hadn't told her ahead of time, he said, because he didn't want her to be put off by "details." Some detail, Susannah thought grimly. And his room was so full of electronic equipment, she didn't see how he could find his bed, let alone sleep in it.

The third surprise was Gus. He had transformed himself. Gone were his beautiful suits, his perfectly pressed shirts, his silk ties, his Italian shoes.

This new Gus, the Gus of Branson, wore tight, faded jeans that rode at dangerously low mast on his hips. His tattered running shoes had seen better days. A black T-shirt stretched across his shoulders, and on the chest, fading gold letters spelled out Sun Studio, Memphis.

Susannah realized she had never seen him in short sleeves before and was startled that he had tattoos. One, across his left forearm, consisted of his first and middle name in misshapen letters: Augusto Jesus. She wondered if he'd done it himself when he was a boy.

A serpent and a bleeding heart were etched into the skin of his right forearm. His arms were hard-muscled with biceps like rounded rocks. They were, Susannah thought, very attractive biceps indeed.

Around his forehead he had knotted an old blue bandana, Apache-style. And, to her amazement, he wore an earring in one ear—a tiny, dangling golden cross. She'd never noticed before that his ear was pierced. How many sides did the man have?

He no longer looked like the Gus Raphael who always seemed to have just stepped from the pages of *Gentlemen's Quarterly*. He looked streetwise, and more than a little dangerous. And to her astonishment, she liked him that way.

"Hungry?" he asked affably. "We've got cooking privileges. Help yourself. Make some toast or something."

"I wouldn't call it a privilege to cook here," she said, wrinkling her nose at the grease-encrusted stove.

"Suit yourself. We'll eat out. But there's soda in the fridge. Sit down and have one."

He rose, went to the kitchen table, and sat down. Taking up tweezers and needle-nosed pliers, he began to work on a tiny piece of equipment.

Curious, telling herself she needed to get used to this new version of the man, she accepted his invitation. She took a can of cola from the refrigerator, opened it, and sat on the edge of the bed, watching him.

"Why are you dressed like that?" she asked.

He lifted one shoulder in a shrug. "I'm a working guy. At the Dusty Lester Show. Assistant sound man."

"How'd you get a job so fast?"

He gave her a wicked smile. "We are the FBI. We are omnipotent."

"Oh."

She watched the muscles in his arms play as he made minute adjustments to the instrument.

"What are you doing?"

"When better bugs are built, yours truly will build them. This bug's for you."

"An electronic bug? For me?"

He nodded. "It goes in a cellophane-tape dispenser. I've got to give you something you can get in and out of there fast. He has the place swept for bugs. Once a week."

"How do you know?"

He crooked a dark eyebrow. "We are the FBI. We are omniscient."

She studied him. He seemed content in this grimy room, tinkering with his bug. She'd never seen him at his work before.

"You like this, don't you?" she asked.

"I *love* this," he said with relish. "It's so sneaky."

Susannah sobered, remembering Laura's warning about Gus's trickiness. She stared at the earring glittering at his ear.

"I didn't know you had a pierced ear."

He shrugged, not looking up. "It comes in handy. Lots of longhairs and musician types here. Helps me fit in."

"And tattoos. I never knew you had tattoos."

She saw his face tighten, grow more guarded. "A misspent youth. I'll get 'em removed. One of these days."

She saw the subject bothered him and veered away from it. "When do *I* go to work?"

"Day after tomorrow."

She was puzzled. "Why wait until then?"

"Tomorrow morning you register with the employment office. Late tomorrow afternoon the local cops take Fish's secretary down. You interview with Fish late morning the next day. You'll be the third one he meets. The first two he won't look at. They're short and round."

He said it calmly and with perfect confidence. She stared at him in amazement. "Now how do you pull *that* off?"

His wicked smile returned. "We are the FBI. We're really cute that way."

The smile made her heart do a small dance. She tried to ignore the feeling. "What am I supposed to do in the meantime?"

He shrugged again, as if he didn't care. "See the town. Take in the attractions. But miss the Dusty Lester Show. What a country ham. God, I *hate* country music."

"Then why did you pick that place to work?"

"It picked me. It's one of Fish's shows, it's closest to his office, and Fish hangs around there almost every night. I've got one earphone for Dusty Lester. But I got another one for our fishy fish, Fish."

He could listen to two different things at once? Her own concentration was excellent, but not to that extent. "What if you get confused?"

"I can't afford to. I never do what I can't afford."

"You're awfully sure of yourself," she said.

His voice was matter-of-fact. "All my life I've had one guy to depend on, little sister. Me. For my sake, I try to be very dependable."

"I don't know if I want to go out by myself," Susannah said pensively. "The traffic in this town is terrible."

He nodded, as if to himself. "Branson's too successful. More tourists than streets. If you'll wait till I finish Billy the Bug, here, I'll take you out. I want to check out Colossal Caverns. That's the one thing I haven't looked at yet. Fish's cockamamy cave."

*A cave.* Susannah shuddered again. Jarod had been forced to leave Laura and Tim in a cave when he went for help. If he hadn't made it, they could have died there. *Caves* were something Susannah found ominous.

SHE SHOULD HAVE suspected the big Harley-Davidson motorcycle chained in front of the motel was Gus's. The next thing she knew, she was on the thing, forced to hug Gus's lean waist. He wove in and out of Branson's infamous traffic, zoomed to the edge of town, and parked in the lot at Colossal Caverns.

Susannah released his waist immediately, if reluctantly. Gus was so hard-muscled that he should not have been huggable, but she'd found, paradoxically, that she liked nestling against him.

She leaped off the bike as if it were an untrustworthy horse and swept off her helmet. Gus took it and hung it from the handlebar of the cycle.

She briskly rubbed her hands together, as if she could wash away the tingling memory of touching him. "Why do you have to have a motorcycle?" she challenged.

He unbuckled the chin strap of his own helmet, which he obviously didn't like wearing. "I'm supposed to be in the music business, a free spirit. It's part of my idiom."

"Your idiom," Susannah repeated darkly. She wasn't sure she would ever understand this man. He was such a puzzling combination of quicksilver and peril, she probably shouldn't *try* to understand him.

And she wouldn't allow herself to look at him—he was too visually stimulating. Instead she gazed up at the garish billboard over the entrance to Colossal Caverns.

You Found It!!! the billboard trumpeted in huge fluorescent-red letters: Colossal Caverns!!!! The Eighth Wonder of the World!! Ozarks' Deepest Underground Lake!! A World of Wonders!!!! See Our Famous Bridal Cave!!

There was an equally garish picture of a bride and groom standing in a forest of white stalagmites and stalactites.

"Ugh," Susannah said. "Who'd get married in a cave?"

"Underworld types?" Gus teased.

"Very funny."

He dismounted the cycle, swinging his long leg over it. He knocked the kickstand into place and hung his helmet beside hers. He strolled over to her and took her arm in a brotherly gesture. There was no reason to tremble, but she did.

Together she and Gus strolled to the cave's entrance. Dusk was falling, and except for them, the parking lot was deserted. The mouth of the cave was barred by a padlocked chain-link gate. A small gift shop and visitors' center stood empty and locked.

Placards and photos filled the shop's windows, showing views of the cavern, the various chambers, the lake, and bizarre formations of stone. There were several portraits of wedding groups in the Famous Bridal Cave.

"Looks like the sort of place where Laura and Jarod should get married," Gus muttered.

Susannah withdrew her arm from his, annoyed and hurt. Would Laura always fascinate him? "Are you going to think about her for the rest of your life?" she demanded, perhaps more sharply than she should have.

"Probably," Gus said, his expressive face going glum. "What's it to you?"

"It's *nothing* to me," she replied, turning from him. But she felt empty and helpless. She had never fascinated anyone. She supposed she wasn't the sort.

She gazed moodily at the picture of the Ozarks' Deepest Lake and shivered. The still, dark water struck her as forbidding.

"Are you cold?" he asked.

She was surprised he had noticed her shiver. "Yes. No," she said. "Not really. It was breezy on that bike. I've never ridden a motorcycle before. I wish a nice, closed-in car was part of your 'idiom.' Why couldn't you be a nice conservative sound-man if you have to be one?"

Gus shrugged. "I dunno. It's like being an actor. It's like this is a part, and this is how I feel this part. It feels right. I can't explain it."

She cast him a wary glance. His profile was sharp against the darkening sky. "If I'm supposed to be such an—exquisite thing for Fish, why am I supposed to be attracted to you? Your current persona is a tad on the grungy side, frankly."

He turned to her, with his superior one-sided smile. "You love the animal in me. Repressed types like you always want a guy who walks on the wild side. Beauty and the Beast."

Susannah looked away from him, glad it was growing dark, because her face was burning. "I'm not repressed."

"Yeah. And I'm not in America."

"I'm *not*," she insisted, setting her jaw. "You haven't the faintest idea."

He shrugged. "All right. I haven't got the faintest idea. But at any rate, Fish is surer to stay away from you if you've got a boyfriend with rough edges. I'm grungy, but I'm yours, baby."

In all of Susannah's life, no man had ever called her "baby." That Gus did so made her start shivering again.

"You *are* cold." He made a move as if to put an arm around her.

Susannah stepped away, eluding his touch. "No. I'm just nervous, that's all. I—I memorized all that stuff you sent. My 'biography' and everything."

He didn't seem bothered that she'd avoided his casual embrace. "Good. We kept it as close to your real life as possible. Your daddy being a minister and all. Fish'll like that. He likes them to seem ladylike. Proper."

She nodded unhappily, seeing herself through his eyes: *repressed*, he'd said. *Ladylike. Proper.* She wasn't repressed—was she? Did he not understand her? Or did she, perhaps, not understand herself?

She tried to steer the conversation to more neutral ground. "I suppose you'll want me to change my hairdo. To look like his other women. I can do it."

He shook his head. "Naw. Too obvious. I even want you to wear the glasses to the interview. Make him ask about the contacts. Make him suggest the hair. He will."

Susannah pushed her glasses up her nose self-consciously. "How can you be so sure about everything?"

"It's easy. I'm cocky."

*You can say that again*, she thought, and turned away, looking at the entrance of the cave again. Even in the fading light, the billboard was blindingly gaudy. Why, she wondered, did people always have to take natural wonders and tart them up so cheaply?

"What would he say, your daddy, if he saw you now?" Gus asked. She had the peculiar sensation that he was studying her.

"He'd probably tell me to go home, right now."

"Strict?"

She shrugged and put her hands into the back pockets of her jeans. "I'm sure Laura told you."

"I want your version."

She stared up at the sky. The moon was rising and a few pale stars twinkled. She didn't imagine her father was looking down, watching over her. Her idea of the afterlife was more abstract, less comforting than his had been.

"He was strict, all right. He was incredibly strict. But— lovable. He was so lovable I could never resent him. Not for long."

"And you wanted to please him?"

"Of *course*, I wanted to please him," she said, remembering her father and missing him. "We all did. We loved him."

"Yeah." Gus's voice had gone flat, as if the conversation was starting to embarrass him. "Well, I'm sorry he's gone. The accident and all."

"Thank you," she said, still not looking at him. Her father had been killed in the same wreck that had injured Tim. The accident had badly shaken her faith. Perhaps she would never have dared come on this mad mission with Gus if the accident hadn't turned her world upside down.

Her father had always taught them that the world was ruled with justice and mercy, and that everything had its reason for happening. The accident seemed neither just nor merciful, and she could find no reason for the death and suffering it had caused.

"Susannah," Gus said, sounding puzzled. "You look sad. I didn't mean to make you sad."

"Don't be silly," she said, squaring her shoulders. "You can't even see my face."

"I don't have to. You're standing sad. I won't bring it up again."

She was startled by his sensitivity. She turned to face him again. The gathering darkness made the hollows under his cheeks seem deeper. "No. It's good to talk about it," she said. "It's funny, but none of us has ever said much about it. To each other, even. I guess we were so caught up with getting Tim well again."

"I'm glad he's better. Jarod'll be good for him. I mean that."

She smiled slightly. It was the first time he'd mentioned Jarod with kindness. "I know. But Daddy dying— Well, it shook our world apart in a way. Our mother died young, you know. Tim can barely remember her. Laura had to mother us. In a way, she gave up her youth, helping Daddy. I always knew she'd get married someday—I mean, she's the pretty one, the one people notice—and then I'd stay home and help Daddy. It'd be my turn then. That's how I always saw it. But now—he's gone. I still can't believe he's—gone."

They were both silent for a moment. She thought of how empty the house would seem without Laura and Tim. She thought about her father, marvelously intelligent and good-natured. He'd taught her to play chess; he'd been proud of her mathmatical ability and delighted that she'd chosen to teach.

"Hey," Gus said gruffly, "you're plenty good-looking enough. I mean, lose the glasses and let your hair down—I told you that once—you wouldn't be half-bad."

"Not half-bad?" Her muscles tensed at the backhanded compliment. She gave him a bitter smile. "Please. Don't kill me with flattery."

"Don't be like that," he said, scowling. "You know what I mean. Jeez, Jarod said at first that he thought *you* were better looking."

Susannah turned, staring at him in disbelief. Was he trying to comfort her with lies? "He did not."

"I swear it," Gus said, raising his hand. "He said, 'I think the tall one's better looking.' Those were his very words. Then, unfortunately, he came around to Laura's charms. Honestly, he said you were the prettiest. It's a matter of taste—see?"

Susannah shrugged again, not knowing what to say.

"Now, I personally have never been attracted to tall women," Gus said matter-of-factly. He stared past her, off into the darkening night. "I'm tall myself. Opposites attract. Also, you'd help your case if you didn't come on all the time like your brain was made by IBM. I say this in the spirit of helpful criticism—"

*He's done it again*, she thought in despair. For a moment he had made her feel good; now he was spoiling it, as usual. Blindly she started toward the motorcycle. She would tell him to take her back to the motel, to lock the door between them and to keep it locked. She was crazy to have joined him here in Branson; she never should have done it.

Suddenly he swore loudly in Spanish. Then he swore in English and seized Susannah by the wrist. He pulled her to him almost roughly, and took her into his arms.

She was so startled she couldn't speak. She stared up at him in alarm.

"Act," he ordered, bending over her. "Act. It's Fish, dammit."

He lowered his face to hers just as a set of headlights caught them in its glare. Susannah gasped, but his mouth had already captured hers. His lips moved with seductive sureness upon her own.

His arms around her were so strong that she couldn't have moved away from him if she'd tried. Her breasts were crushed against his chest, and when she gasped again, his tongue entered her mouth, darting like a pleasure-giving flame.

"Oh," she tried to say, but his tongue continued its ravishment, silencing her, bewitching her.

She was dimly aware that a large white car had pulled into the parking lot.

Gus drew back for an instant. He kissed her temple and ran his tongue lightly along the front edge of her ear. "Don't be so stiff. Kiss back. Improvise," he ordered. His breath was warm against her skin.

Then he kissed her again, so thoroughly it was difficult to think. One word echoed hollowly in her consciousness: *improvise.*

She wound her arms around his neck. He had a nice neck, warm and strong. She rose to meet his kisses, pressing her breasts more intimately against his body. She parted her lips, and this time when his tongue entered, her own touched it, shyly at first, then more boldly.

His touch made her quake. Her own daring made her quake harder. She was frightened—terrified, even—but a marvelously intense pleasure surged through her.

She wound one leg around his, a pose she had once seen on the cover of a book.

This time it was Gus Raphael who gasped.

# 4

*¡CARAMBA!* thought Gus Raphael. *Asombroso y pasmoso—* astonishing and astounding! Susannah was creating this havoc in his mind and heart and loins?—Susannah?

She had small breasts, but they were exquisitely soft against his chest. And her mouth—*mío Dios.* All he'd ever noticed about her mouth before was that a lot of smart cracks came out of it. How blind could a man be?

Her lips were warm, full, mobile, and moist, and tormentingly sweet. They were created to kiss and be kissed. Why hadn't he ever *noticed?*

He'd always liked her. He suddenly realized he liked her a *lot.* How had he gotten to like her so much—without even noticing? And how had she, who'd always seemed so untouchable, become so good to touch? So tantalizingly *necessary* to touch? Fireworks were shooting through him.

He wished Fish would get out of the parking lot. He needed to get this woman out of his arms so he could think straight and reassess the situation.

He also wished Fish would never leave the parking lot. Who needed to think? His body was reassessing the situation just fine, thank you. And his body loved it.

He held her tighter, kissed her harder.

*But Susannah?* he asked himself again. *Susannah—no. Impossible. How could this be happening?*

Then she'd wrapped her leg around his, an action so unexpected, it had left him painfully breathless. The movement tilted her pelvis closer to his, and he felt an irresistible rush of desire. His groin burned and his heart began to do an insane flamenco dance.

He was half relieved, half bereft, when Fish's car finally backed up and turned around. Its lights swept away, leaving Gus and Susannah in the falling darkness. A moment later, he heard the last of the car's smooth motor as it disappeared up the main road. Immediately Susannah disengaged her leg from his.

He thrust her slightly away from him and stared down at her in disbelief. Her big glasses were askew, and she appeared as dazed and wary as he felt. It didn't occur to him to release her. He held her firmly by the upper arms. She was breathing hard. So was he.

Whatever just happened shouldn't have happened, he told himself. He couldn't desire this woman; he was bewitched by her sister, for God's sake.

Why was he bewitched by Laura? Because she had such a passion for life, he thought, shaken. Why had he never noticed the same passion concealed in her cool, logical, wry sister?

"Why did you *do* that?" Susannah demanded, her voice tremulous. Her hands rested on the shoulders of his black T-shirt, and his skin pulsed beneath her touch.

"It was Fish," he said, struggling to breathe more evenly. "It was Fish's car."

She shook her head in apparent confusion, gripping his shoulders more tightly. "How could you tell? I didn't even see it until you . . . grabbed me."

"It's that damn white Cadillac," he breathed. "You can't miss it." He resisted the urge to take her glasses off and kiss her again.

"But why did you *do* it?" she persisted. "Grab me like that?" Her lips were trembling, and she looked so vulnerable, Gus suddenly hated himself without knowing why.

And now that he thought about it, he didn't exactly know why he had seized her so impetuously. Or why, when he had kissed her, he had done so with such unaccountable emotion.

"Instinct," he said, feeling his way toward the truth. "I didn't want him to—notice you. We're on his property, after hours. I didn't want him to stop, ask any questions. He thinks we just came here to neck, he leaves us alone."

"Why? Why shouldn't he notice me?"

Good Lord, she actually was shaking. Had he frightened her? Offended her? Responded too strongly to her pretense of desire? Did she feel something for him, too? *Susannah?*

He shrugged, as if to tell her that nothing of importance had occurred. He struggled to get his thoughts in order, his feelings under control. "Look," he said. "It was a gut-level thing, an ad-lib, that's all."

"Well," she said, "if you were going to kiss me, you didn't have to kiss me like *that.*"

"You didn't have to wrap your leg around mine, either," he said defensively. "Do you know what that does to a man? You shouldn't go around doing that, Susannah. You'll get yourself in trouble."

He looked down at her in confusion. *Santa Maria*—Jarod had been right. She was a pretty girl, a beautiful girl in her way. He'd never let it sink in before. *Why?* he asked himself. *Why?*

Suddenly he realized he was still holding her. He released her and moved away from her to gather his thoughts and calm his body. She'd gotten him into a damned embarrassing state—Susannah, of all people. He ran a hand through his hair.

Laura hadn't kissed like that. Laura *couldn't* kiss like that. Laura was an emotional person, but not a sensual one.

Who would have expected Susannah to be the more physically responsive? Laura, for all the fire in her personality, kissed almost . . . demurely. He stared into the darkness, recalling Laura's embraces. It seemed he could no longer remember them as clearly—or as fondly—as he should.

"What's the matter?" Susannah asked. "Why won't you look at me?"

"I'll look at you in a minute."

"What's wrong? Didn't I do it right?"

His heart still hammered. "It's hard to imagine you doing it more right. But if fate should ever drive us to do this again, *don't* do that thing with your leg, all right?"

"You told me to improvise," she said defensively.

He gave her a disapproving glance. "Where'd you ever learn a trick like that?"

She looked slightly hurt. The moon had risen and gleamed on her hair. He had a wild desire to turn around, pull all the pins out of that glorious hair, and . . . *No, no, no,* he told himself. He looked away again.

"Look, could we just go back to the motel?" she asked, her voice weary with resignation.

"I've got to feed you," he muttered. "We'll eat first." He'd take her for a steak or something—what could be more ordinary? Things would return to normal. He'd forget this ever happened.

"No," she said with firmly. "What if Fish should walk into the restaurant? I don't want you throwing me down on the table and ravishing me in the French fries."

"Fish never eats in restaurants. It's one of his little quirks. And you need to eat. You're so thin."

*But still so nice to hold. ¿Qué pasa? What was happening? What?*

He took her to dinner at a quiet restaurant on the outskirts of Branson. It was a homey place with candles in yellow glasses on red checkered tablecloths. Scenic pictures of the lake hung on the walls, along with stuffed and lacquered bass.

All through the meal he kept stealing suspicious glances at her. He wasn't going to get involved with this woman—or any woman—on any case. Never again.

He'd made that mistake once—with Laura. His job had been to beguile her, to get a little information from her. Instead he'd fallen for her, and to keep on seeing her he'd had to keep on lying. It was that, or blow the case.

He hadn't blown the case; instead he'd lost the woman. He'd known better than to mix business with pleasure. But he had, and he'd been paying for it ever since.

By all that was holy, he wouldn't make the same mistake twice. And not with Laura's sister, for God's sake. Most certainly, not with her sister.

SUSANNAH DIDN'T KNOW if it was her imagination, but Gus seemed to be looking at her differently, almost mistrustfully.

*He's lost all respect for me,* she thought miserably. She shouldn't have kissed him back with such fervor, but he himself had kissed with such intensity. . . .

Her insides did a strange little quivering dance when she remembered his lips on hers. Her thighs tingled and went weak. Until Gus had come into her life, Susannah had never been fascinated by a man. And until tonight, when he had touched her, she had never been truly swept away by desire.

She tended to attract cool-blooded, soft-bodied, polite men—the sort Tim unkindly but correctly called "nerds." They usually wore glasses, clip-on ties, and had pen protectors in their shirt pockets.

On the whole, they had been about as warm and lively as the stuffed bass that hung on the resturant walls. They'd awakened nothing in her but a faint boredom. The men she noticed—more exciting men—never noticed her in return.

Nothing had prepared her for Gus Raphael. And because she was shaken, she made herself more aloof and rational than usual.

"Why do you suppose Fish showed up at the cave just when it was getting dark?" she asked in her best tone of intellectual curiosity. "You said he usually hung around Dusty Lester's show at night."

Gus stared into his coffee. "Who knows? He's strange."

"Was he alone?"

"I couldn't tell. Maybe. Maybe not."

"A cavern is an odd thing to *own*," she mused, tracing a check on the tablecloth. "I wonder what one costs?"

He shrugged, not meeting her eyes. "I never priced one."

"It's not as cost-effective as the theaters," Susannah said, settling her glasses more firmly on her nose. "I mean, at best, he could only sell 640 tickets a day, and you say they're low-priced. How much?"

He shrugged again. "Five bucks a head. Two-fifty for kids."

Susannah gazed unseeingly at the lake pictures and distracted herself with mathematics. "A medium-size theater can seat a thousand people. Say an average ticket is twenty dollars. Six nightly shows and a matinee? He could make, maximum, $120,000 a week. But the cave, at the most, could only give him $19,000—chicken feed to him. Why bother?"

Gus sighed and gave her a tired look. "Susannah, when God gave the command to go forth and multiply, he didn't mean ticket sales, and he didn't mean at suppertime."

"Excuse me," she said. "I was just indulging in a little economic theorizing, that's all."

"Tomorrow night I'll eat with an adding machine. A cheaper date, but all the same laughs."

The comment wounded. She knew she was trying to hide behind a facade of rationality, but she didn't know how else to protect herself from her feelings. "I didn't come up here for *laughs*," she said rather stiffly.

"A wise decision, since we aren't having any."

She unfolded a pamphlet she'd picked up in the restaurant lobby. There'd been two racks filled with tourist brochures and she'd taken one on Colossal Caverns.

"Look," she said, frowning. "This says that two years ago they discovered another series of caverns connected to it. They're still being explored. This isn't the kind of fast development Fish should be pursuing. He should be turning money around more quickly than that."

"Eat your broccoli. Eat your potato."

Susannah ignored both her broccoli and her potato. "It's not even a very interesting cave. This doesn't mention any unusual formations except for that nasty-looking lake. And that Bridal Cave. The stalactites are fairly good, but the stalagmites are disappointing. Nothing spectacular."

"Stalagmites, stalactites—who can tell them apart?" Gus grumbled. The cooler she was, the more contrary he seemed.

"I can. But my point is this: this cave-tour business isn't cash-intensive. Plus, the maintenance and development problems have to be highly specialized. Why doesn't he stick with what he knows—shows? Why does he want this cave?"

"Maybe he got a deal on it," Gus said impatiently. "What are you getting at? That's there's something sinister about this cave? Hey, don't let your imagination run wild."

Rebuffed, Susannah lifted her chin and stared at him with resentment. He stared back. He might be wearing his faded T-shirt and jeans, but his dark features still seemed aristocratic to her—aristocratic and mocking.

She had an irresistible urge to wipe that supercilious look from his face. "Oh. Excuse me. That's *your* department, isn't it? Letting your imagination run wild."

His haughty expression faded. He looked annoyed and defensive. "What do you mean?"

"Isn't that how you ruined what you had going with Laura?" she challenged. "She might have forgiven you for lying to her—after all, it was your job. What she couldn't forgive is how *well* you did it. How *completely* you did it. It was like once you starting lying, you enjoyed it so much, you laid everything on with a trowel."

Gus's head snapped back slightly, as if she had landed a well-aimed slap to his face. His eyes glinted with displeasure. "Touché," he said. "Very good. That hurt. Is that what you wanted? Are you satisfied?"

Susannah studied the emotions crossing his face. She was tired of playing games and tired of not understanding. "No," she said. "I'm not satisfied. I want to know why you did it. I mean you were undercover, but you didn't have to make up such big stories—about being from Spain and being related to a baron and everything. No wonder she couldn't forgive you when she found out the truth. Why did you go so *far*? Didn't you realize it was self-destructive?"

Gus stared at her for a long moment. His one-sided smile appeared again, but it was bitter. "Don't you think I asked myself a thousand times?" He was mocking again, but this time the mockery was directed at himself.

Susannah laced her fingers together and kept her chin high. "All right. You asked yourself. What's the answer?"

He swore softly in Spanish. He glanced away from her. "Did I realize I was self-destructive? No. I don't think I realized anything but the look on her face."

He seemed so regretful that in spite of herself, Susannah felt a wave of sympathy for him. "The look on her face? I don't understand."

He made a dismissive gesture. He looked off into the middle distance as if the truth were visible there, but he didn't like what he saw.

"I told you," he said, sneering at his own words, "every assignment—it's like acting. You find the part that feels right. That whole damned 'Spanish aristocrat' thing seemed right— at the time. And she . . . *liked* it. She'd get such a look on her face. I can't describe it. Nobody'd ever looked at me like that before."

Susannah swallowed. His air of self-blame saddened her, and she wished now that she had never tried to hurt him. "I still don't understand," she said gently.

He cast her an acrid look. "Nobody—certainly no decent woman—ever looked at me like that before. She was so pretty, so full of life—so innocent, so nice."

He tapped his forearm where the crude tattoo spelled out his name. "I don't know. Maybe I thought she wouldn't want the real me. I'm the street punk from Spanish Harlem. The *bastardo*—the *pilluelo*, the *gamberro;* the bastard, the guttersnipe, the hood."

*Street punk*, she reflected, surprised. *Bastard, guttersnipe, hood?*—was that his past? Gus? Elegant Gus?

He sighed in disgust, but then his expression became almost careless. He gave a short laugh. "I never told her that part of the truth. That I'm a bastard. I guessed she had me down for a figurative one, if not literal. I fill the bill on both levels. Well, hey, she deserves better. And she got it."

One of his brown hands rested, palm down, on the tablecloth. Impulsively Susannah put her own hand over his. "I'm sorry," she said. "I really am." She squeezed his hand. "I was being mean. I'm sorry about that, too."

She started to draw her hand away, but he caught it and held it. "No. I was being a jerk. I asked for it."

He linked his fingers through hers and stared at them. "Look—" he said. "I always thought of you like a sister, you know? Let's not spoil it. Things get tense. They'll be tenser before it's over. But let's stay friends, okay?"

*Friends*, Susannah thought, awareness of him running through her; was that all they could be, friends? Couldn't he see the look on *her* face? Or was he paying no attention to her, since as usual, he was lost in his thoughts of Laura?

He shook his head. "Me—I'm too much of a smartass. It gets on your nerves. You, you're just too smart. That gets on mine. But I like you. I always have."

She could think of nothing to say. She, too, stared at their hands, his brown, hers pale.

"What I never expected," he said, his face growing troubled, "was that you could kiss like that. You caught me...off guard."

*I never expected it myself*, Susannah thought. *Until I met you.* "We'd better go," she said tonelessly.

He released her hand. "Yeah," he said. "We'd better go."

They didn't speak again until they reached the motel. And even then, they found they had little to say.

THE NEXT MORNING, they shared a nearly silent breakfast of cornflakes and coffee in the cramped kitchen area.

The night before, Gus had retired to his room, locking the flimsy door just as he'd promised. Now neither of them mentioned the parking lot or their prickly discussion afterward. They sat at the small, cluttered table, avoiding each other's eyes.

Gus seemed ill at ease. Susannah felt self-conscious and eager to escape to her interview at the Branson Busy Bee Employment Agency.

On Gus's advice, she wore her hair down and loose, no makeup, and her tinted glasses. Her blue skirt and white blouse were unremarkable.

"Fish doesn't leave his office during the day," Gus said, pouring himself more cornflakes. "Not usually. You should be safe."

She stiffened with apprehension. "Safe from what?"

He wore his low-slung jeans and a blue-and-white-striped T-shirt that, with his earring, made him look piratical. "Safe from him seeing you. Until you meet him at your interview tomorrow." He poured sugar on his cornflakes.

She pushed her own half-empty bowl away impatiently. "Why does it *matter* if he sees me?"

"I want the element of surprise on our side."

"But why?" she persisted. "Why is it so important?"

He gave her a brief but piercing look. He tapped his stomach. "Instinct. Gut level. It feels right."

Susannah sighed. "I think you want the element of *drama* on our side. *That's* your instinct—to be theatrical."

"Hey, Chiquita, don't knock it. It's kept me alive this long."

There he was. A pirate eating cornflakes, she thought in exasperation. He ought to have a parrot on his shoulder. He ought to have a Jolly Roger fluttering over his head. "You really like it, don't you?" she asked. "Living on the edge?"

"I don't know. I've never lived anywhere else."

She was more puzzled by him than ever.

"What would you have done if Laura had married you? She likes a sensible, meaningful life."

"What would I have done? Whatever she wanted. Somebody should have told me she wanted to run off to the woods and hug trees and live with bears. How was I to know?"

Susannah shook her head and rested her elbow on the table, her chin in her palm. "You'd really give it up—all the intrigue, all the taking chances? *Really?*"

He frowned as if the question annoyed him. "I suppose. I never got the chance to find out, did I?"

She said nothing. Laura was an active, outdoor person, such a creature of the country and nature that she and Jarod seemed perfect for each other. Gus had met her in Hot Springs, when she was away from the mountains, having her fling at city life.

Had Gus even suspected how deep her love of nature ran? Had Laura herself even realized it before Jarod came her way? As for Gus, how could he quit the sort of work he so loved? Could he and Laura have been happy together, had things worked out differently? Susannah didn't know.

She changed the subject. It was too uncomfortable for both of them. "I have to go to my interview. Then I want to see the town. What are you going to do?"

"Tap into Fish's CommuCate system," he said nonchalantly. "Pass the milk, will you?"

Susannah was shocked. CommuCate was an interactive computer service. By modem, Fish could send and receive electronic messages from anyone else in the service. "His CommuCate? I mean, I know you can tap phones. And hide bugs. But tapping his computer mail—is that legal?"

"It's not illegal—completely."

"I mean—" she searched for the right words "—isn't a lot of what you do borderline in the legal sense?"

"Yeah. The milk, please."

She passed him the milk. "So isn't all this listening and bugging and tapping in violation of the constitution? Isn't it breaking the law?"

"Maybe. The law's not completely clear. And you know what?"

"What?" she asked, raising one eyebrow.

"It's never gonna be clear," he said with satisfaction. "It's too complicated. It's not exactly illegal to bug Fish's office. Or tap his phone. Or even his computer service. It's not exactly legal, either. You know the one thing I can't do?"

"What?"

"Open his mail." Gus's tone was disgusted. "The privacy of the airwaves, of *electrons,* for God's sake, is in dispute, but the U.S. Mail is sacred. I could be thrown in the slammer for opening Fish's letter from Publishers Clearing House. That's going to be one of your jobs. Reading his mail—after he's opened it."

"This gets sleazier and sleazier," Susannah said, rising. "I've got to get out of here for a while."

"Hey! We're in the service of our country, here. No remarks. On the surface it may be sleaze. Underneath it's intense patriotism—and other good stuff."

"I know, I know," she said, taking up her purse. "Law and order. Justice and the American Way. But you really do inhabit the Twilight Zone of law enforcement."

"I like the Twilight Zone. Anything can happen."

*So I'm learning,* Susannah thought in near despair.

GUS WAS GLAD SUSANNAH took the car instead of walking. It would help keep her out of sight. He forced himself not to worry about her. She was sensible, resourceful, observant and quick, he kept telling himself. She wouldn't get herself in trouble.

She would need her smarts in a place like this. To Gus, a native New Yorker, Branson seemed like a crazy place, full of rhinestone cowboys with accents that twanged too much. To him, it was hillbilly-ness gone mad.

Gus had no use for small towns—they bored him. Branson was a very small town. Neither did he have any use for tourists. Their gawking, their lollygagging, their need to be amused—all irritated him. Branson swarmed with tourists and had the flashy billboards and god-awful traffic to prove it.

The town had asked for it. In recent decades, Branson had made itself the center of country-and-western music shows. Theaters and more theaters lined its streets and highways.

Gus had done his homework. He knew how important Branson had become. Willie Nelson had played there, and so had Johnny Cash, Merle Haggard, Loretta Lynn, Glen Campbell, Barbara Mandrell, Mickey Gilley, Roy Clark, Ricky Skaggs, Waylon Jennings, Conway Twitty, Kenny Rogers, Pam Tillis, Dolly Parton—the roster of stars read like the Country Music Hall of Fame.

None of this impressed Gus, who believed music had reached its peak of perfection in *Phantom of the Opera*, *Evita*, and *Cats*. Now *those* were music shows.

In Branson, Andrew Lloyd Webber might as well not exist. The music-hungry tourist could start his day listening to banjo-banging at Bubba's Breakfast Hoedown, and go from show to show until far into the night. Broadway it wasn't. If it weren't for the sweet scent of crime in the air, Gus wouldn't be caught dead in Branson.

But he went wherever the Bureau needed bugging done. He called Washington headquarters to check in—something he didn't particularly like doing, these days. He had a new superior, Olivier, who had all the warmth, flexibility and imagination of an ice cube.

Olivier, sounding bored, said things in Fish's organization were quiet—except a snitch in the Missouri area had vanished.

The snitch's nickname was Marty the Mouse because he was always ratting on someone. The Mouse had been supposed to rendezvous with an agent in St. Louis yesterday morning, but he'd never appeared. Nobody could find him. The St. Louis agents were uneasy. Olivier, in his superiority, was not.

Gus grimaced. Marty the Mouse was connected tangentially to Fish's organization; the Mouse knew a lot about its numbers running and prostitution in St. Louis. But the Mouse had nothing directly to do with Fish. There was no real connection. Gus mentally filed the information in case it was more important than Olivier thought.

He spent most of the morning listening in to Fish's phone conversations and recording them. They were routine. He also worked on tapping the computer and got into Fish's ComuCate service with relative ease.

He'd comandeered the dresser of his bedroom for his computer setup. The digital display in the corner of the screen told him the last time Fish had been on the computer was this morning at 9:15. Gus punched the buttons to get access to Fish's private electronic mail.

What Gus had told Susannah was the truth. He couldn't touch the mail Fish got through the postal service. But Fish's electronic mail? That was different.

She was probably defensive about computer privacy because computers were her field. It was hard to get a handle on Susannah. Sometimes she was sophisticated; other times, naive. Often she was so logical it boggled him, and other times he sensed unplumbed depths of emotion in her. Like last night, when she'd been talking about her father and the accident . . . or when they'd kissed—*Stop thinking about her*, he told himself irritably.

"Aha!" he muttered aloud. There it was, Fish's "mailbox." The screen announced three pieces of electronic mail waiting to be read. Gus checked out the first.

It was addressed to Fish from somebody named Maude Ann Hawkins. The first words jumped off the screen and hit him where his adrenaline lived: "Glad the mouse is disposed of."

Gus's nerve ends prickled. *Mouse?* Marty the Mouse was missing, and Fish was getting E-mail about a mouse being gone? A knot formed in Gus's stomach.

The rest of the note was unpleasantly cryptic: "Good trees get ruined when mice chew bark. Affirmative on mole trap. Moles can be ruinous. Gardening would be so lovely without the vermin. Vegetables doing well this year. Flowers, also. And you? Love, Maude Ann."

He moved closer to the edge of his chair and reread the note. Throughout his system, alarms were ringing.

First there was the business about the mouse. Then the "mole trap."

*Mole* was slang for a spy within an organization, one who had tunneled inside. With foreboding, he thought of Susannah. When she went to work for Fish, she would be just such an operative. But nobody in Fish's organization could know about her yet. It wasn't possible.

He pulled up the second piece of mail to the screen. It was from a Linda Lee Schipperhoffen. "Hello!" it began cheerfully. "I saw your note down on the Singles Bulletin Board. I don't wish to sound immodest, but for years people have told me that I look *Just* like Audrey Hepburn. I am five-foot-seven and weigh 169 pounds—I look like Audrey with *curves!* I am a little older than you mentioned, but I look good for my age! And, yes, I am into 'fun and fantasy'! Your new friend, Linda Lee."

Gus gritted his teeth. Fish was cruising the electronic bulletin boards, where people posted public notes. He must be shopping for an extra Audrey by E-mail, for kinky correspondence. Dirty old lecher.

He ground his teeth harder and hoped this didn't bode trouble for Susannah. He'd never heard of Fish trying to harass one of his lookalike harem, but that didn't mean it couldn't happen.

Annoyed by Fish's crazy fetishes, he pulled up the third piece of mail. "Well, Maude Ann," he murmured. "Fancy meeting you again."

Maude Ann's first note had been sent late last night. This one was newer, dated ten-thirty this morning. "Yes, the lettuce has been exceptional this year. So it's true that a saucer of beer will draw slugs to it, and they will drown. I thought it was only a folk tale. The begonias are something, but the apples seem to have blight. Happy gardening—Maude Ann."

Gus frowned. Was Maude Ann for real?

Between forays into bulletin-board naughtiness, was Fish having an exchange on the joys of gardening? Fish had a garden up at his big house on the lake—it was *possible*. But was it *probable*?

Was all this garden jargon some kind of cockamamy code? If so, why bother? And why send any compromising message by computer? Fish should know such mail could be intercepted. Gus had tapped into the system on the off chance the man would get cocky or careless.

Yet in both notes, "Maude Ann" had mentioned death—first of a mole, then of slugs. And then there was that damned business about the mouse being gone. It could all be innocent, of course. It could all be coincidence.

But Gus didn't believe a great deal in innocence, and he didn't trust coincidence. He'd let Olivier know about the messages, and he'd keep his eyes open.

He set up the computer's printer to copy everything in Fish's mail and to print automatically any message that Fish would send from now on. The knot was still in his stomach. *Damn!* He hoped he hadn't dragged Susannah into something more dangerous than he'd expected.

He rose and paced the cramped room while the printer hummed and clicked. His thoughts kept returning, almost compulsively, to Susannah.

He couldn't help it. She was always asking him such off-the-wall questions. Like would he have given up this work for Laura? It made him wonder what he'd be doing now if Laura *had* accepted him. Living on a chicken farm in Arkansas? Repairing television sets in Hot Springs? God forbid.

Or would she have come to Washington with him? Would she have been happy there? He doubted it—not if her idea of a good time was tromping through the woods. Could she have stood having Gus out in the field, gone for sometimes weeks at a time? Laura was a little—well—*possessive*. And she wasn't nearly as open-minded as Susannah. Or as intellectually curious. Now, Susannah would probably *like* a city full of monuments and museums and libraries. . . .

He shook the thought away. It was too bizarre. But another of Susannah's questions kept haunting him in a darker way. It had kept him awake last night. It had niggled at him all morning. It troubled him now.

Susannah was right. She'd asked something nobody in the FBI, including himself, had thought to ask.

Why did Fish have *caverns*, of all things? They weren't making much money. They couldn't. So what was the point?

A man could hide a lot of things in a cavern. Any number of things. He might even hide a missing Marty the Mouse. Why had Fish's Cadillac shown up at the cavern last night? Had it had a special cargo of Mouse in the trunk?

"Baby," he breathed, as if he could send Susannah the message by telepathy, "be careful. We'll both have to be careful, beautiful. Very, very careful."

# 5

SUSANNAH STAYED AWAY from the motel until it was time for Gus to go to work; this was the night he was to start with Dusty Lester. Then she returned to the rooms and went to bed before he came home. But she couldn't sleep.

She heard him come back shortly before midnight, using the private entrance to his own room. He cracked open the door between their rooms.

He stood there for a long time. She sensed he was staring at her. Her body tensed, but she kept her eyes squeezed shut, pretending to sleep. Was he thinking of speaking to her, of coming to her? And if he did, what then? She didn't know, and her uncertainty made her heart pound harder.

But he didn't speak, he didn't draw near. He eased the door shut, and she heard the lock click. He was keeping his promise, and she supposed she was relieved.

The next morning, he acted oddly at breakfast. He was subdued, and he kept giving her furtive glances, his expression unreadable.

"What's *wrong* with you?" she asked at last.

He was eating cornflakes again. Cornflakes must be his idea of a gourmet breakfast, because he had three more boxes in the cupboard. She'd nibbled at a piece of dry toast but wasn't hungry.

He set down his spoon. "What do you mean, what's the matter?"

"You keep giving me these looks—like you're worried."

"Okay. I'm worried. I wonder if I should have dragged you into this."

"Now's a fine time to start worrying. I'm due at his office at eleven o'clock."

He made a dubious gesture. "I got into Fish's CommuCate system yesterday."

Susannah crooked one eyebrow. "And? You smelled a rat?"

"No. I smelled a mouse."

"What?" she asked with perplexity.

Briefly, he told her about Marty the Mouse and the enigmatic notes from Maude Ann Hawkins about "gardening." He included the details about the mole and the drowned slugs. "I don't like it," he said, his face stonier than before. "If you want out, get out. Now. While there's time."

Oddly, Susannah felt no fear. Instead, a prickling surge of excitement swept through her. "Wow," she said softly. "This is *interesting*."

Gus gave her an incredulous look. "Interesting? Excuse me, I'm talking death here. I'm talking mayhem."

"You know what I mean," she said. "I knew there was something funny about that cavern business. It doesn't add up with everything else. I'm going to—"

"Keep your nose out of that cavern."

Susannah was too swept up to pay attention "—find out more about that cavern. Oh, I like this. This is like a bonus."

"Susannah," he said, warning in his voice, "this is not a 'movie of the week.' This is reality. I'm concerned about your safety."

"I'll be perfectly safe," she insisted. "I'm not a reckless person. You know that."

He frowned. "Yes. But—"

"Besides," she said, allowing her more rational side to take over, "the whole thing may be coincidence. You said so yourself. You could be worrying over nothing."

"I know, but—"

"You're basing your premise on insufficient data."

He scowled. "I *hate* it when you talk that way—'a premise based on insufficient data.'"

"If it's a coincidence, there's nothing to worry about," she said with conviction. "If it's not a coincidence, you're lucky—more's going on here than you expected."

"Stop being logical. Be sensible instead," he ordered.

"I am being sensible. You're being paranoid. I presumed you trusted me to do this." She picked up her toast and took another bite.

"I did trust you—I do," he said. "But there's more. On CommuCate he's trying to getting a little E-mail chat going with somebody who looks like Audrey Hepburn. He wants it to be a dirty little E-mail chat. If this guy puts the move on you—"

"You said he wouldn't."

"We gotta allow for a margin of error. If this guy puts the move on you—"

"I can *handle* him, Gus," Susannah said calmly. "Besides, you're having me take a bug into the office. If I have trouble, you could be there in a minute."

"And blow our cover," argued Gus. "Besides, he could sneak up on you—soundlessly, like a cat. He could put a rag full of chloroform over your face. You'd fall over, and he'd have his way with you—"

"Gus!" She fought down a smile. His imagination was out of control again, but she rather liked having him act so protective. It made her feel so warm and snuggly that she had another bite of toast.

"It could happen," he insisted.

"Your imagination's running amok again."

"Yeah? Well, yours isn't running at all. I want to consider every possibility. This guy's a bit of a nut case, you know."

"He can't be any worse than you," Susannah countered. "Creeping up and chloroforming me—really. You sound like some nineteenth-century tract on white slavery."

He gave her a disapproving glance. "Hey. I've seen the world, Chiquita. You haven't. It isn't a pretty place. Trust me on that point."

Susannah felt rebuffed. He was right, of course. He was a worldly man, extremely worldly. She was the opposite. But she intended to hold her ground.

"I'm not afraid," she said, pushing the toast aside again.

He studied her, disapproval on his face. He crossed his arms, which made his lean muscles ripple. "I know," he said with an unpleasantly sardonic crook of his mouth. "You're not afraid. And that's what's starting to scare me about you, baby."

*Baby.* She couldn't help it. Some primitive part of herself loved it when he called her "baby."

He swore softly in Spanish—a complex curse she couldn't understand. Then he poured himself more cornflakes.

TWO HOURS AFTER breakfast, she knocked on Gus's closed door, ready to go to her interview with Fish. Gus couldn't help it. When he saw her standing there, he felt an irresistibly pleasant ache in his chest and groin.

*Damn!* he thought. *She looks great. Who wouldn't fall for her? Fish, prepare to be hooked.*

She was dressed in a simple dark yellow sundress he had picked for her. Gus knew clothes, and knew this dress quietly but emphatically said "class act." She had on the gold necklace with the one large fake pearl, the pearl earrings, the low-heeled white shoes he'd chosen.

*My God, she can be beautiful when she tries.* And he wondered, once again, why he had never noticed before?

"Do I look all right?" she asked. She didn't seem as confident as she had earlier.

"You look okay," he said gruffly. "The eye makeup—you got it right. That's good."

She seemed to relax a bit. Behind her big glasses, her eyes were carefully made up, emphasizing their largeness, their uptilted angle, their long lashes. She'd darkened her brows slightly, accenting their winglike curves.

Her mouth was glistening coral pink, and her perfume drove his mind excitingly down forbidden paths. The scent was "Always." He'd picked it for her because it seemed right at the time. It was more than right; it was so perfect it agonized him and made him slightly dizzy.

"You're sure you want me to wear the glasses?" she asked, still seeming nervous.

He nodded. He found he was having trouble speaking.

She touched her hair, which was severely swept back, as usual. "I can change this. Make it softer, the way he likes it."

He shook his head. "No. I don't want you to look too perfect." He looked away from her.

"Should I drive? It's such a short way. Maybe I should walk."

"I'll drive you," he muttered.

She looked surprised. "But *why?*"

"Because," he said, still not looking at her, "I told you. We're a couple. We need to be seen together. It's for your own protection."

"Drive that short a way?" she asked skeptically.

"We'll take a long way. Go up to the lake and come back. It won't look like we came straight from here."

"I still think we look weird together," Susannah mused, looking him up and down.

He glanced at his tight, faded jeans, his tattered running shoes. "Yeah? Well, it *feels* right," he said. "In this scenario, you're one of those chicks who puts all her money on her back—clothes and stuff. I'm the one who makes you happy when your clothes are off."

He cast her a furtive look and saw he had made her blush. He was sorry and wished he'd kept his mouth shut. "It's a part," he told her defensively. "It's a set of parts we play."

"Because it feels right to you?"

"Yeah."

"And because you always trust your instincts."

"Yeah."

She looked at him for a long, measuring moment. He met her gaze, wondering if she was going to lose her nerve at the last minute and go home, be safe.

"Well," she said dryly, pushing her glasses up on her nose. "All the world's a stage. Let's go play our parts."

He looked her up and down. No, she hadn't lost her nerve. Not a bit. Damn, she was something.

But all he said was, "Yeah. Let's play our parts."

SHE FOUND HERSELF holding her breath when he pulled into the parking lot of Fish's office. He stopped the car and switched off the engine. "I'll wait for you here. You got the bugs?"

She nodded, her mouth set determinedly. She had the bugged cellophane-tape dispenser in her white shoulder bag. In addition, she wore another bug fastened inside the belt of her dress. Gus had told her it was small but powerful. He could monitor her from the car while he seemed to be listening to a Walkman headset.

The tape dispenser was to be left, at her first chance, in Fish's office. She must let its presence seem so natural that Fish would never notice it. She understood she might not be able to put it in place today; it might be too soon.

A short, squarely built man with close-cropped blond hair and pale eyes came cutting across Fish's parking lot.

Susannah saw Gus tense. "That's Epperson," he said. "One of Fish's buddies. He hangs around the Dusty Lester Show. He knows me. Look natural. And gimme a kiss."

Susannah glanced at the man named Epperson, whose face was dour and whose body was powerful. He gave off an aura of menace. She tensed.

"No—" she started to protest.

But Gus was already leaning toward her, and his hand framed her jaw. His voice was soft, beguiling. "Just a little one, Chiquita. For luck. I won't even mess your lipstick. For luck. *Buena suerte.*"

Lightly he pressed his lips to hers, so gently it was as if a butterfly had landed there, but a butterfly, for all its delicacy, that intoxicated her with sensuality.

His hand on her face was seductively tender. His mouth barely touched hers, yet it lingered as if he was reluctant to restrain himself. Then, just when it seemed he might deepen the kiss in spite of his promise, he drew back.

His eyes shuttered. "Okay," he said, his voice suddenly businesslike again. "Go get him."

Susannah's mouth trembled slightly, and her cheeks burned beneath the carefully applied rouge. "Right," she said, struggling to breathe normally. "Go get him."

She got out of the car, swung her bag over her shoulder, and holding herself tall, walked past the man named Epperson and toward the entrance of Fish's building. Behind her she heard Gus's voice call a lazy greeting to Epperson.

*I'm really here. I'm really doing this,* she said to herself as she entered the lobby.

Although the building was only two stories, it had an elevator with a brass door. She pressed the button. The doors opened and she commanded her knees not to tremble.

She felt hollow, almost disembodied by the time she reached the second floor and stepped off the elevator. A receptionist's desk of golden oak dominated the entry area.

In front of the desk, bizarrely, was a miniature replica of "The World-Famous Dancing Fountains." Five small fountains changed their heights and shapes as colored lights played on them, changing their colors, as well.

The receptionist was an extraordinarily thin young woman with a gaminelike haircut. She had large eyes, a longish nose, but hardly any chin to speak of. She wore a chic summer suit of pale green.

When she saw Susannah, her wide eyes grew wider. She glanced at the clock on the wall, then back at Susannah. A hopeful expression crossed her face. "It's eleven o'clock," she said. "You wouldn't happen to be the woman from the Busy Bee Employment Agency, would you?"

"Yes," Susannah said briskly. "I'm Susannah Fingal. I brought my résumé and my letters of recommendation. Do I need to fill out a form?"

"Do you know computers?" the receptionist asked dubiously, as if Susannah were too good to be true.

"I have a major in computer science and a minor in business," Susannah said. "I taught for two years in Memphis, but my fiancé's working here. I need a job that pays better than teaching. The agency said—"

"Oh, Mr. Fish pays well, very well," the girl supplied, almost too quickly. She pushed an application form and a ballpoint pen toward Susannah. "Fill this out. Then I'll tell him you're here."

Susannah sat down, crossing her legs at the ankles. She took a copy of *Country Music Scene* magazine to use as a lapboard and filled out the form, quickly and efficiently. She was amazed as the falsified information flowed from her pen. It gave her a pleasant sensation of power.

When she finished, the receptionist nodded curt approval and switched on the intercom. "There's a Miss Fingal here to see you from the Busy Bee Employment Agency," she said.

The answer was a rather ill-tempered mumble that Susannah couldn't make out. The receptionist nodded again and looked at Susannah. "Mr. Fish will see you. Just go through that door."

*Just go through that door*, Susannah thought fatefully. Once she went through it, she would no longer be herself. She would enter a world of deceit, spying, and very possibly danger. Anxiety surged through her.

But when she rose from her seat, her movements were sure and poised, her step unfaltering. She opened the walnut door and stepped inside.

The office was darker than the reception area—all the blinds were shut. The first thing Susannah saw was another model of The World-Famous Dancing Fountains, this one larger. Seven miniature fountains played up and down, changing colors to recorded music. The song was an orchestrated version of "Moon River."

The fountains danced before a large desk that was unoccupied. It was, she supposed, the desk of the arrested secretary.

On the walls hung rather florid oil paintings of Fish's country-music stars and several framed Gold records. She counted four computers in the room, one at the desk and three others at their separate stations.

The carpet was dark green and so thick that it seemed to swallow up the heels of her shoes. She stood very straight, glancing nervously about the room. Then the door to Fish's inner office opened, and the man himself appeared.

Susannah forced a smile to her face. Fish didn't so much as glance at her at first. He seemed engrossed in studying a sheaf of papers.

He was a small man, perhaps an inch or two shorter than herself. He was slightly plump, his face had a doughy softness, and his hair, brown shot through with gray, was thinning.

He wore gray pin-striped trousers, no suitcoat, a white short-sleeved shirt, a scarlet tie and black suspenders. He had a potbelly and an air of self-importance.

At last he raised his eyes and looked at her. He had cold, pale eyes that looked sleepy, almost dreamy.

But the eyes widened when he saw Susannah, and their dreaminess vanished. They became almost preternaturally alert. They studied her face for a long moment, then ran up and down her body with obvious gratification.

His soft lips stretched into a smile that made Susannah want to recoil. *He's nasty,* she thought. *A very nasty man.*

But she didn't flinch, and she kept her polite smile in place. "Mr. Fish?" she said brightly. "I'm Susannah Fingal. From the Busy Bee Employment Agency."

She had her résumé and application in her left hand. She extended her right to him—a businesslike offer of a handshake.

Instead Fish set his papers down on the desk. He took her hand in both of his, moving closer to her than necessary. His hands were soft, warm, and unpleasantly damp.

"Miss Fingal," he breathed, gripping her hand more tightly. "Miss Fingal. I'm so pleased. Come into my office, my dear. *Please.*"

Keeping her hand between his own, he drew her through his open doorway and led her to a large couch of black leather. "Sit," he said. "Please. May I fix you something to drink? Coffee? Tea? A soft drink? Sherry?"

The couch was so soft and cushy that Susannah had the fleeting sensation that it would swallow her. But it did not, and at least, when Fish turned to his bar, he had released her hand.

"No, thank you," she said. "I never drink stimulants." She didn't know why she said it; she loved coffee. It had *seemed* like the right thing to say.

The answer seemed to please him. He stepped back, and his eyes ran up and down her body again. Susannah felt another wave of repulsion.

"I hope you won't be bothered if I have a little something," he said, rubbing his hands together.

"Not at all," she replied.

He went to the bar, opened it, and poured himself a small glass of cream sherry. He downed it in two gulps, closed the bar and turned his attention to her once more. He kept smiling a disturbingly gentle smile.

He came and sat beside her on the couch. He reached and took her application and other papers. His hand trembled slightly. With a sickening realization, she knew that he was shaking from suppressed excitement.

"My," he said, poring over her application. "My, Miss Fingal. This *is* impressive. Impressive."

"Thank you," she said. She folded her hands demurely in her lap and hoped he wouldn't reach for her. She distracted herself by counting computers. There were five.

Fish opened the folder containing her counterfeit résumé and letters of recommendation. He licked his lips. He nodded as he read. He made a small grunt of pleasure.

Susannah scanned his office, which was large, and, like the secretary's office, too dark. To her dismay, she saw yet another, still-larger replica of The World-Famous Dancing Fountains.

They played before Fish's desk—nine small fountains, rising and falling and changing colors. The same music played as in the secretarial office. For some reason, they made her flesh creep.

"Miss Fingal?" Fish's voice was slightly breathless.

She turned her attention to him, smiling coolly. "Yes?"

"You seem to have dropped from heaven in my hour of need. Your background seems perfect. May I ask you a few professional questions?"

"Certainly."

"Are you familiar with the Word-Wise system for word processing?"

"Intimately. Also WordStar, WordPerfect, and PFS WRITE."

"How about accounting? Can you use the Peartree software program?"

"Peartree, Account Action, Balencia, and Cratchett."

"Desktop publishing?" he asked, rubbing his hands on his knees. "What system do you prefer?"

"I'm best with Print X-Press," she said. "But I can learn almost anything quickly."

"Jet-Quill?" he asked, still rubbing his knees.

"Oh, yes. Jet-Quill's quite good," she said. She made a minute adjustment to her earring. He watched with apparent fascination.

"You can do spreadsheets, schedules, files?"

"Yes."

He gave a long sigh that was too sexual for Susannah's comfort. He gripped his knees until his knuckles paled. "Now—do you mind if I ask you a few personal questions?"

She resisted the urge to grit her teeth. "Not at all."

"Your résumé says you were a teacher in Memphis. What brings you to Branson? And to apply for *this* job?"

She sat straighter, cocked her head slightly. "I'm engaged. My fiancé found work here. We want to get married—but a teacher's salary doesn't go very far."

Fish leaned toward her slightly, a strange light in his pale eyes. "You and your fiancé—are happy? Are suited?"

"Perfectly," Susannah said with a shy smile. "I mean he's not the most intellectual of men. But we're very . . . compatible. I'm satisfied, yes."

Fish swallowed with apparent difficulty. He smiled. "It's important to be compatible. A satisfied woman is a happy woman, and a happy woman is a happy worker. Are you a happy worker, Miss Fingal?"

Susannah cast her eyes down modestly. "I like to think so. And I'd want to keep my employer happy, too."

Fish sucked in his breath, a small, wet sound. "You make a nice appearance, Miss Fingal. You are—ladylike. I like that."

"Why—thank you."

"And your family background?"

"My father was a minister. My mother was a teacher. They're both . . . deceased."

"My poor dear," he said. "You're almost alone in the world, aren't you?" He was leaning so close that she could feel his breath on her bare shoulder. Mentally she cursed Gus for buying her a sleeveless dress.

She shrank back from Fish, but kept her aplomb. "I have my fiancé. And I hope to find satisfying work. I *need* to find work. Work means a great deal to me. I want to be . . . of service to someone."

"I *like* your attitude," he said earnestly. Sweat was breaking out on his upper lip. "I like your resume, your background, your—bearing. I thought I'd never find anyone to equal my last secretary. But that loss seems a blessing in disguise. You seem, possibly, to *excel* her."

"You flatter me," Susannah said and pretended to be prettily flustered.

"I pay high wages, Miss Fingal. I pay excellent wages."

She kept her eyes downcast. "The agency said as much."

Fish's voice altered subtly. "I seek the perfect woman, Miss Fingal. But I myself am far from perfect."

"No mere mortal is perfect, Mr. Fish," she said in her best Sunday-school voice.

"Least of all, me," he replied. He took his hands from his knees and began to pick nervously at his fingers, worrying hangnails. "I'm far, far from perfect. I must admit that I am in some ways—eccentric."

Susannah watched in perplexity as he continued picking his fingers. He raised one hand to his mouth and bit off a particularly stubborn hangnail.

She tried not to wince. "Eccentric?"

He'd resumed picking at his fingers and couldn't seem to stop. "I'm somewhat—nervous," he said. "High-strung."

"Nervousness often goes with intelligence, Mr. Fish."

"Yes. Indeed. Well, I simply mean to be frank. Sometimes I will make—rather odd requests. You mustn't mind. Think of it as part of the job."

"Odd requests?" she asked, raising her eyebrows.

"Don't get me wrong," Fish insisted. "I don't mean anything . . . improper. No, no . . . never improper. Perhaps just a little strange. Nothing to alarm you in the least. Or your fiancé. Not at all."

She eyed him warily. "Could you be a bit more specific?"

He gritted his teeth and seemed to force his hands back to grip his knees again. He took a long, quavering breath. "Appearance—is very important to me. I hope you won't be insulted if I ask if you have contact lenses?"

*Score one for Gus*, Susannah thought, and struggled to keep her expression neutral. "As a matter of fact, I do. I'm just not too used to them yet."

"Would you be willing to wear them to work?"

"Well, certainly, Mr. Fish, if you'd prefer."

He exhaled, then took another deep breath. "And your hair. Your hair is quite lovely, Miss Fingal. An extraordinary color. Somehow I'd never imagined auburn. It's quite—I don't know how to say it—so unexpected, so right, so new to me—"

"Yes?" She found she was inching away from him again, and made herself be still.

"Yet the style is so—*severe*. I'm going to give you the name of a hairdresser. Miss Teagle of Klassic Kuts. Tell her that I sent you and that you'd like 'the usual.' It'll be charged to the office. It's a style—of which I'm fond. Not altogether different from yours. But softer. It would be a great kindness to me if you'd comply with this—rather personal preference of mine."

*Score two for Gus.* She gave Fish a weak smile. "You're obviously a successful man," she said. "You deserve to have your office environment exactly as you like."

"Miss Fingal, I have a third request. Please don't think of this as harassment in any way. I would rather die than harass you. It's just another little—eccentricity. There's nothing prurient in it."

"Yes?" She kept her smile, insincere as it was, in place.

Fish began to tap his feet nervously. Now his forehead as well as his upper lip was filmed with sweat. "So excuse me for asking: Are you wearing panty hose?"

She tried to keep the shock from registering on her face. "Actually—I am."

Fish's feet tapped harder. "A well-dressed woman should always wear silk stockings," he said from between his teeth.

"Real ones. I can't abide panty hose. It would please me if you would wear the . . . other sort of garment."

She stared at him in astonishment. *Well, Gus, if you were going to miss one, this was the wrong one to miss. It's a doozy. Garters and stockings, is it?*

Fish stopped tapping. He stared at the floor and looked solemn. "When I was married," he said, "I had a large wolf-hound puppy. I loved that dog. He was in the chewing stage. He . . . unfortunately choked to death on a pair of panty hose my wife had left drying in the bathroom. I . . . haven't been able to tolerate panty hose since then."

Susannah clenched her hands more tightly together in her lap. She kept her face as composed as she could. "I see," she said, not believing a word of the story.

"Knowing that I'm near panty hose all day long fills me with—repulsion and sorrow. It would be a mercy to spare me that. A kindness, that's all."

"I would certainly want to spare you pain," she said carefully.

"Miss Fingal," Fish said, his cold eyes glittering as he raised them to hers, "you're a woman of rare accomplishment and understanding. The job is yours."

Susannah smiled widely. In spite of her dismay at how strange the man was, she felt triumphant that she had succeeded. Elation flooded her.

He offered his hand, and she had no choice but to take it in a handshake. Immediately both his hands closed moistly over hers.

"When do I start?" she asked.

"When *can* you start?" he asked, licking his lips.

"Tomorrow?" she suggested, praying he'd say yes.

He agreed eagerly. "Tomorrow."

She managed to withdraw her hand and rise to her feet. "Oh, I'm so delighted," she said. "I can't wait to tell my fiancé. Oh, this is wonderful, Mr. Fish."

Fish struggled to his feet. He started to walk her to the door, but she hurried ahead of him, as if too happy to restrain herself. "I can't wait to tell him," she said. "He's waiting for me. Oh, it's just too wonderful."

"Indeed, it *is* wonderful," Fish said, eyeing her hungrily.

And then his phone rang. Susannah gave silent thanks. "I'll let myself out," she said gaily. "And see you tomorrow— bright and early! This is *so* exciting."

"Yes, yes, it is," said Fish. Then reluctantly he picked up his phone, but he kept his gaze fixed on her until she let herself out.

As soon as she closed the door, she couldn't repress a sigh of relief.

"You got it, didn't you?" said the receptionist as Susannah passed her desk. She didn't smile when she said it.

Susannah put her hand to her chest as if to still her beating heart. "I can't believe it. I *needed* this job so much. And he pays so well."

"Yeah," said the receptionist, still unsmiling. "Well, we earn it, believe me. My name's Ginger, by the way."

Susannah nodded in greeting, but let her smile fade slightly. "What do you mean—we earn it?"

"*Him*," Ginger said, nodding in the direction of Fish's office. "Oh, he never hurts you or anything. He never even touches you. It's just he's so—yuck. But don't worry. He's really harmless. So long as you've got a strong stomach."

Susannah shrugged and said, "Well, we're working girls. We do the best that we can, I guess."

"Tell me about it," Ginger said sourly. "Well, welcome to the garter-belt brigade."

"What?" Susannah stared at her in surprise.

Wordlessly, Ginger turned her swivel chair so that her legs were free of the desk. She pulled up the short skirt of her suit. She wore silk stockings and a lacy white garter belt. She gave Susannah a sardonic look.

"Yes—" Susannah sucked in her breath "—I sort of wondered—about that."

Ginger pulled her skirt back into place, but her expression remained unhappy. "Don't worry. He likes to have a little inspection now and then."

"An inspection?"

"Just a little *peek*," Ginger said sarcastically. "Like I say, he's basically harmless. But he can get on your nerves. I say at this salary, to hell with the nerves. Anybody tell you what happened to his last secretary?"

Susannah swallowed. "Not . . . exactly."

Ginger frowned and lowered her voice to a conspiratorial whisper. "She turned into a klepto. She got arrested. And you know why I think she did it?"

Susannah shook her head and waited.

Ginger cast an ominous glance in the direction of Fish's office. "I think he drove her to it. I think she did it to get away from *him*. She was, like, a nervous sort, you know? So don't let him get to you. Survival of the fittest, and all that."

Susannah nodded somberly. "Right," she said.

"I knew you had the job if you wanted it the minute you stepped off the elevator," Ginger declared cynically. "You look like Audrey Hepburn, sorta. He's got a thing for her. I look kinda like her, too, except for my chin. *He* offered to pay for a chin implant for me. Can you imagine?"

"Plastic surgery?" Susannah's eyes widened.

"I said, 'Thanks, but no thanks.' I don't want anybody cuttin' on *me*. I mean, you gotta draw the line somewhere."

"Right," Susannah said again. She glanced at her watch. "Oh—I should go. My fiancé's waiting for me."

"Fiancé?" Ginger echoed, giving her a measuring look. "Maybe you better break some of this to him gently. He's got nothing to worry about. Not really. He's not the jealous type, is he?"

"Oh, no. Not at all. He's . . . very open-minded, really."

"Good," said Ginger. "And am I *glad* you showed up. He's been a wreck since Nora's been gone. A real wreck. And nuttier than usual."

Her phone rang and she picked it up. "Denton Fish Enterprises, Unlimited," she said. "How may I help you?"

Susannah forced herself to smile and waggled her fingers goodbye. Ginger waggled back, looking bored, then turned her attention to the call.

Susannah didn't bother with the elevator. She fairly flew down the stairs and out the lobby of Fish's building. Her heart was beating so fast that she felt like a runner who has reached the euphoric state and is going full speed on a pure, delicious, adrenaline high.

She couldn't wait to see Gus. *It had worked! It had all worked perfectly!* She had never before felt such intense excitement. She had never before felt so completely alive.

*I love this. I love this with all my soul.*

# 6

BREATHLESS, SHE hurried to the parking lot and let herself in on the passenger side of the blue Ford.

"Did you *hear*?" she said excitedly, as soon as the door was safely shut behind her. Gus was putting his fake Walkman earphones back into their case. "He *hired* me. It worked."

"I heard you, all right," he said with a brooding sidelong look. "Laid it on a little thick, didn't you?"

Oh, but Gus certainly looked good after Fish's flabbiness and pasty, pale-eyed face. She was filled with delight that all his strength and Latin intensity were on her side. She hardly noticed his tone or that his expression was less than happy.

"I go to work *tomorrow*. Did you hear?"

"I heard." His jaw was set. He turned on the ignition.

"He bought it all," Susannah said, shaking her head in awe. "He only threw me once—that business about panty hose. But I guess I brought it off. Ha! For a minute I believed you knew everything—but you didn't. I bet you wish you'd known about the panty hose—don't you?"

"I knew," he said tonelessly and backed the car out of the parking space.

Her euphoria dissipated. She stared at him as if she hadn't understood him correctly. "What?"

"I knew about the panty hose," he muttered, not looking at her. He concentrated on easing into the heavy traffic.

She frowned in disbelief. "You *knew*?"

"Yeah. Did it ever occur to you that I didn't buy you any panty hose in Hot Springs?"

She straightened in her seat, her posture almost militant. "No, it did *not*. Why didn't you tell me?"

He still didn't look at her. "I thought it might put you off."

"Put me off? Are you crazy? Do you know what it was like in there with him? For him to spring that on me—without warning?"

"I wanted your reaction to be natural."

"My natural reaction would have been to hit him on his male-chauvinist-pig head," Susannah said with spirit.

"I wouldn't have asked you to do this if I didn't think you could keep your cool. You kept it well enough."

"Well enough?" she fumed. "Don't kill me with praise. That was *rotten* not to warn me. And now I have to go out and buy a garter belt. God. How humiliating."

"No, you don't. I've already got 'em. At the motel."

"You got them?" she demanded. "You knew all this, you went ahead and got them, and never said a word to me?"

"You're a nice girl," he said sarcastically. "A minister's daughter. What would you have done if I'd said you were gonna have to flash a little thigh from time to time? So he's got a thing for—a certain type of lingerie. It's nothing to be alarmed about."

"I ought to beat you with your 'certain type of lingerie,'" she gritted.

"Oh, happy day," he snidely declared. "I've always wanted to be flogged with a garter belt. No. Actually I haven't. That's Fish's fantasy, not mine."

"I have to flog him?" Susannah asked in horror.

"No, no," Gus said impatiently. "He'll just want a peek at your thighs each day. And he may ask you to do something, like reach for something that'll make you show some leg. Give himself an extra peek. It's no big deal."

"No big deal? Well, they're not your thighs and not your legs."

He ignored the comment and concentrated on the traffic. He smiled to himself, almost bitterly. He was in a prickly mood, and she couldn't understand why.

She stared out the window, her pulses still racing from her encounter with Fish. Gus was heading out of Branson, and the traffic was thinning. "Where are we going?"

"To the lake. We'll buy some burgers and have lunch there. I want you to chill out a little. Then I'll take you to get your hair done."

"Chill out?" she demanded. "Why?"

"Because I've got a feeling you like this too well. You're on a high. You need to slow down, stay cool."

Susannah's heart contracted. "I thought I did fine—"

"You did okay, you did okay," he admitted. "But don't *over*do it, all right?"

"What do you mean?" she asked, pained. "What did I overdo?"

He cast her another look. It fairly smoldered. "The Southern accent, for one thing. Your accent got a lot heavier with him—honey chile. Why?"

Susannah was taken aback. He was right; she had laid her accent on thicker—she'd hardly been aware of it, but she'd done it. "I—I don't know," she admitted, searching for the reason. "It . . . *felt* right."

"Oh, God," he said, with something akin to despair.

"Well, what's wrong with that?" she asked righteously. "You say it all the time—and it's true. It *felt* right."

"Just don't make him like you too much, Scarlett. Those accents are potent. How'd the South ever lose the lousy war? Why didn't they just send all you women out to sweet-talk the enemy?" His tone grew mocking, "Why, ah do de-clare, ah just want to keep mah employah happy, Mistah Fish."

"I wasn't that bad," she said defensively, because she knew she hadn't been.

"I'm just telling you this for your own good," he grumbled. "Don't get him too excited, that's all."

"What did I say that was exciting?" she challenged.

"It wasn't just what you said, it was the way you said it: 'I just want to be of *service*.' 'I would certainly want to spare you *pain*.' You just have to fulfill some of his fantasies—not all of them."

"I think you're making too much of this," she said and crossed her arms.

"And I'll tell you another thing—I didn't appreciate the crack about me not being an intellectual type. What was *that* for? I happen to be plenty intellectual. Just not about intellectual stuff."

She tossed her head. "I thought I was supposed to give the impression you were the physical type. You Tarzan, me Jane Austen. Wasn't that your scenario?"

His fingers tightened on the steering wheel. "I'm worried about you, that's all."

"Don't. I did what I had to do."

"Yes. But you *liked* it. Didn't you?"

She raised her chin. "Yes."

"Don't like it too much," he warned. "There's no thrill in the world like it—except sex. I'm telling you: Don't get cocky, and don't get careless. For your own good."

"I understand," she said and studied his profile. And suddenly she felt as if she *did* understand.

It was dizzying, like a revelation. She understood Gus Raphael and what made him tick. This mercurial, paradoxical man truly loved living on the edge. It gave him that same feeling that had so elated her in the office—that of being completely alive, alive in every atom of one's being.

*I know you,* she thought, studying his handsome face. *I know you, and I'm like you. I'm so much like you it scares me.*

The realization stunned her. Guiltily she stopped looking at him—because she liked looking at him too much.

The lake came into view. He sped up and turned the car onto a scenic drive that ran uphill, then pulled into the first lookout. The lake spread beneath them. A summer haze glazed its surface. Beyond rolled the low mountains, green with summer.

He switched off the engine.

She was afraid to look at him. She stared out at that impossibly blue and placid lake. "I thought you were going to get something to eat," she said.

"I forgot," he said tonelessly. "Are you hungry?"

She tried to give a casual shrug, but was too tense. "No. Are you?"

There was a beat of silence. "Yes," he said and reached for her. "Oh, God, yes. Come here, Chiquita. Come here."

She didn't know exactly how it happened, except that it came about so quickly and easily, it seemed absolutely inevitable. It *had* to happen.

She was in his arms, raising her lips to his. He kissed her with such sweet ferocity that some lonely part of her died.

It made no sense to kiss him, and yet it made perfect sense. Something—sanity, perhaps—should hold them apart. Yet it would have been easier for her to defy gravity than to deny the attraction he had for her.

His mouth moved against hers—warm, uninhibited and intoxicatingly desperate. Susannah kissed him back as recklessly as he kissed her.

His tongue penetrated her mouth, boldly tasting and taking. And she welcomed him—loved him doing it. She sank deeper into his arms, and he pulled her against his hard chest. His hands moved across her back, as if tactilely savoring even its subtlest curves.

She wound her arms around his neck. He gasped and kissed her bare shoulder. His hands moved to her waist, gripping her so tightly that it was her turn to gasp.

Hotly, he kissed her collarbone through the fabric of her dress, then the hollow between her breasts, then, even more hotly, the tip of each breast. His hands moved to her hips, then her thighs, with long, hungrily exploring strokes.

She arched against him more passionately, and he dragged his lips from her breasts to her throat. He kissed her, open-mouthed, at the pulse point throbbing excitedly there, making her half faint. He nuzzled her ear, making her faint almost completely.

She ran her hands down his shoulders to his arms, to feel their hard contours. Then she kissed his arm, right above the tattooed serpent. Gus inhaled sharply and grasped her shoulders, raising her so that her face was level with his. Her coral lipstick had made a blurred smear across the sensual curves of his lips.

His mouth was pained, and his hooded eyes looked drugged with desire. "Chiquita," he said, his voice strained. "We gotta stop this. I don't even know how it started. Laura never—Laura never—"

She stared at him in stunned disbelief for a second, then jerked free of his grip. "Oh, *Laura*," she said miserably. She put her hand over her eyes and leaned her forehead against the window. Her hair had come partly loose, but she didn't care, didn't try to repair it. She was struggling too hard not to weep.

"Is that what happened?" she asked bitterly. "For a minute you had Laura back? You couldn't get her, so for a minute *I'd* do?"

"No." He reached out, touching her arm. She flinched feeling utterly devastated and betrayed. Worse, she had betrayed herself.

"*No*," he repeated, anger in his voice. "That's not it."

"Then why'd you do it?" she asked, her hand covering her eyes.

"I did it because I couldn't help it. I don't know why. I had to do it."

"Why?" she demanded unhappily. "*Why?* It's not fair."

"Because," he said, his voice somber. "It happened... because."

He touched her arm again. Again she flinched, but this time he grasped her just above the elbow. "Look me in the eye, Susannah," he said. "Come on. Don't cry. Please don't cry. Look at me. Please."

He gripped her more possessively. Half frightened, half resentful, she turned to him, teary eyed.

"It happened because you understand," he said, almost accusingly. "You know what I mean. Don't you?"

She knew what he meant: She had been hypercharged with energy from her encounter with Fish. She'd felt the thrill she knew he felt in his work. She understood him. And he knew it, and understood her in return.

Wordlessly she nodded. A tear spilled onto her cheek, and she hated the feel of it, its wet heat on her cheek.

He shook his head, as if he were almost as bewildered as she was. He raised his free hand, reached gently under her glasses, and wiped the tear away with his thumb.

"There's more," he said, settling his hand on her bare shoulder. A disgusted expression crossed his face. "I was jealous," he said with reluctance. "I didn't like Fish talking to you like that. I didn't like you making up to him—even a little. I hadn't expected that. I was . . . *very* jealous."

She looked at him warily. "You—jealous of me?"

"Yeah," he replied, his eyes on her lips.

"But," she said shakily, "you're in love with Laura."

His hand tightened on her shoulder. For once in his life, he seemed to have trouble finding words. "I . . . could have been wrong about that," he said.

Her heart leaped with impossible hope. "You loved her for years," she said, her voice trembling. "You wanted to marry her. You said you'd love her forever."

"Susannah—" He took a deep breath, and once more seemed at a loss for words. Pulling his hands away, he locked them on the steering wheel and stared out at the lake. "I gotta think," he said. "We've gotta think. I mean, I'm *surprised* by

this. How'd I get you into this? How'm I gonna get you out?
Look—when this is over—"

She held her breath, watching him. He was so obviously
in conflict with himself that she was amazed. His face was
taut and the muscles in his arms were tensed.

"Yes?" she breathed. "When this is over?"

"When this is over," he said grimly. "Then we talk about—
us. About you and me. Because you really did, Chiquita, you
took me off guard."

"I . . . did?"

"Look," he said, a muscle in his cheek twitching, "I came
to my senses long enough to realize I shouldn't make love to
you at high noon in a public place in a car. Especially one
with—goddamn!—dual bucket seats."

"Make love to me?" she echoed weakly.

He ran his hand over his hair. "Oh, that's where it was going. And we can't do that."

Susannah could think of nothing to say. With a surge of
guilt she realized what he said was true. If circumstances had
been different, they probably *would* be making love. She
would have been helpless to resist.

Embarrassed, she took off her glasses. She stared down at
them in her lap, bending and unbending the earpieces.

"I do not," he said from between his teeth, "get sexually
involved with a woman on a case. I do not. It's not—professional. I never have. I never will."

He took another deep breath. "I never made love to your
sister, you know that? I don't know if she told you that. I
wouldn't. It wouldn't have been right."

She looked at him again, startled. He was staring out at the
lake. She had always assumed he had made love to Laura; he
seemed like such a sexual person.

"Maybe that's why I carried the torch for so long. You
know. The unattainable. Oh, hell."

*I'm attainable. I'm altogether too attainable. It probably
scares him.*

He made a tense gesture with one hand. He kept staring at the lake. "When this is over . . . When this is over . . ."

"When this is over—what?"

"I don't know," he said, looking troubled. "I guess we'll see, won't we?"

"Will we?"

"Yeah," he said, not glancing at her. "We will. But for God's sake, Susannah, make me behave. I gotta take care of you, see? We can't make this any more complicated than it is. It's too dangerous."

She shook her head, not understanding. "But you said it wasn't dangerous. Not really."

His gaze met hers, jarring her to the marrow of her bones. "Baby," he said quietly, "it's always dangerous."

*NOW WHAT HAVE I DONE?* Gus thought once they were back at the motel. He'd taken Susannah to the hairdresser, and her hair looked okay, he guessed, in a retro-sixties way. But he liked it better loose. He remembered, back in Arkansas, when Laura and Jarod were hunting for Tim, seeing Susannah with her long hair down.

Now she was in the next room, curled up on her bed with a book, of course. She'd brought a damned nightcase full of books with her.

If he got up from his recording equipment and computer, he could go in, take the book out of her hand, and let her curl up with him instead. His thoughts were so lecherous they put him in physical pain.

But this was *Susannah*, he kept telling himself in disbelief. How had this happened to him? Why hadn't he seen it coming? Or *had* he?

Was that why he had gone back for her, brought her here? But this was Laura's sister, for God's sake. It was practically incestuous, wasn't it? Yet Laura had never made him feel like this. Never. He'd tried to tell that to Susannah. But he didn't know how.

He didn't know how to say anything to her, dammit. He didn't because he himself didn't yet understand what he felt. He'd meant what he'd told her, though; they couldn't get sexually entangled while working—they'd start flying too high. They'd lose their edge.

He had to stay focused. So did she. In the meantime, how did they go back to small talk after what had happened between them? Now it was more important than ever to keep her safe, because it somehow felt as if she ought to be *his*.

He grumbled to himself, he swore eloquently in Spanish, but he couldn't get her out of his head. He tried to concentrate on monitoring Fish's phone calls from his tapes. They were boring as hell.

He sat, listening to the tapes on his earphones, and idly he punched up the computer buttons to tap into Fish's E-mail. Nothing new. No more gardening hints from Maude Ann Hawkins. No more would-be Audreys applying for the position of electronic pen pal.

And Fish—from the lack of printouts on the computer—had not communicated with anyone by that system, either. Gus swore and listened to a call Fish had logged shortly after Susannah had left his office. He was griping to a printer about a recent batch of posters for the Waltzing Fountains.

The conversation ended. There was a moment of silence until the next recorded call, which had come in three minutes later. The time flashed on the recorder's digital clock.

On the tape, Fish answered the phone. The caller identified himself as Lem Colter. Gus's ears pricked up. Lem Colter was the live-in boyfriend of Nora Geddes, Fish's secretary who'd been arrested.

Gus turned the volume up. Lem Colter had a low, whispery voice, and he sounded hesitant.

"I want to thank you, Mr. Fish," Colter said, "for posting bond for Nora."

"I was glad to do it," Fish said bruskly.

There was a moment's pause. "Nora got your notice that she's fired. Listen, Mr. Fish, she's very hurt. I am, too. She needs that job. We need that money."

Fish's voice grew cold. "I gave her a month's severance pay. It was more than generous."

"Mr. Fish, Nora isn't a criminal. She's got a little problem, is all. She needs *help*."

"See that she gets it."

"She needs your support, Mr. Fish," Colter wheedled. "It ain't right to fire her."

"My secretary must be above suspicion," Fish said stiffly. "Nora stole. I paid her well, but she stole. I consider myself—betrayed."

"Mr. Fish, it ain't right. Also, I got notice today that *I'm* fired. I been working backstage at the Waltzing Fountains for two years, Mr. Fish. I didn't do anything wrong. Why am I fired? Because of Nora? This ain't *right*."

Fish was not moved. "You got severance pay, too. I think it would be best for you and Nora to leave Branson, Colter. Our relationship is over. And now, good day. I have to—"

"Don't cut me off, dammit," Colter said, his voice suddenly fierce. "This isn't right. Nora and I put up with a lot from you. I turned my eyes the other way a long time. I even tried to help you about—you know. You're the reason she got so nervous. Look, give us our jobs back. She'll get help. She never took anything very big—except for that jewelry, a couple CDs. It was all *little* stuff."

There was a beat of silence. When Fish spoke it was in a controlled snarl. "Colter, Nora's and my relationship was—deteriorating. I overlooked it too long. Now I have no choice. If she steals from stores, she could steal from me. I can't chance that. Good day."

"No! Don't hang up. She never stole anything from you. But wait—she did 'borrow' something. Something you'd be interested in. She copied some papers. Private papers."

"What?" Fish's voice went chillingly cautious.

Colter sounded almost desperate. "Some private papers.
Nora's seen a lot goin' on in that office, Mr. Fish. That's another reason she's . . . nervous. I told her she needed insur-
ance. In case you ever pulled something like this. You want
us to leave Branson? Fine. But we're gonna need traveling
money, Mr. Fish. A decent amount."

"What papers are you talking about?" Fish demanded in
the same malevolent tone.

"I'll put it this way: the papers you'd least like to have fall
into the wrong hands, Mr. Fish. I'll let you use your imagination."

Fish was silent for a long moment. "How much do you
want?" he asked at last.

"A hundred thousand," Colter said, bold now. "A hundred thousand dollars is what we want. And we want it *now*."

"Precisely when do you mean by 'now,' Mr. Colter?" Fish
asked.

"Tonight. I'll be out of this town plenty fast, then. Nora'll
leave as soon as she's been before the judge. You can kiss us
goodbye. But you'll do it fair, you'll do it right, by God."

"Fair," Fish repeated. He put soft malice into the word.

"Yeah," Colter said. "I want to meet you. I'll tell you when
and where."

"No," Fish said smoothly. "I'll tell you. I'll send someone
to make an appointment. Where are you?"

Gus cursed under his breath. *Make the appointment now.
So I can hear it, dammit. Say it.*

"I'm not home," Colter said. "I'm at the outlet mall. The
one by your office. At the pay phone by the toy store."

"Stay right there. I'll send someone."

Gus swore again and looked at his watch. The call had been
made hours ago. It was almost three o'clock. Who knew
where Colter was by now, or what Fish's emissary had told
him? Gus's only hope was that Fish's next call might tip him
off.

Colter said, "Make it fast," then hung up.

Fish had wasted no time in making another phone call.

"Yes?" said a voice.

"Randolph?" said Fish. "I want you here immediately."

"You got it. See you."

Gus swore again. Randolph, he knew, was a nondescript man who worked behind the scenes at the Dusty Lester Show. He'd struck Gus as treacherous.

Fish's next call was made less than a minute later. It was to someone he didn't call by name, but who had an Eastern accent.

"Black bugs," Fish said cryptically.

"*Don't* spray unless necessary," answered the voice.

"Yes," said Fish.

"Be careful. Too much spray can harm you."

"Yes," Fish said again and hung up.

"Damn," muttered Gus. Blackmail, black bugs— What in hell *was* this? He listened through the rest of the calls on the tape, hoping for more information, but there was nothing.

He took off the headphones. He'd call the local police to keep an eye out for both Colter and Nora Geddes. He didn't quite know what was going down, but he didn't like it. Nobody had counted on *this.*

Gus phoned the Bureau first, to get an okay. He got Olivier's assistant, Brightman. He felt lucky. Brightman could think fast, make a quick decision.

"We got a blackmail threat coming down on Fish from a guy named Colter," Gus said. "Fish's ex-secretary's boyfriend. He says he's got something that's worth a hundred thousand. He wants the money tonight. Call the locals?"

"Affirmative," Brightman said. "But be discreet. Just surveillance. No busts until we get a better picture."

"Right."

"By the way, how's the girl?" Brightman asked, meaning Susannah. "Good as you thought?"

"Too damn good," Gus said. "Yeah. Perfect. Listen: Anything new about Marty the Mouse?"

"Nothing. He's like fallen off the edge of the earth. His girlfriend's hysterical. She thinks something's happened. Could be right. It doesn't smell good."

"No."

"But we don't know that it's got any connection with you down there. Olivier's not excited. He never is. But keep your eyes open. Any more of those garden notes?"

Gus told him about Fish's call about the black bugs.

"Interesting," Brightman said with scientific coolness.

"Listen, if this *should* get rough," Gus said, "I'm gonna pull the girl off it right away. She's not a pro, you know. I mean she's really smart, but she's not a pro."

"Olivier wouldn't like that," Brightman cautioned. "You know that. We got her where we want her. Keep her there as long as possible."

"Right. I'm just saying—"

"I know what you're saying. And you know what Olivier would say. Listen—don't get hinky over her. Repeat: Keep her there as long as possible. Over and out, Raphael—I got a call on another line."

"Don't get hinky," Gus mocked after he hung up. "If I was any hinkier I'd hink myself to death."

He dialed the local police and asked to talk to Lieutenant Bobby Chelsea who was his liaison on the case.

"Look," Gus said. "We need a little discreet surveillance on Lem Colter, Nora Geddes's boyfriend. On her, too. We've got something—"

"Repeat that," Bobby Chelsea demanded. He had a deep Southern voice. It reverberated ominously. "Say that again."

Gus sighed with impatience. "We need discreet surveillance on Lem Colter—"

"I don't think so," Bobby Chelsea said grimly. "Lem Colter's not going anywhere. He's dead."

Gus's skin went cold. "He's *what?*"

"Dead," Chelsea said emphatically. "He was crossing the highway down by the outlet mall. A drunk hit him."

*No.* "What are you telling me?"

"I'm telling you a drunk hit him, killed him. Eleven-forty this morning. He's dead, he's a stiff, he's bagged."

"Gone?" Gus demanded, incredulous. "You say this is an accident?"

"We got nothing else to call it, Raphael. The driver's in the drunk tank right now. He admits it."

Gus shook his head. He couldn't believe it. "Who is he?"

"A guy named Dunwoody. New in town. Looking for work. A loser. Now—why were you concerned about Colter?"

Gus explained, as tersely as he could. "Listen, Chelsea, I don't like this. Colter threatens Fish with blackmail—thirty minutes later, Colter's dead? It's an accident? I'm not buying this."

"It's all I got to sell. He's dead, and we're holding the guy who did it. He's cryin' and prayin'. I'd be cryin' and prayin', too, in his shoes."

Gus gripped the receiver more tightly. "Nora Geddes," he said from between his teeth. "Keep an eye on Nora Geddes, then, dammit. Before some 'drunk' hits her, too. And run a check on this 'drunk's' prints."

"You're paranoid. But if you want it, you got it."

Gus hung up. He felt as if somebody had punched him in the stomach, hard. *Santa Maria, what's happening here? It's turning crazy.*

He dialed headquarters again. This time he wasn't as lucky. Olivier was back at his desk. Gus told him the news. Olivier was as emotionally detached as ever. "Odd," he said. "Sit tight."

"What do you mean, sit tight?" Gus protested. "I got a woman here to worry about. An *inexperienced* woman."

"You wanted her. It wasn't my idea. Don't complain. Brightman says she's in place. Keep her there. Does she know about this? About the blackmail? About Colter being killed?"

"No."

"Does she know about Colter at all?"

"No."

"Don't tell her about the blackmail. Don't spook her."

"Don't tell her? Listen, I got an obligation—"

"You got an obligation to your country. You got an obligation to the law and to this organization. We've got everything in place. We're poised and ready. Don't screw with it."

"I can't hold out on her," Gus protested. "It's not right."

"Look—you want her as safe as possible? Keep her as coolheaded as possible. The less nervous she is, the better off she is, right?"

"Right, but—"

"So mention Colter's dead. She'll hear about it anyway. Don't say any more than you have to, dammit. Keep it to yourself. For her own good."

"But—"

"Consider it an order, Raphael. Are you hung up on her or something?"

"I'm *concerned*."

"Then do her a favor. Keep her in the dark, she's better off. That, I repeat, is an order."

Gus hung up the phone. He felt as if something inside him had broken and was cutting him. Once he had lied to Laura because he had to, because it was his job.

Now he was doing it to Susannah.

And something was *wrong* in Branson. He could sense it. Something dangerous, and it was coiling tighter and tighter around them, like a cobra. He *felt* it. He *knew* it.

But he went to the door, unlocked it, and told Susannah that Lem Colter was dead. It was an accident, he told her. Nothing to worry about.

He was an excellent liar when he wanted to be.

And she believed him. "If that's what you say, all right," she'd said at last. "I trust you."

*I trust you.*

Nobody should trust him. Nobody.

## 7

"WHY ARE YOU SO . . . gloomy?" Susannah asked during supper.

Gus had gone out and brought them back Chinese take-out food. For a man bearing moo shoo pork and fortune cookies, his mood seemed impossibly grim.

He picked at his food, saying nothing. Finally he pushed it away, rose, and made himself a plain peanut-butter sandwich on white bread and opened a can of cola. Looking both angry and remorseful, he took a bite of the sandwich.

"What's wrong?" she demanded. "Something's bothering you. Is it this Colter business? It is, isn't it?"

"No," he replied. He managed to say it acerbically, even with peanut butter in his mouth.

Susannah was puzzled. She knew he was worried, deeply worried. If not about Colter, then what? Was it because of their scene by the lake? Did he regret it?

She attempted to clear the air. "You told me not to worry about Colter. You said it's an accident. If that's true, then what's wrong? Tell me. And we've got perfectly fine food here. Why are you eating peanut butter?"

He didn't look at her, his expression bordering on hostile. "I *like* peanut butter."

"But with no butter or jelly or anything?" she asked with distaste. "Why?"

"Because that's how I always eat it." He took a long pull from the cola can.

"The only supplies you've got are cola, coffee, peanut butter, milk, and cornflakes," she said. "Don't you think that's . . . odd?"

"No," he said and looked irritated that she would dare ask.

"Well, I'd think a man like you—I mean, the way you usually dress—would be a gourmet. You'd like fine wines. Things like that. Not cola out of the can."

He shrugged. "Off duty I can be a gourmet. On, I want soul food."

She raised a dubious eyebrow. "Peanut butter and cornflakes are soul food?"

"They're *my* soul food, all right? What'd you think: I grew up on tacos and Spanish rice or something?"

His response piqued her. "I don't think in stereotypes," she countered. "And I don't know anything about how you grew up. You never talk about it. Why?"

"Don't ask."

Susannah lost patience, and threw down her paper napkin. "Dammit, Gus, I *am* asking. Why are you being so mysterious? Is that why you told Laura so many lies? Because you don't want to tell anybody the truth?"

He finished his sandwich and wiped his mouth with the back of his hand. He stared at her, his face unreadable. "I don't think I've ever heard you swear before. You shouldn't swear. You're a nice girl. That's one of the things I like about you. You're a nice girl."

"What about you?" she asked, her frustration mounting. "Were you a nice boy?"

"Do I *look* like I was a nice boy?" he asked with a sarcastic nod at his tattooed arms. He rose from the table and went to the cupboard.

"No. Now what are you doing?"

"I want a bowl of cornflakes. You object?"

"No," she said, pushing her own food away. She was no longer hungry. "Don't talk. See if I care." She crossed her arms and stared unhappily at the dirty window.

He sat down with his cornflakes, and she heard the crunch when he took the first bite. *I thought I understood this man,* she thought fatalistically. *I'll never understand him.*

There was a moment of tense silence, broken only by his crunching of his accursed cornflakes.

"All right," he said at last. "You wanna know about me? Why I eat like this? I don't *know* why I eat like this. It's how I ate as a kid, is all. This is what I ate. This."

Reluctantly, she glanced at him. "That's all?"

"Look," he said, his lip curling slightly. "I lived with my grandma. She worked in a factory. She was gone all the time. She'd leave me food I could fix. This."

"Cornflakes and peanut butter?" Susannah said in horror. "That's all?"

"Hey. She didn't have a lot of choice. And she wasn't so crazy to have me around, frankly."

"And your mother?"

He poured more milk on his cornflakes. "We never talked about her."

"Don't you know anything about her?" Susannah asked, her anger forgotten. Her sympathies were always easily evoked.

"Yeah." He cocked his head cynically. "She was a junkie. She died when I was sixteen. Hepatitis, the death certificate said. Probably from needles."

"I'm sorry," she said, which seemed a supremely inadequate thing to say. She studied his dark face, which at times seemed gaunt, and at other times handsome, and more often seemed both at once.

"Would you like to know about my father?" he asked with sarcasm. "So would I. I've got no idea, except he was probably Puerto Rican, too. This face—a hundred-percent home boy, right?"

"It looks like a fine face to me," she said tightly.

"I tried to be all home-boy here, too," he said, putting his fist over his heart. "I hung out. I stole. I was the best thief in my gang. I fought. I cut a couple of guys in my time. All right—you want the whole truth? I shot a little smack, too. Only it musta been bad stuff, 'cause it made me sick, is all. I didn't like it. Lucky me."

Tears came to her eyes. "All right. I understand. You don't have to talk about it."

"No. You *don't* understand," he said. There was anger in his voice, but whether toward himself or her, she couldn't tell. "Maybe you should. 'Cause you should know exactly what you're getting tangled up with, Chiquita. It'll give you second thoughts. To tell the truth, you ought to have 'em. I ain't country club."

Angry at herself, she forced the tears back. "All right," she said. "So what happened? How'd you escape your life of fabulous crime?"

"The hard way," he said, his face stony. "I got shot."

"*Shot?*"

"Yeah. My gang and another gang, we...fought. Bad. The cops came. There was shooting. I got shot."

"Where?"

"The gut."

She winced. "How?"

"A cop," he said with strange passion. "He nearly killed me. Instead he saved my life."

"How?"

His mouth slanted, and frown lines appeared between his brows. "His name was Pete Domingo. And he felt *guilty.* So he took me, like, under his wing. I got out of the hospital, he took me home with him. My grandma said, 'Take him. He's *un demonio*. He's yours.'"

"And...he changed you? Did he have a family?"

"He had a wife. They didn't have kids. No, they didn't *change* me," he said contemptuously. "Not just like *that.* You think I got no character? I ran away a million times."

Susannah looked away from him in despair. "How did you change, then? Because you must have."

He gave her a sarcastic smile. "He felt so guilty, he made himself be patient, poor bastard. You know what I used to do at their house? I'd take things apart. Their radio. Their toaster. Their television. Their telephone. One time their electric stove."

"And *that* changed you? Electronics, I mean?"

He frowned and shook his head. "I don't know. Christ, I was only thirteen when they took me in. All I'd eat was peanut butter and cornflakes, and I stole from them.... I really was an animal."

"Gus," she said, her throat tight, "you were only thirteen. How did they get through to you? How did they help you?"

He shook his head again. "Hell, I don't know. Maybe they had me exorcised in my sleep or something. Secretly, I was kind of impressed he was a cop. Secretly, I got to like her—a lot. She got me nice clothes. I liked that, too. And there were always cops over at the house. And some of 'em were, like, righteous dudes. Very tough, you know? And bloods—like me. I saw people like me could have *authority*. Be somebody, you know?"

She nodded although she knew nothing of city policemen. She tried to imagine how policemen had appeared to his young, cynical eyes.

"When I was fourteen," he said, "Pete's cousin comes to visit. This man was FBI. I was *really* impressed. I mean, this was a class act. This was something."

"He was . . . kind?" she ventured. "He encouraged you?"

"No," Gus said. "He was actually an arrogant fart. But— hey—I was *into* arrogance, you know? And he was into electronic surveillance and all, and I thought, hey, I can do *that*. I'd say, show me how to do this. He wouldn't. So I'd try it on my own. And know what? I could do it. I got obssessed by it. And by the FBI. So here I am. So what else you gotta know?"

She studied him. He'd regained his self-mocking air. He pushed away his cereal bowl.

"What happened to them?" she asked. "Your . . . foster parents or whatever they were?"

His face didn't soften. "Pete died a year after I got out of the Academy. Maria, she's still in Manhattan."

"You stay in touch?"

He looked almost offended. "Of course. You think I'm an ingrate? Yeah. I go see her every Christmas. And Valentine's Day, and Mother's Day, and her birthday, if I can. And if I can't get there, I call her and stuff. Last Christmas I gave her a trip to San Juan. She says, 'It's too much, too much.' I tell her, 'For you, nothing is too much. You're a saint.' It's true."

She managed to smile, glad he had someone. And somehow, she wasn't surprised at either his generosity or his sentimentality.

"So," he said, slapping the table, "that's the stinking story of my life. I should have had violins behind me when I told it. It would have been more poignant and all."

"Did you . . ." she hesitated. "Did you ever tell Maria about—how you felt about Laura?"

For a moment, he didn't answer. "Yeah. I told her. Just after we'd met."

"And?"

"And she said she was glad I'd finally found a nice girl. I'd never been interested in nice girls."

"And . . . when it didn't work out?"

She lifted her eyes to his. He gave her a funny, self-conscious smile. "She said she'd pray for me. That I'd find another nice girl."

"Oh." She rose and started to clear the table.

He crossed his arms. The look he gave her was almost challenging. "You. You're a minister's daughter. You must believe in prayer, right?"

She made a helpless gesture. "I used to. After the accident—my father and Tim—I don't know anymore. . . . What about you?" she asked. "When's the last time you prayed?"

He looked momentarily taken aback, then shrugged casually. "A long time ago. A long, long time."

"When?"

His face grew solemn, thoughtful. "When I was shot, I guess."

A frisson of terror chilled her. She thought of him, little more than a child, lying in the street in his own blood. "What did you pray?"

"To die," he told her. "I prayed to God to let me die."

A pain shot through her chest. "But He didn't."

"No," Gus said. "He didn't."

She turned to the counter and set down the remains of their supper.

"I've got to go to work," he said.

She nodded. She didn't turn. She heard him rise from his chair. She heard him move behind her. She felt his nearness at her back.

He slipped his arms around her waist, and she suddenly felt faint with feeling for him. He drew her close, he rested his chin on her shoulder, his cheek touching hers. He did nothing else. He merely held her. She closed her eyes and held her breath.

"When this is over—" he said softly in her ear.

But he didn't finish the sentence, and neither did she. They simply stood, close, his arms around her.

And then he had to leave. "Be a good girl," he said, kissing the nape of her neck. "Lock the door between our rooms tonight. Promise me."

She nodded. But it was a promise she didn't want, at all, to keep. "I promise," she said, and had to bite her lip.

She locked the door that night when she went to bed. She heard him when he came in, after midnight, using the separate entrance. She could feel his presence so strongly on the other side of the door that it was eerie, like a clairvoyant experience.

But he didn't knock at her door. He didn't try the lock. He didn't call to her.

ONCE AGAIN, WHEN THEY rose in the morning, they found themselves awkward with each other. Once again, they had a nearly silent breakfast. Gus had cornflakes, and she found she was having them, too, as if they were sharing some strange, secular communion.

He let her walk to Fish's by herself, and she was more nervous than she admitted. Her new hairstyle included bangs, which she kept wanting to brush out of her way. She wore her contacts and struggled not to squint. She missed her big glasses, which always felt to her like a safety barrier between herself and the world.

She wore one of the dresses Gus had chosen for her. It was expensively simple. Dark green with short sleeves, it had a tight waist and a full skirt. Her makeup, Gus had assured her, was impeccable. The problem was that when she looked in the mirror she didn't recognize herself.

But, she thought, stepping into the lobby of Fish's building, she wasn't *supposed* to be herself. That was the point.

Pinned beneath her belt again was the tiny bug that could pick up Fish's voice when he was in the same room with her. In her purse was the tape dispenser containing the stronger bug, the one Gus wanted in Fish's office.

Well, if he wanted it in Fish's office, she would, by God, get it there. Somehow she knew she would.

Once again, when she pushed the elevator button, she experienced a rush of excitement so strong it was almost sexual. Although she was nervous, she was also exultant.

Once more she had the same unbidden thought that had assailed her yesterday: *I love doing this. It makes me feel alive.*

She stepped out of the elevator and into the reception area. Ginger hadn't yet arrived. It was still five minutes until nine o'clock. But the miniature fountains were already spouting and changing colors.

Susannah opened the door to Fish's outer office, where she was to reign. The fountains before her desk were also already at play. The piped-in music echoed softly—an orchestral version of the score of *My Fair Lady*.

She was surprised to see Fish in the room, sitting at her desk, going through its drawers. But she hid any emotion she felt behind a sweetly wide smile. "*Good* morning, Mr. Fish," she said.

Fish seemed strangely startled to see her. He sucked in his breath and his expression grew vaguely trancelike. "Miss Fingal," he breathed.

"On the job and ready to start." She cocked her head like an extremely eager-to-please early bird.

He stuffed something into a large manila envelope, licked the flap and sealed it. He set the envelope aside, then rose. He looked her up and down, pleasure kindling in his cold eyes.

"*Miss* Fingal," he repeated, his voice low. "You are a vision. A vision. Thank you. You're kind. Very kind."

Susannah smiled more shyly. "Kind?" she echoed, as if she didn't understand.

Fish stepped from behind the desk and came to her side. He took her by the arm. She battled her urge to flinch.

He stared into her eyes. "You've granted my foolish wishes," he said. "Your eyes . . . Without those glasses, your eyes are almost as lovely as *hers*."

"Hers?" Susannah said weakly.

"The woman who ate breakfast at Tiffany's," Fish said reverently. "And your hair—your hair is nearly perfect. But you must stop at Miss Teagle's every day before coming here. Have it combed out so it's quite perfect. She's open at eight-thirty. It's on the company tab."

*This man really is insane*, Susannah thought, watching, warily, as his eyes seemed to eat her up.

He raised his hand so that it hovered perilously near her hair, almost, but not quite touching it. "That color," he said, his voice strained. "Why did no one ever think of that color before? Oh, Miss Fingal, I want you to be very happy here."

"I'm sure I will," she breathed, praying he wouldn't touch her.

"I'll do everything in my power to see that you are," he said ardently. Then he dropped his hands and took a step backward. He clasped his hands behind him, squared his shoulders, and looked at her knees. "And I hope you won't take it wrongly if I ask about . . . the other? You know?"

He rocked slightly on the balls of his feet. He gazed more fixedly at her legs, her skirt.

"Oh—that," she said as primly as she could. "Yes. It's . . . taken care of."

Fish rocked again slightly. He wet his upper lip with the tip of his tongue. "I'm not a suspicious man. But, uh, would you grant me a little . . . a very little inspection?"

Susannah felt her smile growing more sickly. But she reached down with one hand and grasped the hem of her dress. *I can't believe I'm doing this,* she thought, but started to lift the skirt.

"No!" The sharpness of his command made her wince. She paused.

Fish's body grew tense, and he licked his lip again, his eyes locked on her hand. "Slowly," he cautioned. "Slowly."

She set her jaw gamely. With teasing slowness she lifted her skirt until Fish could see the top of her stocking and the black straps of the garter belt.

He nodded stiffly when she had raised the hem high enough. She stopped. He stared for fully forty-five seconds at her thigh.

Then he nodded again. "Thank you," he said, his voice tight. "Thank you."

Then he wheeled away without another word, and picked up the envelope from the desk, walked into his private office and closed the door behind him.

*Dirty old man*, Susannah thought, her face hot with resentment. No wonder Nora Geddes's nerves had snapped.

How demeaning to be subjected to Fish's "inspection," day after day.

The door to the outer office opened, and Ginger peered in. "Ga," she said, staring at Susannah. "You're early. And you look fabulous. Hey, you look almost *too* good."

"What do you mean?"

"Hey," Ginger said with a sly smile. "Don't drive him out of his mind, okay? If you don't watch it, you might put him right over the edge."

"What edge?" Susannah asked, eyeing Ginger carefully. She wasn't sure whether or not the other woman was kidding.

"You know," Ginger said with a wicked toss of her head. "The *edge*."

Mentally Susannah uttered a word she had never said and would never say aloud.

GUS HEARD WHAT GINGER said, and he used the worst word he knew. He spoke to Susannah even though he knew she couldn't hear. "Stay cool, baby. Cool. Stay cool for me, okay?"

Then he swore again. He'd been swearing all morning.

He'd sworn at Bobby Chelsea of the Branson police. "I don't care if that drunk's prints aren't on file anyplace. Keep checking, dammit."

"Look, Raphael," Chelsea had protested, "we've gone to the central computer, national. But we have to stand in line. If the information's there, we'll get it eventually."

"Screw eventually. I'll lean on D.C. I want it now. And if you don't get it outta this country, try Canada."

"Canada?" Bobby Chelsea almost howled. "What you want, boy? I call in *Mounties?*"

"You heard me. You watchin' Nora Geddes, for God's sake?"

"Yes, we're watching Nora Geddes."

"And?"

"And nobody's come around her. She took a cab to the mortuary to see her boyfriend. She broke down and cried. The funeral director had to call a doctor, get her a sedative, drive her home."

"You keeping watch on her full-time?"

"Yes, dammit, full-time."

The exchange grew more tense and less polite. When Gus hung up, he said, "What a bubba."

He dialed headquarters and talked to Olivier, telling him to do whatever it took to speed up the fingerprint search on the drunk that had hit Colter.

"Don't go off on a tangent," Olivier said coldly.

"I'm not on an effing tangent. And what's coming in from St. Louis? On Marty the Mouse?"

"I can tell you in one word—nothing."

"He's still missing."

"Affirmative."

"The Mouse was going to rat," Gus said between his teeth. "Who was he was gonna rat on? And about what?"

"He was being mysterious," said Olivier. "He acted as if he had something big. Probably exaggerating."

Gus grumbled something under his breath.

"One thing at a time," Olivier advised blandly. "What you got there? Anything on his phones? On his computer?"

"Nothing on the phones. CommuCate isn't working since early last night. Can't get into the system. It's down."

"What's wrong?"

"I called them. It's technical. You got me any information on who Maude Ann Hawkins is—or isn't?"

"We're working on it. Be patient."

"Patient? We're the effing FBI. We're supposed to have this stuff at our fingertips—"

"Whoever she is, she's been sending these things from a public library in Passaic, New Jersey. I tell you, we're working on it."

"I hate public libraries. I *hate* them," Gus muttered. Libraries were fine as long as people put only books and records in them. But then some insane progressive wanted computers and computer services like CommuCate. Any crook in America could walk into a public library and zap a message anywhere about anything—including murder.

A red light began to flash on one of Gus's recording machines. It meant that Fish was using his private office phone. "Look," he pleaded with Olivier, "get me some information, will you? I'm getting extra-strong vibes on this. Extra strong."

"Drink less coffee," Olivier said.

Gus hung up. "Jerk," he said, glaring at the phone as if he could somehow curse Olivier with the evil eye.

He snatched up an earphone and listened in on Fish's current phone conversation. Fish was again haggling with the printer about the posters for the Waltzing Fountains. At last he hung up.

"Cheapskate," Gus grumbled. He put aside the earphone and took up another connected to another recorder. It was the wire to the bug Susannah wore in her belt. He wanted to see how she was doing. It was nearly eleven o'clock.

"...brought some fresh office supplies for the laser-printer station," Susannah was saying her voice echoing like a spirit's in his ear.

His spine tensed. He drew in his breath and picked up a second earphone, the wire to the big bug, the one in the tape dispenser. He could hear exactly the same thing on that wire, only louder.

"You're efficient, Miss Fingal," he heard Fish say, the voice coming in stereo, from each earphone, from each bug.

She was doing it, he thought with tense satisfaction. She was getting Billy the Big Bug right in the inner sanctum. It had taken her only slightly more than two hours.

"Chiquita," he said, listening and shaking his head, "you are good. You're the only one I can depend on."

*Oh, baby, baby,* he thought, his heart tightening with excitement. *Oh, yes. Oh, yes.*

"Miss Fingal," said Fish in a silky voice, "I have a special job for you."

"Certainly," said Susannah—too eagerly for Gus's taste. *If he wants to look up your skirt again, I'll kill him.*

"I don't know if you're aware of it," said Fish, "but your, uh, predecessor's had something of a tragedy."

Damn! Gus thought. What was this? Why was Fish bringing up Nora Geddes? Was he going to talk about Colter's death? Would it shake up Susannah? Would she be caught off guard?

But Susannah's response was careful, measured, polite. "A tragedy?"

Fish sighed. "I had to let her go on short notice because, well, frankly, she had trouble with the police: She was arrested, in fact. Poor girl. She needs help, actually. But I simply couldn't trust her in such a responsible position with her, uh, problems unresolved."

"Sometimes business and compassion conflict," Susannah said politely. "It's sad."

"She left some things behind, in her desk—your desk, now, actually," Fish said. "I put them in this envelope."

"Yes, sir?"

"Tell Ginger to take this over to her on her lunch hour, will you? I'd send it by courier, but that's so impersonal. I can't ask you to do it, of course. It would be insensitive to send her own replacement on the errand. For *both* of you. I must think of your feelings in this, too."

"Oh. Why, thank you."

"Poor girl," Fish said with sympathy. "Her troubles seem to come in bunches. She's had a personal loss, as well. I just read of it in the morning paper."

*I bet,* thought Gus, gritting his teeth.

"I'm sorry to hear it," Susannah said with just the right amount of regret.

*Good for you, baby. Good.*

"Phone the Ye Olde Azalea Florist Shoppe," Fish said. "Have a nice arrangement sent for the Colter service. Large, but not vulgar. Dignified. On the card, have them put, 'With Deepest Sympathy from Fish Enterprises.' Have them send it to the Berryman Funeral Home. Can you remember all that?"

"Yes, sir." Susannah seemed to hesitate a moment. "I hope her loss wasn't someone . . . close to her."

"A close friend, yes, I'm sorry to say," Fish said with apparent sadness. "But these things happen. In the midst of life—death."

There was a short silence, as if once again Susannah was hesitating. "Had this friend been . . . sick?" she asked.

Gus tensed so hard his muscles went ironlike. *Don't push it!* he thought. *Back off. Now. Don't make him suspicious.*

But Fish's response was smooth and immediate. "No. Car accident. The traffic in this town, it's no wonder."

Susannah gave a murmur of agreement.

Gus held his breath. *Don't ask anything else.*

"I'll take care of it right away," she said.

Gus exhaled with relief. *Now,* he prompted silently, *get out of his office.*

For a moment or so, there was nothing except a blurred static coming over the earphones, with music playing in the background.

Then he heard only the music in his right ear, from the big bug in Fish's office. But in his left, from the bug on Susannah's bra, he heard her voice, brisk and efficient, on the telephone.

"Yes?" she said, more naturally than he could have prayed for. "This is Miss Fingal of Fish Enterprises. I'd like a sympathy arrangement sent . . ."

*Yes,* he thought desperately, *that's it. The florist first. And look in the envelope. Look at it before you give it to Ginger. Look in it, baby. Be careful—but look.*

He was willing her to do so, to do so carefully and quickly. He willed it so hard that his stomach knotted and his heart seemed to have jumped into his throat.

*The envelope, baby. Look in it!*

IN FISH'S OUTER OFFICE, Susannah sat, calmly repeating Fish's order to the florist.

While she talked, she picked up her letter opener and without hesitation slit the envelope open. Gus would want her to look inside. She could feel it.

Her only course was to act boldly. She had a drawerful of envelopes such as this. She would simply throw the open one away and reseal everything in a new one.

Fish might, of course, open the door before she was done, but that was a chance she had to take.

"Yes," she said to the florist. "Let's just double-check all that, shall we?"

And as the clerk repeated the order, Susannah looked into the envelope. Its contents jolted her.

Her heart began beating too fast, too hard.

# 8

THE CONTENTS OF the envelope hadn't just come out of Nora Geddes's desk. Fish must have merely made a show of cleaning out the drawers.

Susannah told the florist everything sounded fine and hung up. She gritted her teeth. Feeling herself going shaky, she willed her nerves to be steady.

In the envelope was money—a lot of money. Twenty-dollar bills were done up in packets. She calculated there must be fifty bills to a packet and there were twenty packets: $20,000.

There was also an airline ticket in a red, white and blue envelope. Susannah gritted her teeth harder, prayed Fish wouldn't catch her, and opened the ticket envelope.

The ticket was one-way to Denver, Colorado. The airline was U.S. Eagle. The flight was number 207 out of Springfield, Missouri. There was a change of planes in St. Louis to U.S. Eagle flight 119. The ticket was made out to Nora Geddes. She was to depart at 2:05 p.m. today.

*Today?* Susannah thought, alarm rising. If Nora Geddes left, wasn't she skipping bail? Shouldn't she be staying in Branson until her hearing? Was Fish encouraging the woman to run? Why?

Quickly Susannah memorized the flight numbers. She focused her concentration as sharply as she could and memorized the serial numbers of the top bills on three of the packets as well.

*I have to remember this,* she told herself desperately. *I must. But hurry! He can walk in on me any minute.*

Quickly, she took another envelope from her desk drawer. She transferred the ticket and money into it, then sealed it. She thrust the slit envelope into the wastebasket.

Her heart banged madly. She must get word to Gus as soon as possible. She would use the phone and ask that he come get her for lunch, but she was suddenly paranoid. Did Fish tap his own phones? Wouldn't it seem more natural if Gus called her?

She must seem as artless as possible. She rose from her desk, went into the reception area and handed the envelope to Ginger, giving her Fish's orders.

"Oh, Gawd," Ginger said with a sullen expression. "I don't want to face her. It's embarassing. Her stealing and all? Plus Lem getting killed. You know her boyfriend got killed, didn't you?"

Susannah nodded but tried to look blank. "Yes. I heard...a little bit about it."

"I'll have to say I'm sorry," Ginger said, her mouth petulant. "But I'm not. She should have dumped him. She probably wouldn't have *been* in this mess if Lem had stood up for her. If he'd supported her."

"What do you mean?" Susannah asked, trying to sound casual. "If he'd supported her?"

Ginger tossed her head. "I'm not even going to talk about it," she said darkly. "Just hope you *don't* find out."

Susannah stared at Ginger expectantly. But Ginger ignored her, as if determined to say no more.

*She wants to talk*, Susannah's instincts told her. *And she will talk, sooner or later. She just wants to seem important. She's playing games, that's all.*

"Ginger?" she said beseechingly. "What . . . ?"

"My lips," Ginger said with asperity, "are sealed." She nodded uncharitably toward Fish's office. "If I'm going to have to run errands for *him*, then I'm going to take an early lunch hour. Screw it."

She picked up her purse, pushed away from her desk, and stood. "If I was Nora, I'd just get out of this place. For good."

*Maybe she is,* Susannah thought. But she continued to seem bewildered. "Boy," she said pensively, "I hope my fiancé comes and takes me for lunch. I'm ready to see a familiar face and just relax—you know?"

Ginger pushed the elevator button. "Yeah," she said, unsmiling. "I know, all right."

"I really hope he'll show up," Susannah said, praying Gus was listening and that he would understand. The ticket and the money seemed of enormous importance, and Nora Geddes, if she used the ticket, was due to leave in less than three hours.

She only hoped that Gus would get the message.

GUS GOT THE MESSAGE, loud and clear. She'd slipped it in naturally; he was impressed. *Damn,* he thought, she was better than he could have hoped.

He gave her a minute or so to get back to her own office. Then he took the earphone from his ear, reached for the telephone and pushed the buttons of her number.

She answered on the second ring. "Denton Fish Enterprises, Unlimited," she said in her clear, bright voice. "Miss Fingal speaking."

"Hello, Miss Fingal," he said, sounding lackadaisical about it. "Wanna do lunch?"

"I'd *love* to," she answered. She said it just right—not too eager, not too gushy.

"I promised you burgers by the lake the other day. I didn't quite—deliver. Want to try again?"

"Absolutely."

"I'll be there at twelve sharp. I'll pick you up at your office."

"I could meet you outside."

"No," he said. "I'll come up for you."

He smiled slightly and hung up the receiver. He would go
to the office because he figured it was time that Fish got the
strong impression that Susannah was, completely and without compromise, the property of one Augusto Jesus Raphael, a very bad dude.

Fish needed to remember that. It would keep him on his
best behavior with Susannah, and that was necessary, for
Fish's very best behavior was none too good.

WHEN GUS STROLLED INTO Susannah's office, he did so with
slow insolence, like a tomcat on its home turf.

Fish had been standing behind Susannah as she sat at her
desk, showing him the record of ticket sales on her computer
screen. He had wanted, he'd said, to make sure she understood the system at Fish Enterprises. But he'd seemed more
interested in hanging over her, breathing on her neck.

She *felt* the difference in him the moment Gus appeared.
Fish tensed and edged back, away from her.

Relief washed over her. Gus had changed little about his
appearance. He wore the faded low-slung jeans and running
shoes so tattered they were a joke. His black T-shirt stretched
nicely across his wide shoulders, but was otherwise unremarkable. In his ear was a gold stud.

He gave Susannah a slow smile, one that was, in fact, quite
gentle. Yet every atom of his being seemed to exude subtle
menace. Susannah sensed it, and she knew that Fish could,
too.

Fish stepped away from Susannah and stood a few feet
from her side. Gus walked up to him and thrust out his hand
in greeting. It was a perfectly ordinary gesture. But, somehow, it carried a clear hint of threat.

Fish instinctively understood that implied threat; Susannah could see it in his face. He took Gus's hand and shook it
with pretended warmth. But wariness played across his features.

"Mr. Fish," Gus said affably. "I seen you 'round. I'm Augie Raphael. I work at the Dusty Lester Show. Pleased to meet you. I'm the fiancé of her—*la belleza*. The beauty." He gave Susannah a proprietary smile.

"Denton Fish," Fish said. He withdrew his hand, looking uncomfortable. Everything in Gus's manner seemed friendly and respectful enough, yet at the same time radiated warning.

*How does he do that?* Susannah regarded him with wonder. *Oh, I like it when he does that.*

"You're—a lucky man," Fish said, rubbing his hand as if Gus had squeezed it too tightly.

"Yeah." Gus shrugged. "Can she go? Or you got more stuff for her to do?"

Fish pushed back his cuff and glanced at his gold watch. "It's one minute after noon," he said. "Lunch hour is officially here. I must relinquish her."

"Thanks." Gus reached for Susannah's hand.

She gave it to him gratefully, gazing up at him with what she hoped seemed like adoration. She felt, in truth, that she didn't have to pretend to be starry-eyed.

With her free hand, she reached for her purse. Gus drew her to her feet and away from her desk, leading her to the middle of the floor, as if for a dance. He looked her up and down with such an air of possessiveness that her heart gave a pleasant shiver.

"She looks nice, eh?" Gus addressed the question to Fish, but didn't take his eyes off Susannah. "You got good taste, Mr. Fish. Her hair and everything. I always told her she should wear her contacts. Yeah. I like it. *All* of it."

He glanced at her legs and then at Fish. Susannah stiffened. Gus was telling Fish that he knew about the garter belt and "inspections," that he had given his permission for things to go that far, but no further.

Fish seemed to understand. His cold gaze met Gus's and held it. "Indeed," he said, clasping his hands behind him. He gave a noncommittal smile. "Well, be off, the two of you. Have a pleasant lunch."

"Thank you, Mr. Fish," Susannah said with her most innocent smile. And then Gus led her out of the office.

Neither of them said anything in the elevator or out on the street. They maintained a taut silence until they got into the Escort. Gus started the car and edged into the traffic.

"The envelope," he said, flashing her a dark glance. "You looked inside. Right?"

"Right," she said. Quickly she told him about the money and the one-way ticket to Colorado. She gave him the flight numbers, the time of departure, the time of arrival in Denver. She told him the serial numbers of the three bills, and wrote everything down on a scrap of paper before she could forget.

"Maybe I should have copied all the serial numbers," she said worriedly. "I was afraid to take the time. I was afraid to put anything on paper while I was there."

"You did fine, you did perfect," he said, pulling the car into the parking lot of a supermarket. "I gotta make a couple of calls. I'll be back in a few minutes."

She nodded, her face sober. She knew that he must call Washington with this information; he must notify local authorities, too. She wondered whether they would stop Nora Geddes or let her slip away.

Gus switched off the ignition. He leaned toward her. "And Chiquita," he said, softly but with great intensity, "you really were good. You did great."

He kissed her on the lips. It was a short kiss, but she sensed a turbulence behind it that shook her to her marrow. Then he was out of the car, striding away. Her eyes followed him to the pay phone on the outside wall of the supermarket.

He made two calls. Each time he spoke with an air of contained ferocity, and his face was as serious as death.

Within five minutes he was back in the car, his expression still tense.

"What are you going to do?" she asked, as he steered into the traffic again. "Will you let her go?"

"We have to," he said grimly. "If we pick her up, we'll tip off Fish. I don't like this."

"Why?"

"Because I don't understand it. Why's he doing it? Why's she? She'll get herself in trouble."

"Maybe it's like Ginger said," Susannah offered. "Maybe she just wants to get away from it all. Maybe too much has happened, and she can't cope."

"She's gonna miss her boyfriend's funeral? She lived with the dude six years."

"Maybe she can't face it."

He shrugged as if he didn't agree. "I don't like this," he repeated.

"So what's going to happen?"

"They'll tail her from here to Springfield, but won't stop her. There'll be a man waiting in Denver. To spot her. Keep an eye on her."

"And then?"

"Pick her up when all this is over. See what she knows or doesn't know."

"What does this whole thing mean?"

"I don't know," he said. "I've gotta think." He lapsed into worried silence.

He stopped at a Dairy Queen on the edge of Branson. Watching him come back to the car, she wondered if he was the only man in America who could look stormy and sexy with his hands full of burger bags.

He got back in the car and they drove on to the lake. He chose a different spot from yesterday, and she wondered if he did so to avoid memories of what had transpired between them before. Strange things were breaking in the case, and she knew that they both must stay cool and undistracted.

She tried to eat but didn't feel hungry. She gazed meditatively at a French fry. "Gus?"

He was eating slowly and staring at the lake. It lay as placid and deeply blue as the day before. "Yeah?" he said.

"Did you hear what Ginger said about Lem Colter? That she didn't like him? That he didn't stand up for Nora Geddes? That she might not be in trouble if he had?"

A frown line had formed between his brows. It deepened. "Yeah. I heard."

"What do you think *that* meant?"

"I don't know. It's the first I heard of it."

She sipped her cola. When she spoke again it was with deliberation, her voice thoughtful. "Fish said something about his relationship with Nora deteriorating. That her trouble with the police was the last straw. What was going wrong between them? Do you know?"

A second frown line appeared between his brows. "No. I don't."

She was silent a moment. She stirred the ice in her drink with a straw. "You've got someone else on the inside, don't you?" she said. "Besides me, I mean. Somebody's been feeding you information from within, haven't they?"

He glanced at her. If he was startled, he didn't show it. "Of course."

"Who is it?"

"I can't tell you." He glanced away again. He took another bite of hamburger and stared at the lake.

She kept stirring the ice. "All right," she said. "I think I understand. The less I know, the better, right? One less secret to keep."

He exhaled a long sigh from between his teeth. "Yeah."

"Whoever is inside, whoever is talking, can't be that close to the center or operations, right?" she asked. "Or he—or she—would have known what was going wrong between Nora and Fish. It's probably someone at the Dusty Lester Show, isn't it?"

He looked at her again. "Don't try to figure it out, all right? For your own good."

Her eyes held his. "I'm just...supposed to trust you? Even if you don't tell me everything?"

A muscle in his cheek twitched. "You got it."

She took a deep breath, wanting to know more, wondering how much she could ask. Her hamburger was only half-finished, but she wrapped it up and put it back in the bag.

She stared into her unfinished drink. "Why did you do what you did in Fish's office? *How* did you do it? I can't even describe it. You were so macho. It was like you gave off vibrations."

He shrugged. "That's all. I gave off some vibes."

"Why?"

"So he'll keep his distance. I don't want him to like you too much."

"Why?"

He looked at her unhappily. His eyes were midnight dark in the noon brightness. "Because *I* like you too much."

Her heart seemed to leap, leaving her feeling dizzy.

"I want to protect you, *querida*."

She felt even dizzier.

He leaned toward her, his body taut. "Listen," he said, "if it ever seems—even *seems*—like this could get ugly, I pull you out of it immediately. I send you back to Arkansas. You gotta trust me on that. Do you?"

She nodded, her emotions churning. "What if I wouldn't go? I'm *not* scared, Gus. I'm really not. I—I like it."

He touched her cheek. "I know you do."

She put up her hand, lightly touching his. "This business gets right inside you, doesn't it? It makes your blood sing."

"Your blood sings. Exactly."

Then Gus was bending closer, both his hands framing her face, and she was leaning toward him, raising her lips to his.

But he didn't kiss her. At the last minute he drew back, but his fingers lingered on her face.

"Look," he said, regret in his voice, "I can't do this. I gotta take you back to that damn office. Maybe I'd better stop trying to eat lunch with you. I always want to have you for dessert. And that's *prohibido*. Don't make me lose my head, Chiquita."

He released her.

She cast him a glance that was half grateful, half resentful.

He didn't seem to notice. He hardly spoke as they drove back to the office. When he pulled up in front, he leaned over and gave her another of his short, hard, intense kisses. Her heart did a cartwheel.

"Take care of yourself," he said against her lips. "Because you're mine, understand?"

*Because you're mine,* he'd said. Did he mean it? Her heart did another cartwheel.

"Is this part real?" she asked, her mouth trembling. "Or are you just pretending? Because you're supposed to be my lover? And because it seems right—at the moment?"

"We can't answer that now," he breathed. "We answer it later. Now we can only play it as it lays."

He kissed her again.

THAT AFTERNOON IT seemed to Susannah that everyone who came into Fish's office looked suspicious.

At least four men from the Dusty Lester Show appeared, and she couldn't help wondering if one of them was the informant who was secretly feeding Gus information.

The first, Epperson, looked too cold-eyed and self-serving to be concerned with anything except his own well-being. The second, a ferret-faced stagehand named Randolph, looked too bland to ever consider the difference between right and wrong. The third, an assistant manager called K.K. Kordiner, seemed too cheerfully egotistical to care that right and wrong existed.

Finally, there was Dusty Lester himself, a large, bluff man in an expensive powder-blue Western suit and a matching cowboy hat. Dusty Lester was the sort of man who prided himself on being a "good ole boy." He labored so hard to be sincere that insincerity oozed from him as if he were a snail leaving a trail of slime in its wake.

"Fish—you got yourself a new little darlin'," Lester brayed when he came into the office. "Honey, I'm gonna hug your neck. Ole Fish, he's been like a brother to me. Welcome to the family, sugar baby. I always hug family."

He'd swept down on her as she sat at her desk, giving her a smothering hug and a wet kiss on the cheek.

After Lester left, Fish stared after him in contempt. "He's a consummate ass. I apologize for him. Once he had talent. Now he's become a caricature of himself. But the tourists love him."

Susannah smiled feebly and straightened her dress. She still felt enfolded in the cloud of Dusty Lester's personal fragrance, which seemed partly musk, partly saddle soap.

"He oversteps himself," Fish mused, his expression unpleasant. He kept staring at the door through which Lester had disappeared. "Constantly, he oversteps himself. Ignore him, my dear."

Susannah nodded. She patted her hair to make sure it was in place. "There's one in every crowd," she said.

Fish gave her a thin-lipped smile. "I doubt if he'd paw you if he knew about your fiancé. Your 'Augie,' is it? He has—an air. He doesn't seem a man to be trifled with."

Susannah blinked innocently, not having expected him to mention Gus. "Well," she said with a shrug, "he's Latin. You know what they say."

Fish's gaze traveled to her lips and settled there. "No. What do they say?"

Susannah felt slightly rattled by the hunger in his look. She shrugged more elaborately. "You know—Latin blood, Latin temperment. Jealous. Protective. *You* know."

"Ah," said Fish, his eyes still trained hypnotically on her mouth. "Ah. Passionate. I can imagine."

Then, abruptly, he wheeled and entered the inner sanctum of his office. A few seconds later, Ginger peered in.

"Alone?" she whispered.

Susannah was so paranoid by this time, she hardly knew what to say. "It seems so."

Ginger slipped inside. Her pixie-style bangs were mussed, and she brushed them angrily back into place. Her lipstick was smudged. "I forgot to warn you about *him*," she said, with a nod over her shoulder. "Dusty Lester. Mr. Hands."

Susannah made a face. "He's disgusting."

Ginger nodded. "Right—but get used to it. He makes me sick. He's supposed to be Mr. Family Entertainment. He's always singing about puppies and little children and putting flowers on his mother's grave. But once he's off that stage, no woman under eighty is safe."

"Mr. Fish acts as if he doesn't like him. Why does he tolerate him?"

"Beats me," Ginger said, adjusting her collar. "He can't sing for sour apples, if you ask me. But he's got Fish's biggest theater. Go figure."

Susannah figured. The fewer people that attended the Dusty Lester Show, the more empty seats. The more empty seats, the more ticket sales Fish could fabricate, and the more money he could launder. But she kept her face blank.

"Show business," she said philosophically. "Who can understand it?"

She changed the subject. "How was Nora Geddes? Was it awkward seeing her?"

Ginger frowned and shook her head. "She seemed in shock. Like a zombie. I didn't stay long. I mean, I wanted to wave my hand in front of her eyes and say, 'Nora? Is anybody home in there? Yoo-hoo.'"

"That's sad," Susannah said.

"Hey, she's better off without that Colter jerk," Ginger said, curling her lip. "Working for Fish got on her nerves. I think she would have quit. But *he* wouldn't hear of it. No, if anything, Colter wanted her to get closer to Fish. Ick. Ugh."

Susannah's eyebrows rose in suprise. "Closer? How?"

"Honey," Ginger said with a superior smile, "you don't want to know. Well, at least she's safe from all that now."

*"Safe?"* Susannah echoed warily.

"And I'm safe. I mean, like my boyfriend's understanding—up to a point. But after that, he's jealous. Very jealous. Is yours? Your boyfriend? Jealous, I mean?"

Susannah nodded gravely. "Oh, yes," she said. "Well—sort of." She didn't even know if she was lying.

"Good," said Ginger. "Just hope he stays that way. Well, like I said, Nora should be safe now. Which is what makes it so strange."

Susannah's heart skipped, but she kept control of her expression. "Why? What's so strange?"

The phone in the reception area rang.

Ginger looked irritated by the interruption. "She seemed . . . scared. Scared numb. Not sad, like you'd think. Yeah. She looked really, really *scared*."

In the reception area, the phone kept ringing. "I gotta go," Ginger said. She left.

Susannah wanted to run after her, to shake the truth out of her. *What could Nora Geddes be scared of? And why?*

# 9

GUS WAS WORRIED. Fish was receiving and making strange calls.

At 3:55, that afternoon Fish made a call on his private line. The conversation was terse and cryptic.

Fish kept saying the same incomprehensible phrases: "Seven-eleven," "Snake eyes," and "Boxcars."

The man on the other end of the line sounded reluctant, even alarmed. Fish became more insistent. "Seven-eleven," he repeated relentlessly. "Snake eyes. Just do it."

The back of Gus's neck prickled. *What the hell?* "You're sure?" the other man asked. He sounded dubious, nervous. "Snake eyes?"

"You heard me," Fish said and hung up.

Gus swore. What the devil had *that* meant?

He had little time to wonder. Hardly thirty seconds lapsed before Fish was back on the line, making another call.

"Hello," said a voice. Gus recognized it. He'd heard it yesterday, the man with the Northeastern accent.

"We've taken care of the black bug problem," Fish said. "Partly."

"*What?*" the voice demanded, sounding incredulous.

"Almost."

There was an eloquent pause. "This is unexpected."

"It has to be done. One down. One to go."

"Are you spraying? Spraying is dangerous. You have to keep your hands *clean*."

"I am," Fish said testily.

"If you overspray, you won't have anything left."

"I," Fish said, his voice cold, "am nothing if not careful."

"If you'd been careful, the problem never would have come up," the other voice said acidly. "You could have nipped it in the bud. A little more preventive maintenance at that end is in order."

Fish had gone silent. He did not answer.

"Discretion," hissed the other voice, "is not only the better part of valor. It's the better part of everything. When lilies fester, what will weeds do? Take over, that's what."

"That's what I did. I weeded." Fish's tone was defensive.

"It's better if there's no place for weeds to grow. Understand? Get your act together."

"There's no problem," Fish said, more defensive than before.

"Really? See that it stays that way."

Fish had hung up.

*"Damn,"* Gus muttered savagely. The tenor of the conversation spooked him.

*One down, one to go.* Was he talking about Colter and Nora Geddes? Colter was dead. Was Nora next? Was that why Fish was spiriting her out of town, to lead her to her death?

Once more, Fish gave Gus little time to think.

The CommuCate system was working again. Two minutes after the call, Fish was on his CommuCate line, sending E-mail to Maude Ann Hawkins. "The pests are as good as gone," he had written. "Who was the philosopher who said it's necessary to tend one's own garden? That's what I've done. You do the same. The weather is favorable, and I intend to keep everything watered."

Gus gritted his teeth in frustration. *He's trying to defend himself. What in hell does he mean that he'll keep things watered?*

He glanced at his watch. It was a little after four. Nora Geddes should be on the last leg of her trip to Denver. Why had Fish given her the ticket? Did he still have some feeling for the woman, but want her at a safe distance? Or did he have something more sinister in mind?

Within minutes, Maude Ann Hawkins was on the CommuCate system with a reply. Gus read it with foreboding.

"I can't caution you too much about excess spraying. It can harm the environment. Try to keep your garden pest-free by natural means. It's safer. I hear you have a new ornamental fern inside. I trust that this one will give you less trouble. Try paying a little less attention to it. Sometimes one ruins a plant with too much attention."

*Goddam! What's going on?* Gus's nerve ends were going crazy with warnings. All this babble about pests and pesticides was about hits, about murders. He'd swear it. He could *feel* it.

And the "new ornamental fern," he realized, had to be Susannah. Although he was glad Fish was being warned away from Susannah, he didn't like her name coming up. Not at all.

He had always relied on his instincts, and his instincts told him that he'd come into this assignment with insufficient information. The thing was turning into one goddamn huge can of worms, and the worms were pale, wriggling, and lethal.

Susannah shouldn't be involved. She was an amateur—naive and untrained. Moreover, she was in the most sensitive position in the whole operation and as such, the most at risk.

He was going to pull her out. He called Olivier. Tersely he explained the phone conversations, the exchanges of E-mail.

"This is interesting," Olivier said with his usual cold-blooded objectivity. "But it's all theory. You can't prove anything. You've got nothing that'd stand up in court. A good defense lawyer'd make mincemeat out of what you've got."

"Yeah?" Gus challenged. "What I've got is a *feeling*. These boys aren't talking about any goddam garden. You know it, I know it. You got Marty the Mouse gone in St. Louis. You got Colter dead here. You got Nora Geddes splitting. These boys make people *disappear*, Olivier. And they're not amateurs. They've done it before. I can *feel* it."

"Feelings prove nothing," Olivier retorted.

"Yeah?" Gus said combatively. "Okay, answer this. Fish is part of a big organization, right? The Midwest operation, right? How many people connected with that operation have disappeared lately? Since Fish came to Branson?"

Olivier was silent.

"How many?" Gus persisted. "Just tell me that."

Olivier sounded thoughtful when he spoke. "Are you talking friends of the organization? Or foes?"

"Friends *and* foes," Gus answered. "Tell me, dammit. How many have just . . . vanished in the last three years?"

"About six," Olivier said dispassionately. "That we know about."

"Counting Marty the Mouse?"

"No. Not counting Marty the Mouse."

"All foes?"

Olivier hesitated a moment. "No. One friend. But we thought he was going to roll over. Come to our side."

"But he didn't roll over?"

"The only place he rolled was out of sight," Olivier said in his dry voice.

"Listen," Gus pleaded. "You got six people vanished—just disappeared. What does this tell you? They've got to vanish to someplace, right? Why not here? Fish's got a cave. It's full of nooks and crannies. He's also got a lake in it. It's deep as hell. What's he got it for? It doesn't make the organization any money."

"You're saying Fish is involved with these disappearances?"

"That's what I'm saying. Hey, it's a possibility."

"You've got no *proof*, Raphael. None."

"Is Marty the Mouse gone—or not?" Gus argued.

"Marty the Mouse could be sitting in Samoa drinking gin rickeys, for all we know."

"Is Colter dead—or not?" Gus retorted.

"He's dead. By accident. That's the official opinion."

"Yeah? Well, it's the most convenient damn accident I ever heard of—"

"Have you checked with the local police lately, about your 'suspect,' about your drunk?" Olivier asked.

Gus exhaled sharply. He'd checked, all right. But Branson's finest hadn't uncovered anything.

"All right," he admitted. "They can't find his prints on file in the U.S. So what? I told them to check Canada, but they're sitting on their duffs—"

"Yeah, well, maybe he's *got* no record. If you want to kill somebody, there are simpler ways to do it than have a drunken Canadian ram him. This driver could get charged. You do a hit, you don't throw your hit man to the fuzz, let them put him on trial."

"Why not?" Gus argued. "It's perfect. Who'd suspect? He'll cop a plea, pay a fine, get a suspended sentence, go his merry way. You want to kill somebody and not arouse any suspicion? Tell me a better way to do it."

"You should write mystery stories. The guy was legally *drunk*, Raphael."

"Yeah? Give me a couple of shots, and I could pass as legally drunk. I could run down whoever I wanted and walk away with no more than a slap on the wrist."

"No," Olivier said with finality. "You can't turn a disappearance into murder. You can't turn an accident into murder. That's that. This garden jargon is...curious, but what's it prove? Nothing. Would it hold up in court? No."

Gus knew that tone and hated it. Olivier was the most stubborn, close-minded, logic-bound lunkhead on the planet.

"Look," Gus said from between his teeth, "whatever this means, it's something we didn't expect. I want to pull the girl out of it. She's got to be safe."

"The girl stays *on*," Olivier said with exaggerated patience. "You're the one who recommended her in the first place. She's not at risk. Nobody's at risk here. This is money laundering. It's not murder one. She's inside, where we need her. She stays inside."

"I say we pull her out," Gus practically snarled.

"You pull her out, I'll bust you," Olivier warned. "I'll have your badge *and* charge you with obstructing justice. You do *not* put this investigation in jeopardy."

"Listen, Olivier—" Gus began, a dangerous edge in his voice.

"No," Olivier interrupted. "*You* listen. We can have a very tight case here—or we can blow it because you get goosey. What is it with you and this woman? You're as crazy as Fish, you know that?"

"I have this very strong intuition that something's wrong here, that it's not what we thought. That we've got possible murder here—"

Olivier cut him off coldly. "I'll tell you where to put your intuition. Maybe that kind of voodoo counts on your native island, Raphael, but this is the FBI, not the zombie jamboree."

Gus exploded. "You're talking about Haiti, you arrogant asshole. I'm Puerto Rican, but I was born in Manhattan. I'm as American as you are, you son of a—"

"You have your orders," Olivier said coldly. He hung up.

Gus swore. He rose and kicked the dresser, he kicked the door, he kicked the leg of the bed. He punched the wall as hard as he could, which was a mistake. The wall was a slab of cheap sheetrock, and his fist went through it. That angered him, so he punched it twice more.

His fist was bloody when he stopped. He swore again. He called Olivier every name he knew, in both English and Spanish.

He forced himself to calm down. Then he went into the bathroom and washed the blood from his hand.

He returned to the bedroom and sat down in front of the computer monitor. He glanced at his watch. It was almost five o'clock. Susannah should be home soon.

*Home*, he thought ironically. Home was where a person should be safe.

He didn't give a damn. He'd make her leave, he'd get her out. It didn't matter what Olivier said or what he threatened. Gus could feel danger, he could smell it coming. He would get Susannah out of its path.

FISH KEPT SUSANNAH overtime. To her disgust, he ended the day with another of his "inspections." First he'd called Ginger into his office, then, after dismissing her, Susannah. He'd coyly hinted that he wanted to see her legs.

Once again she'd slowly raised her skirt. Fish's eyes crawled over her with obvious pleasure. She tried to keep her face expressionless, but she felt used and dirty.

She was still burning with resentment when she climbed the rickety stairs of the motel. She unlocked the door and pushed it open.

Gus stood there. Without preface, he took her by the arms, his face taut with suppressed anger. "Pack up," he said. "You're going home."

She went still as a stone. She stared up at him without comprehension. "What?"

One hand gripped her shoulder so tightly it hurt. "I said, 'Pack.' I want you out of here. I'll give you money for a plane ticket. Just leave."

"I can't leave—I just *started*."

"Congratulations," he said from between clenched teeth. "You've also just finished."

"What is this?" she asked, trying to push away from him. "Are you mad because Fish looked at my legs again? It's all right—really. I don't like it, but it doesn't hurt me. It just makes me more determined to get the goods on him."

He shook her slightly. "You're going home," he repeated, more grimly than before.

All day she had suppressed anger. Now it flared. "Don't you manhandle *me*," she warned. "Don't you dare."

He shook her again, harder. "I'll dare anything I damn well please. Pack. You're out of here."

Acting instinctively. Susannah clenched her fist and hit him on the chest, hard.

He sucked in his breath, and his face became almost cruel. "Don't fight me, Chiquita."

Rebelliously, she hit him again. He grunted with displeasure. "I'll tie you up and carry you back to Arkansas, you little—"

The phone rang, and he froze.

"What's going on here?" she demanded, trying to wrest free.

The phone rang again but he didn't move. He stood, every muscle tensed, holding her prisoner.

Susannah tossed her head in frustration. "Let me go," she ordered. "And answer the phone, you knucklehead."

He gripped her more tightly as the phone rang for the third time. Then he released her. He strode into his crowded room, picked up the reciever. "What?" he demanded.

Rubbing her shoulder, Susannah followed him as far as the door. She leaned against the doorframe, watching him resentfully. What was wrong with him? He'd been like a man possessed.

"What?" he was saying. "*What?* Oh, *Jesucristo*."

Susannah's nerve ends prickled in apprehension. She stopped rubbing her shoulder and studied Gus's face. It was etched with fury and despair and disbelief.

"She wasn't on the flight to Denver?" he was saying. "Then where the hell is she? Did she change her ticket?"

Susannah's flesh went cold, her blood went cold; it seemed the very center of her bones went cold.

*Nora Geddes hadn't arrived in Denver? Where was she? What had happened?*

Gus alternately cursed and asked questions. When he hung up the phone he sat on the bed and raked his hand through his hair.

"What's happened?" she asked, watching him warily.

His dark eyes flashed. "Nora Geddes wasn't on the Denver plane. We've lost her."

Her stomach lurched in alarm. "Lost her?"

He nodded. "She got as far as St. Louis. Chelsea's man saw her board the plane in Springfield. But in St. Louis—she disappeared."

"But—but what happened?"

He shook his head and kneaded the back of his neck.

"One of three things. Maybe she screwed up and missed the plane. She'll turn up, safe and sound."

She studied his face. His expression was so stern it frightened her. "You don't believe that—do you?"

He rubbed his neck again. His eyes held hers. "No. I don't."

"What do you believe?"

"Maybe she wanted Fish to lose track of her. He was sending her to Denver, so Denver was the last place she wanted to go."

Her heart pounded, and the pulse in her throat hammered. "Do you believe that?"

He looked away, scowling. "No."

Her blood thrummed harder. "What do you believe?"

"She was never meant to get to Denver. Somebody intercepted her."

"Why?"

He raised his eyes to hers again. "Maybe she knew too much." He gazed at her for the space of three hectic heartbeats. "I'll tell you the truth," he said quietly. "I don't think Lem Colter's death was an accident."

"But the police—"

"The police," he said in contemptuously.

"They said it was an accident."

He rose. Restless, he began to pace the cramped confines of the room.

She watched him warily. "*You* said it was an accident."

He stopped pacing. He looked her up and down, as if she were hopelessly naive. "Hey," he said, "I *lie*. If you don't believe me, ask your sister."

The mention of Laura hurt her more than she thought possible. She turned her face away.

"Listen," he commanded, "I've been eavesdropping all afternoon. Something's wrong here. Something heavy's going down. I want you *out* of it."

She said nothing, still trying to sort out her emotions about Nora Geddes's disappearance.

*Maybe she's fine,* she thought. *Maybe he's right—she's just on the run from Fish.*

Gus had the phone in his hand. He was punching numbers.

*Lem Colter's death has to be an accident,* Susannah told herself. But an evil imp seemed to be whispering in her ear: *What if it's not? What if Fish had him killed?*

Gus's voice was terse. "Olivier? I *know* you're home. Yeah, I consider it an emergency—Nora Geddes never made it to Denver. Hell—how do I know? Maybe elves stole her."

She watched him out of the corner of her eye. He seemed impatient with the man called Olivier. "Of course I checked on that," he said irritably. "Yeah? Well, maybe somebody stopped her before she could get to Denver."

He sighed harshly. "I know it's the worst scenario. I'm *not* imagining things, dammit."

He listened for a moment to Olivier. His expression grew more bitter. "Damn straight, buddy. I'm sending her home.

She didn't sign on for anything of this—this magnitude. Yeah? Well, I'll give you my badge myself, you son of a bitch, and you can put it where the sun don't shine. You think I care? You think you *scare* me, Olivier? *I* say she goes home, and you can take a flying—"

Olivier must have interrupted him. Gus stopped in mid-sentence, his upper lip curled. "Oh?" he said sarcastically. "Oh, really? Really? That's very interesting, Olivier. I'm fascinated. Phaugh."

He slammed the receiver down, then looked over at Susannah. "Pack," he said.

She took a deep breath. "No," she said and stood taller.

He raised one dark eyebrow. "You're going home."

"No," she retorted, crossing her arms. "I'm not."

He took a step toward her.

She lifted her chin in defiance. "If I leave so soon, it'll look strange, suspicious. And you won't have anybody close to Fish. You wouldn't even know Nora Geddes was gone yet—if it weren't for me."

He took another step closer. "Susannah—"

"No," she said emphatically. She gave a curt nod in the direction of the telephone. "*He* doesn't want me to go. That Olivier person. I could tell."

Gus's jaw clenched. "Olivier's a jackass. Rocks have more imagination. If I brought him Nora Geddes's body with a knife through the heart, he'd stare at it and say, 'How do you know she didn't fall on it?'"

"How would you know?" she challenged.

He gave her a snide smile. "Don't you start, too."

"It's a good question," she said. "How do you prove any of this? That Colter was murdered? That somebody stopped Nora Geddes from going on to Denver? You're guessing."

"I'm a hell of guesser, baby. And I've got vibes that this is not the place for you to play Junior G-Girl."

"I'm not playing. You told me I was good."

"I lied about that, too."

She shook her head. "No. I am good. You just don't want to admit it."

His smile was cynical. "Don't flatter yourself. You're an amateur."

"If I'm such an amateur, maybe you won't want to be bothered with *this*," she said, just as cynically. She reached into the neckline of her dress, withdrew a folded piece of paper and held it toward him.

"Oh, cute," he sneered. "See what Mata Hari's done now? What's this, a signed confession?"

"Look at it," she said without emotion.

With a cavalier shrug he took the paper and unfolded it. As he read it, his superior smile died. Susannah, feeling vindicated, breathed more freely.

He raised his eyes to her in disbelief. "This is a printout of Fish's receipts for the Dusty Lester Show for last week—the real receipts. How did you get it?"

"I have my amateurish ways," she said, cocking her head.

His expression grew earnest. "Susannah—*how* did you get this? This is exactly the sort of stuff we need to make the money-laundering charge stick. A record of the real receipts. To compare with what he'll claim came in."

She shrugged. "I *know* it's important. That's why I brought it."

"How'd you get it?"

She made an impatient gesture. "I was in and out of his office all day. I saw him going over all this just before five. I saw his handwritten records, too; but he shreds them. He was putting this on the computer. I saw the heading and the date."

"And?" He was still frowning in disbelief.

"And when he went into the bathroom, I went to the computer and hit the Print Screen button. It printed everything that was showing on the screen. It only took thirty seconds or so."

His eyes narrowed. "Weren't you scared? That he'd come out and find you?"

"A little," she admitted. "But I was careful." She held her head high. "I can get more. I know I can. You've got to let me. You can't stop me when I'm this close."

His expression grew regretful. "Chiquita, this man is dangerous. I didn't think so, at first. But I was wrong. I can feel it."

"If he's dangerous, let's take him out of the game," she pleaded. "You can investigate the rest later. But for now, I'm right *next* to him. I can get everything you need to put him away for the money laundering. I know I can."

His face went stony. "No."

"He doesn't suspect a thing about me. I'm in no danger. I'll be careful. I won't take any dangerous chances."

"No."

"Maybe I can find out what the trouble was between Fish and Nora Geddes. Ginger wants to talk. I know she does. But who'll she talk to if I'm not there?"

His expression didn't change. "No."

"Listen," she said. Desperation tinged her voice. "If you really think something happened to Nora Geddes—if you think Fish made her disappear—I may be able to find out something. I'm there. I *see* things. You can only listen."

"No."

"Lem Colter," she pleaded. "If Fish did have him killed, there's got to be a way to trace it to Fish. Somebody'll be paid. Such things can't happen in a vacuum. I may be able to find something you can't."

"No."

"You'll get in trouble if you make me leave. I could tell. From the way you talked to that...Olivier person. *He* wants me here. Aren't you afraid to break orders?"

"No," he said. And she saw from the set of his mouth that he meant it.

"It's safe," she said, imploringly. "Let me stay on a week. Just a week, and I can have so much information in your hands that—"

"No!" His sharpness cut her off.

She stared at him, hoping she didn't look as bewildered as she felt. "Why?" she asked. "Why? I can take care of myself. You said you believed in me. What happened?"

"Things change," he muttered. "People change. I thought you wouldn't be distracting. You are. It's hard to concentrate when you're around."

A muscle twitched in his cheek. His eyes were coldly somber. "You remind me too much of your sister," he said. "If I act—interested, it's because I think of her. If I hold you, I pretend it's her. If I kiss you, I wish it was her. Go home before I take you to bed—thinking of her."

Susannah drew her breath in a painful gasp. She leaned against the doorframe, stunned. She thought she'd never seen a face as cruel as his had become.

Somehow, he managed to make his expression colder, crueler. "You think you're hot, but you're bush league. You take stupid chances; it makes me nervous. This case is turning out to be very big. I don't want you screwing it up. So go home. And give my regards to your sister. I'd rather have her in my imagination than you in the flesh. Accept No Substitutes—that's gonna be my motto. Sorry, little sister."

She couldn't breathe. The blood burned in her cheeks.

He gave her a slow, one-sided smile. "I almost jumped your bones. Out of wanting *her*. So pack up your stuff, Chiquita. I gotta go to work. Be gone by the time I get back. I don't want to have sex with you out of boredom and charity. Your sister wouldn't like that. She wouldn't like that at all. When I think about it, neither would I."

He moved past her and toward the entrance of the suite. He picked up his wallet and stuffed it into the back pocket of his jeans. He picked up his motorcycle helmet. He paused, his other hand on the doorknob. He looked at her one last time, over his shoulder.

"*¿Comprendo?*" he asked, his voice full of insolence. "I'll condense it to one word: scram. Be gone when I get back."

She could say nothing. She only watched him with stricken eyes.

"*Adiós*," he said, and left her standing there alone.

HE GOT BACK SHORTLY after midnight. Her car, the Escort, was still parked in front of the motel.

She couldn't still be here, he thought wearily. He didn't think he could handle it anymore.

Maybe she left the car behind because she left everything behind. She couldn't have stayed. He'd seen the look on her face. He'd hurt her badly. He'd had to. It was the only way to keep her safe.

Maybe he'd make it up to her someday. If she'd let him. He couldn't think of that now. He couldn't think of anything except getting this rotten job over and done with.

But when he climbed the delapidated stairs, he saw that the light was on in his room. She *can't* still be here, he thought again. He wanted her far away, safe from Fish, safe from him.

But when he opened the door, she was standing there in his room, waiting. His heart contracted painfully. She was barefoot. She wore denim shorts and a plain navy blue T-shirt. She must have had her contacts in, because her big glasses were missing.

She'd let her hair down. She had washed it. It was natural and free of hair spray. It fell to her shoulders in thick, auburn waves.

*Oh, God*, he thought helplessly. *Why did she let her hair down?* Didn't she know what it did to him inside?

He met her eyes. They were beautiful eyes, but stubborn and fearful and full of questions. Her face was pale. She wore almost no makeup. She stood, her back to the wall, staring at him. She clenched and unclenched her fists nervously.

*I think my heart just broke*, he thought. *I can't take this. I can't.*

He had never seen her in shorts before. She had long legs, slender and smooth. Her breasts looked small and vulnerable under the soft cloth of the shirt. He wanted to take them in his hands. He wanted to lift her shirt and kiss them until she begged for mercy.

He looked away tiredly. "I told you to go," he said.

"I started to. But then—"

He shut the door behind him. He locked it. "Don't make me say it all again," he said, shaking his head. "I don't want to have to say it again."

She stood straighter, but she kept clenching and unclenching her hands. "You didn't mean it," she said. Her voice shook slightly.

He couldn't help it. He raised his eyes to meet hers. "Susannah—"

"You didn't mean it—what you said." Her heart was beating so hard, he could see it, making her shirt quiver between her beautiful breasts. She raised her chin. "You were lying. Weren't you?"

He found it hard to swallow. He knew what was going to happen. There was no way to stop it.

"You're not safe with Fish," he said, his voice taut. "You're not safe with . . . me."

"I am," she retorted.

*Oh, God,* he thought. *I'm getting lost in her eyes. Lost.*

"I'm safe with you," she said. "Maybe I'm safe only with you. It's the only place that feels . . . right."

"No," he muttered. He looked her up and down, from her shiny auburn hair to her slender bare feet. "No. See, if you stay—"

"If I stay?" she interrupted.

"If you stay—" He couldn't finish the sentence. He wanted her too much.

"Yes?"

She didn't move. She stayed, her back to the wall, staring up at him.

"Yes," he said and stepped toward her. "Yes." He put his hands on her shoulders, the ran them slowly down her arms and took her hands in his. Setting them on either side of his belt buckle, he wrapped his arms around her gently, carefully, as if the moment was so fragile it might be broken by the wrong gesture.

But no gesture seemed wrong. He ran his fingers through her long hair. He bent and kissed her on the mouth. She had a full mouth, sweet and cool and tender, and it opened to his. He tasted her as if she were honey.

He was so aroused that he ached for her. Her hands tensed on his belt. He gasped and kissed her until he thought that perhaps he was dying.

# 10

SUSANNAH'S HANDS tightened on his belt. Gus kissed her with such intensity that she felt faint.

His hands were under her shirt, caressing her bare breasts and stroking their tips until they ached with yearning. Then his mouth was upon them, teasing first one, then the other.

He straightened and his face hovered above hers, and his dark eyes devouring her, making love to her. "I want to feel my skin naked against yours," he said, his voice tight. He drew off his T-shirt, let it fall to the floor.

He had a flat, hard, smooth chest. A white scar slashed across his midsection, like a lightning bolt. Over his left nipple was another tattoo, a small red heart pierced by a dagger.

She pressed her lips against it, then touched his scar.

"You'll make me crazy," he whispered, raising her face to his. "I think you have already."

She smiled shyly at him. Slipping off her T-shirt, she dropped it beside his on the floor. Then, self-consciously, she hid her nakedness against his bare chest.

"No," he said in her ear. "I want to see you. Because you're so beautiful."

He held her at arm's length, gazing at her hungrily. With his fingertips he traced the nipple of first one breast, then the other. Then he ran his hand up and down her spine, making her shiver.

"I've imagined this," he said. "In my mind I've undressed you, looked at you, touched you, just like this."

She looked away, experiencing another wave of shyness. Her hands fluttered upward, trying to hide herself again.

"No," he cautioned, catching her hands. "In my mind, I've already kissed you all over. Here," he said, kissing her right shoulder. "And here." He kissed the left. "And here." He turned her and kissed her nape.

"Everywhere." While his hands caressed her breasts, he kissed her between the shoulder blades and then up and down her backbone until she shivered.

Weak with desire, she closed her eyes and leaned her head back against his chest. She was almost unbearably intoxicated by the pleasure of his touch, the warmth of his bare flesh against hers. *Gus*, she thought, *I've loved you for so long— and I love you so much.*

His hands moved lower, unsnapping her cutoffs, sliding them and her panties off and they fell to the floor with a rustle of soft fabric. He kissed the curve where her throat met her shoulder, as he stroked her stomach, hips, and thighs.

His touch was sure, sensitive, urgent. When his fingers found her most sweetly aching parts, desire mounted, shuddering through her.

Just when she thought she would die of wanting him, he turned her to face him and lowered his mouth to hers again. Once more he placed her hands on either side of his belt buckle. His touch conveyed his hunger, and her heart leaped, craving to satisfy his need and her own.

His fingers guided hers to undo the belt, unzip his jeans, to touch him until he gasped, his mouth hot upon her own, his bare chest brushing the tips of her breasts.

Then he was as naked as she, and Susannah was dizzily aware of how lean and beautiful his body was. She looked at him with happy wonderment, and when he kissed her again, it was with such hot-blooded need that she could think only *Yes, yes, yes.*

He led her to the bed and drew her down beside him, taking her into his arms. His mouth, supple and teasing, moved from her lips to her throat, from her throat to her breasts, to her stomach to her thighs.

Only when he had driven her past every limit of desire she had ever imagined did he prepare to enter her, and she arched to him in readiness. He paused only long enough to make sure that sex between them was safe.

Then he made love to her, slowly and fiercely and completely. She lost herself in his need and his giving, and she found herself as well, becoming one with him.

When it was over, she lay in his arms, shivering with happy exhaustion, her eyes damp with tears.

He felt the tears against his chest.

"Why do you cry?" he asked softly.

"Because I'm happy."

"Good. Good."

She leaned over him so that her hair spilled down silkily, curtaining them off from the rest of the world.

She stared at his face, so complex, so contradictory, so passionate. She touched his lips. He kissed her fingertips.

He ran his hands over her bare arms. "I said terrible things to you," he whispered.

"Yes." She touched his mouth again. He had a beautiful mouth.

"I didn't mean them."

"I know."

"We've broken all the rules," he said. He kissed her fingertips again.

"I know that, too."

He shook his head. "It couldn't be helped. I wanted you too much."

"I wanted you, too."

"If it meant dying, even, I would have had to make love to you. I would die for you. Do you believe that? It's true. I would die for you."

She laid her finger against his lips. "Shh. No. Don't say such a thing. Talk about living, not dying."

"Living," he said. He raised himself and kissed the hollow of her throat. His warm arms enfolded her. "Do you know I'm going to make love to you again?"

"Yes."

"Yes," he said. He drew her to him and brought her lips to his. "Yes."

SHE AWOKE IN HIS ARMS, and sighed with happiness as she snuggled against his shoulder. Wakening in response, he nuzzled her neck. She turned to nibble softly at his nipple, which hardened beneath her lips.

He cupped her tingling breasts and rained kisses on them. Then he stroked her, gently, sensually as if she were silk.

They were learning each other's bodies, learning the infinity of ways in which they might please each other. Susannah was aglow with love for him. She had not thought it possible to reach the same peaks of pleasure she had reached the night before, but she was wrong. Inevitably and gloriously, they made love again.

And once again they lay, spent, in each other's arms. She wanted to stay there—her face against his chest, her legs entwined with his—forever. All too soon, he raised himself on one elbow and stared down at her. "I want you to go home," he said, his face somber. "I'll come for you when this is over."

"No," she said, caressing his jaw. "I *can't* leave you now. You need me, you know you do."

He took her hand in his. "No, I have bad feelings. I want you home. I want you safe."

"I am home," she insisted, squeezing his hand. "I am safe."

"No. I should never have gotten you involved."

She laid her cheek against his bare shoulder. "But you did. I don't want to leave. I'm *happy* here."

"You don't understand," he said.

"You have to let me stay," she said, holding him tighter. "You *have* to. It's the only way I'll know."

"Know what?"

She found it hard to say the words. "That you . . . care for me."

"*Care* for you?" he asked, his mouth crooked with disbelief. "How could I not love you? How could I not see you were so—"

She drew back and put her hands on either side of his face. "Don't send me away—please. Don't you see? It'll be as if I failed, I wasn't good enough."

His expression grew pained. "Susannah—"

"It's as if I've been waiting all these years for *life* to happen to me. It didn't. Not until you."

"Susannah—"

"Here with you...it's been the best time of my life. To leave it—to leave you—don't ask me that. Please."

He stared down at her. He nodded, almost reluctantly. "It's been the best time of mine, too. The craziest, but the best."

"Do you mean that?"

He kissed her. "I mean it. But this—you and me—it turns the world upside down. All the rules are broken and I feel like we're living on borrowed time."

"If you meant what you said—about me, about being over...my sister—then prove it. Break the rules for me, Gus. Please. You said you never did it for anyone else. Do it for me."

"Oh, God, Chiquita. I've already broken them."

She wound her arms around his neck. "Gus . . ."

He lowered his head and kissed her. She kissed him back with all the need and love in her heart.

When he broke the kiss, the look in his eyes was troubled. "You want to stay that much?"

"Yes. Oh, yes."

His expression became more unhappy than before. But he he kissed the hollow of her throat. He gazed at her and smoothed her tumbled hair. "Then, stay," he said. "But stay *safe*. Be careful. Take no chances. Promise."

"I promise," she said. He took her into his arms and held her, simply held her, as if he was afraid to let her go.

SHE SKIPPED BREAKFAST because she needed to put herself in Miss Teagle's hands, to have her hair teased and lacquered back into the style that Fish liked.

Miss Teagle was a weary-looking woman in her fifties. A cigarette was always burning in her ashtray.

"You're certainly bright-eyed today," Miss Teagle muttered when Susannah sat down. "Glad somebody in this cruel old world is happy."

*It shows,* Susannah thought, staring at herself in the mirror. *I'm in love, and what people say is true: It shows.*

But she told herself to be a little less rapturous, to start thinking with her head again, not her heart. "I'm just glad to have found a job as good as I did," she said.

"Huh," Miss Teagle muttered cynically. "Nora Geddes was excited about that job, too, when she started. Well, *that* changed. She was a nice girl, once. That Fish person, he drove her to it, if you ask me."

Susannah's nerve ends prickled, and her euphoria dwindled. "What do you mean?"

Miss Teagle shrugged and brushed Susannah's hair. "You got a natural wave. It could be real attractive if you didn't always wear it pulled back."

"What did you mean about Nora Geddes?" Susannah asked, wincing against Miss Teagle's ministrations. "Mr. Fish drove her to *what*?"

"To stealin'," Miss Teagle said. She took a quick puff from her cigarette, then began to thrust pins into Susannah's hair. "I mean, you could see her gettin' more nervous all the time. She was afraid. You could see it at the end."

Susannah shifted uncomfortably. "Why was she afraid?"

Miss Teagle shrugged. "First off, he's weird. This hairdo nonsense, for instance. Not that I'm complaining—he pays his bills. But, sheesh! The fountains and the garter belts and the strange ideas—"

"Strange ideas? What strange ideas?"

Miss Teagle adjusted the hairpins, her face stony. "She was never, like, specific. But I got the impression that Fish asked her to do something she thought was really wrong. She didn't want to, but her boyfriend was tryin' to get her to go ahead and do it. Then Fish got—well—displeased with her. But he didn't let her go. The man was obsessed. I mean, really *obsessed*. With her looks. Just with her looks."

Susannah shuddered, and her good mood began to vanish.

"I'm no gossip," Miss Teagle said flatly. "I'm tellin' you this for your own good. She was happy once, too. But it changed. Fish changed it. You ask me, that's why she had her problem. Hell, she even stole from *me*."

Susannah's eyes widened in surprise.

"Yep," said Miss Teagle gloomily. "A comb once. A damn *comb*. Like I wouldn't have give it to her if she asked? Once a bottle of shampoo from a display. I saw her."

"You didn't stop her?"

"I felt sorry for her. And it was such little stuff. The drugstore next door? Yeah, she hit them all the time. Finally they just started billing her for things at the end of the month. Her boyfriend payed. He should have helped her. Well, he's gone now. She's rid of them both. She's better off. I hope she gets her life together."

"Yes," Susannah said. She tried to keep the worry out of her eyes. "I hope she does, too."

"Poor kid," said Miss Teagle, spraying Susannah's bangs. "She had an appointment yesterday. To get her hair cut short. We were going to color it blond, too. A whole new her, see? But she didn't come in. Because of the boyfriend, I guess. But she will."

*No*, Susannah thought, *she won't come.*

"I'm not tellin' you this to scare you," Miss Teagle said, anchoring Susannah's hair with another pin and spraying again. "It's just I'm telling you to be careful. I don't want to see history repeat itself. She used to come in here in the morning happy, just like you. But at the end, she wasn't happy. Not happy at all."

She gave a last squirt of hair spray. "There," she said with grim satisfaction. "You're finished."

ONCE AGAIN SUSANNAH arrived before Ginger. Once again Fish was waiting for her in her office. He was sitting at her desk. The fountains were on, playing to the recorded music. The tune was "I've Grown Accustomed to Her Face."

"Mr. Fish," Susannah said as pleasantly as she could.

"Miss Fingal," he said with satisfaction. "You're a vision today. A vision."

She smiled uncomfortably. She wondered why he was at her desk. Had he been searching it?

He rose slowly. With glittering eyes, he studied her. She wore her pink Givenchy summer suit and a simple white blouse.

"That suit," Fish said admiringly, "it brings out the pink of your cheeks. I never noticed how rosy they are. You look quite . . . radiant this morning."

"Thank you," she said and swallowed nervously.

"Perhaps that's what love does to you," Fish suggested. "Your fiancé—he keeps you . . . happy?"

"Yes," she said, gripping her white purse more tightly. "He keeps me . . . *very* happy."

"He appears, if I may say, to be an extremely physical young man."

"Yes. Well . . . yes."

"He's not the sort I would have expected you to pick," Fish said. His cold eyes kept traveling up and down her body, up and down. "You're so elegant and elfin. He's such a contrast with the tattoos, the earring. Mexican, is he?"

She raised her chin. "He's American. Of Puerto Rican descent."

"Ah. Puerto Rico. The Caribbean. Perhaps that's why he has a hint of the pirate about him. The elf queen and the pirate king. An interesting combination."

"We . . . suit each other," she said. "That's all."

"I hear he's gifted in electronics," Fish said. There was slyness in his tone.

*Oh, God,* she thought, panicking. *He's found the bug in his office. He knows. Somehow he knows about us.*

She willed herself to be calm. "Yes. He's good."

"I can always use good sound-men," Fish said with the same shrewd air. "I'll be sure to compensate him for his worth. I want the two of you to be happy here in Branson."

Susannah felt a rush of relief. Her fear subsided. But at the same time a new suspicion, one she didn't even want to name, was rising about Fish. She tried to push it away.

"You're very kind," she said.

"Not at all," Fish replied. "And now . . . if you don't mind, could we have this morning's little inspection?"

She set her purse on her desk. She bent and started to raise the hem of her skirt.

"No," said Fish quickly. He gave an abrupt wave of his hand. "No. Let's do it . . . a bit differently. Would you mind standing by the wall, facing it?"

*What now?* she thought in frustration. But she smiled and said, "Of course." She moved to the wall and faced it.

"Now," Fish said, his voice tightening, "if you would just raise your skirt a bit . . . very, very, very slowly."

Susannah gritted her teeth. Slowly, using both hands, she raised her skirt to midthigh.

"Ah," said Fish with a pained sigh. "There. Yes, there. Ah."

Her face grew hot. Her heart began to beat hard and angrily. But she had asked Gus to let her stay, she had begged him. This was the price.

To her shame and indignation, Fish kept her standing that way for nearly two minutes. She could almost feel his eyes, crawling over her like bugs.

At last he said, "That will be fine." His voice was thick. He turned and left the outer office, closing the big door behind him.

Susannah ran her hand across her forehead, which was hot. She went to her desk. Fish had left a folder and a box on her desk. She sat and opened the folder. Inside was a scrawled note. "Miss Fingal—I am giving a party a week from Friday to celebrate the third anniversary of the Waltzing Fountains. Please address invitations by hand. Yours, D.F."

The box held engraved invitations. Under the note in the folder were five sheets of names and addresses—a computer printout. She leafed through them and was surprised to see her own name and Gus's, the last entries on the list.

Fish was inviting them to his party? Why? She searched the list. Ginger's name was on it, as well, and beside it that of a man Susannah assumed was Ginger's boyfriend.

All right, perhaps Fish was just trying to be sociable.

She started addressing the invitations, glad to have such a mechanical task. Her mind could drift back to what she wanted to think of—Gus, of being held in his strong arms, of pressing her face to his naked chest, of tasting his warm, mobile, wonderful mouth.

Ginger entered, looking grumpy. "Gawd," she said, "are you early every day? What are you doing? Invitations? Oh, *no*, not another party."

Susannah gave her a suspicious look. "What's wrong with a party?"

Ginger shrugged irritably. "Nothing—if you can dodge *him*. Fish never drinks except at parties. But when he does, he gets friendlier than usual. *If* you get my drift."

Susannah sighed. Fish, sober, was far too friendly. The specter of Fish made more amorous still by drink was too awful to contemplate.

Ginger lowered her voice. "The trouble between Fish and Nora started at a party last year."

Susannah gripped her pen more tightly. "Just what *was* the trouble between Fish and Nora?"

"Don't ask," Ginger said ominously. "If you're lucky—and play it smart—you won't ever have to know."

"Ginger!" Susannah was tired of being taunted with hints.

Ginger ignored her. "I've gotta report in," she muttered. "And you shouldn't come in too early. It just gives you that much more time with him. Besides, he likes to be alone in the morning."

"Why?"

"He goes over the last night's receipts, adds up the take. He likes doing it in private."

Susannah shrugged as if to say one more of Fish's peculiarities made no difference. But her mind was working busily. Fish must be the only person to see all the real attendance numbers.

Each theater manager would turn in the figures and money to Fish. Fish had to keep a record of the real receipts—he *must*—in order to keep his personal records straight and know how much money he could launder. Susannah would give a great deal to see the full record of those real receipts.

Ginger had disappeared through the door to Fish's inner office. Susannah's irritation with the other woman melted. She knew what was happening in the office. Ginger, too, was being subjected to the morning "inspection."

Susannah bit her lip and went back to the invitations.

In less than five minutes Ginger was back, out of Fish's office. Her face was scarlet and the set of her mouth angry. "Something's up. It's the old face-the-wall and lift-it-*slowly* routine. I *hate* it when he does that. That means he'll be weirder than usual all week."

"Are you all right? I didn't know that was . . . unusual."

"I'm fine," Ginger answered sullenly. "But he's going into a major creepy phase. It must be because of you."

"Me?" Susannah asked with surprise.

"He was really bummed out over Nora. *Really* bummed. Then you came along. Now his adrenaline's running high again. Look, take my advice. Don't be quite so perfect—you know? A little imperfection keeps him off-balance."

"How do you mean?"

"Well," Ginger said, tossing her head, "he finds me physically attractive, but he thinks I'm too mouthy. Nora, he found her attractive, but too close-mouthed, and then too nervous. Toward the end, she was really nervous."

"About what?"

"Oh, everything," she said vaguely. "I don't know. My opinion is, the less you know around here, the better. Why go lookin' for trouble?"

Resentfully, she straightened her skirt. "I'm going back to my desk. When he's creepy, I sit there and think of ways to push him down the elevator shaft. He'll buzz for you in a minute. He says he wants you to go to the bank—and the florist. Once a week, he's gotta have a fresh pot of *hyacinths*, for cryin' out loud. They cost a mint."

Susannah smiled weakly and watched her flounce back to the reception area. True to Ginger's prediction, Fish signaled Susannah by intercom to come into his office.

He waved at a rather nondescript leather bag on his desk. "I want you to go to the bank for me. I had one of my security men take in yesterday's receipts. But I want you to deposit some money in my personal account. I've made out the deposit slip. The bank's just across the street."

Susannah nodded and tried not to look at the money bag too curiously. It was beige and of medium size.

"Then I want you to stop by the florist the next street over. They have some fresh hyacinths for me. Mine are drooping. I hate it when my hyacinths droop," he said, his voice full of regret.

He stared almost mournfully at the withering purple flowers on his desk. He had become strangely moody. A volume of poems lay on his desk. It was bound in black leather, and Susannah could see the title stamped in gold on the front: *The Collected Poems of Edgar Allan Poe.*

His desk was otherwise clean. If he had tallied yesterday's receipts, there was no sign of it. A fresh layer of paper, like confetti, lay in the bin of the paper shredder. He must already have tallied the receipts and destroyed the originals.

*He loses no time,* Susannah thought with grudging wonder. *But has he put the records on computer yet? Yesterday he didn't until late afternoon. I'll have to watch like a hawk.*

"Be careful of the traffic," Fish said. "It's going to be a killer today."

She smiled mechanically. "Killer" was perhaps not the most tactful term to use when Lem Colter was still lying in state at the Berryman Funeral Home.

"I'll see to everything," she said. She took the bag and turned to go.

"Miss Fingal—"

She faced him again. He was staring at her legs. A fine film of perspiration had appeared on his forehead. His mouth twitched.

She had the sudden apprehension that he was going to ask to see her thighs again. But, with effort, it seemed, he raised his eyes to hers and smiled stiffly. "Nothing, Miss Fingal," he said and nodded for her to go. He opened his book of poems and stared into it.

"What's he doing now?" Ginger asked when Susannah reached the reception area.

"He's reading Edgar Allan Poe."

Ginger shrugged in disgust. "*That's* a new one. It's usually some James Bond junk when he's in this mood."

*What is this mood?* Susannah wondered. *And why is he so mercurial today? I'll have to notice everything. Everything.*

She got into the elevator. When it reached the bottom and the doors started to sweep open, she immediately hit the Close Door button. With a hiss, they shut again.

Swiftly, keeping her elbow poised next to the Close Door button, in case someone buzzed for the elevator, she opened the bag. She drew in her breath with surprise.

The bag was full of twenty-dollar bills, bound in packets. Hurriedly she looked at the deposit slip. Fish's sprawly writing indicated that he was depositing $20,000. It was precisely the amount she thought that Ginger had taken to Nora Geddes yesterday.

Holding her breath, she scanned the top bill of each packet. She had a good memory, and she relied on it now. One by one, she found the serial numbers she was looking for.

A chill passed over her. This *was* the money that Ginger took to Nora Geddes yesterday. The serial numbers matched perfectly.

But if it had been given to Nora yesterday, how was it back in Fish's possession today? The police had followed Nora Geddes yesterday. She had gone only to one place—the airport. The most logical assumption was that she had carried the money with her.

She had boarded her plane, but at St. Louis she had disappeared. Supposedly the money had gone with her. But the money was back.

How could Fish have the money again—unless he'd had something to do with Nora's disappearance?

Susannah sensed with a horrible certainty about what it meant: Nora Geddes wasn't coming back; and wherever she was, she wouldn't be needing any money.

# 11

GUS CALLED SHORTLY before noon to say he was tied up and couldn't take her to lunch. Susannah could tell he was worried but didn't want to go into details.

"Are you sure you can't get away?" she asked.

She hadn't realized how much she had counted on meeting him. She wanted to tell him about the money and the serial numbers, but even more, she wanted simply to see him.

"I'm sorry, baby," he said, regret in his voice. "I really am."

"I am, too." *How can I miss him so much? We haven't even been apart five hours.*

"I'll see you tonight," he said. Then, gruffly, he added, "I love you, Chiquita."

He didn't have to say that, she thought happily.

"I . . . love you, too," she whispered, clutching the phone more tightly. Her cheeks had gone hot.

"Let's say it again. I love you. Oh, damn, this isn't right. The first time I say it shouldn't be on the phone."

"It's fine," she said softly. "It's . . . wonderful. I love you, too."

"Bye, baby. Take care." His voice was husky and tense.

"You, too," she said.

There was a click. The receiver went dead. She set it down gently, almost reverently. He had told he loved her—twice. It seemed nothing short of miraculous.

"You're blushing like a bride, Miss Fingal."

Fish's voice made her jump. He stood by his office door, staring at her. He was only a paunchy little man with thinning hair, yet the sight of him always chilled her.

"Exchanging sweet nothings with your pirate king?" he asked. He ran his tongue over his upper lip.

"Yes, sir," she said, and looked away. "It won't happen again. I don't usually waste company time."

Oh, Gus was right, she thought miserably; emotion didn't mix with this sort of business. If Gus couldn't meet her, it meant he was accessing important information. She should be doing the same—and with the greatest of care.

When she looked again at Fish, he gave her an eerily angelic smile. "I'd never stand in the way of young lovers," he said. "I'm all for them. They...interest me. Talk all you want to your beautiful pirate."

She smiled guiltily, but could think of nothing to say.

"Perhaps you think it's odd that I refer to a man as beautiful," Fish said, his smile hardening. "Or perhaps you think *I'm* odd to call a man beautiful."

"Oh—no," she managed to say. "Men can have a beauty of their own. M-Michelangelo's *David*, for instance."

"Exactly," said Fish. "And your fiancé has the aesthetics of a certain type—the Latin. I merely remark on it. To comment on your good taste, your insight."

"I . . . see. Thank you."

"He affects a rather rough appearance, but beneath it he has—what?—a certain grace. Elegance, even."

Susannah nodded and stared in embarrassment at her computer screen. "Yes. He does."

"You're an unusual couple. But . . . unusually elegant."

She nodded again and swallowed. "Thank you."

"So when is the happy day?" Fish asked. "The marriage?"

"The marriage? Oh...the marriage." She gave him a smile that she hoped was maidenly and modest. "Well . . . as soon as we can afford it, I suppose. Not for a while, certainly."

His own smile had become fixed, masklike. "It's a shame that money should be an obstacle."

She made a gesture of acceptance. "That's life."

"I see. I see."

He stood, simply staring at her. His smile died, and calculation shone in his eyes. He clasped his hands behind his back. He began to rock on the balls of his feet.

Ginger came in, and Susannah welcomed the interruption. Fish had seemed transfixed, and he'd alarmed her.

"There's a guy out there with a registered letter," Ginger said, jerking her head toward the reception area. "He won't let me sign for it. He says you have to. Should I send him in?"

Fish seemed to come back to himself with a start. He regarded Ginger with something akin to resentment. "No. I'll come out," he said brusquely.

He stalked past Ginger, who gave Susannah a sardonic glance, then followed him.

Susannah gave a long, relieved sigh. She mustn't let Fish catch her off guard again.

While he was out of his office, even briefly, she would peek inside. She had been careful to create an excuse to do so, if the opportunity arose.

She took a letter from her desk drawer. It was a form letter about smoking policies that Fish wanted mailed to all employees. She had purposely set her own printer to print the letter as dimly as possible.

She took the floppy disk from the A-drive slot of her computer, then rose and went quickly into Fish's office.

The copy of Poe's poems still sat on his desk. The fresh hyacinths filled the room with scent. The fountains before Fish's desk rose and fell to the tune of "With a Little Bit of Luck."

On the desk beside the Poe book was a small black book, open at a page of figures. Susannah glanced down at it, warily listening for the sound of Fish's return.

The pages contained neat rows of columns labeled by the weeks of the month. She sucked in her breath: Was this *it?* Fish's handwritten record of real receipts?

She turned her attention to his computer screen. This *was* it, she thought with excitement. He was in the midst of transferring the figures to his computer.

Susannah heard the softest brush of wood against carpet. She stepped back from the desk and pasted a bland expression on her face.

"Miss Fingal?" Fish said, raising an eyebrow. "What are you doing?"

"The printer, sir. It's not working. I was going to use yours to print the new policy on smoking. Or would I disturb you?"

She held the letter toward him. He came over and scowled at it. At the same time, with one smooth movement, he closed the black book and thrust it into his pocket.

Aha! she thought with triumph; she had been right. Fish *did* want the contents of the book kept secret. She was certain it was a record of the company's real profits.

He waved impatiently at the dimly-printed notice. In his other hand he gripped the registered letter so tightly that it was wrinkling. "Did you check the ink injector?"

"Yes. It seems fine."

"Yes, then. Use mine."

Mechanically he hit the Save button of his computer. He took out the disk, put it in a marked cardboard jacket. He went to the wall safe as if in a trance, and opened it.

Susannah watched closely. She saw the first number of the safe's combination—ten to the right—but then his body blocked her view.

He turned around, his eyes strangely dazed. He stared down at the letter still gripped in his hand. A look of pain clouded his face. "Yes," he said vaguely. "Only—leave me alone a minute. My God, what do they want? I'm only human."

"I'll just slip this disk in the computer while I'm here," she said. She slid the disk into the slot as Fish sat down heavily in his chair.

He reached for his letter opener and slit the envelope. "Oh, *drat*," she said with passion. "I think I've run my stocking. And this pair's brand-new."

She bent, reaching under her skirt. She let her thumbnail rake the top of her nylon, snagging it slightly. Discreetly she raised her skirt and surveyed the damage. "Well, it isn't too terrible," she said with all the innocence she could contrive. "Do you think?"

Fish had drawn out the letter and unfolded it. His face was flushed and he barely glanced at Susannah and her exposed thigh. Once more he seemed to have fallen into a trance.

"I'll see if Ginger has some nail polish. That'll fix it," she murmured. She licked her forefinger and dampened the snag so it wouldn't run. "Look at that," she said.

But Fish didn't look. He seemed hypnotized by the letter. It contained only a few words. Susannah did her best to read it out of the corner of her eye.

There were only a few sentences, but she couldn't make them out. She did manage to read one phrase: "Before the end of the week—"

Fish crumpled the letter. He rose and strode to the paper shredder. He smoothed out the letter and read it again, his eyes running back and forth over its few lines.

Then he inserted both the letter and envelope into the shredder. The machine buzzed into life, gnawing the paper to tiny bits. Fish stood and watched, as if stunned.

Susannah let her skirt fall back into place. Clearly, Fish had received bad news, shocking news. Her torn stocking seemed hardly to have registered on him. She wondered, apprehensively, if her move had been too bold.

But he barely seemed aware of her. He turned and acted startled to find her still standing there.

"Miss Fingal?"

"Yes?" She tried to keep her voice bright, guileless.

"Why are you here?"

"To use the printer, Mr. Fish. It's about the smoking-policy notice. I showed you—"

"Oh," he said, frowning. "That. Let it wait. Don't put any more calls through to me today. Admit no callers. Tell Ginger. I need to be alone."

"Of course. I'll just take my disk—"

"Leave it be," he commanded. "I need—to be alone."

Susannah backed away from the desk obediently. "Certainly," she said and left. She let the heavy door fall shut behind her as she hurried to the reception area.

"Mr. Fish doesn't want any calls put through and no visitors admitted."

"Oh, no," Ginger said, wrinkling her nose. "He's gonna sit in there watching the VCR all afternoon. Yetch."

"The VCR? You mean he'll watch a movie or something? I don't think so. He seems...upset. That letter upset him. The registered letter. Do you know anything about it?"

"Nope," Ginger said. "He gets registered letters sometimes. Sends 'em, too."

"When's the last time he sent one?"

"The day you came for your interview."

"To who? I mean—whom? To whom did he send it?"

"Some woman named Hawkins or something."

"Where? Where does she live?"

"New Jersey. New York. She moves around. He sends her a lot of letters. What business is it of yours?"

"None," Susannah said with an innocent shrug. "I'm just concerned. He really seems upset. Quite upset."

"So he's upset," Ginger said without sympathy. "Big deal. He'll sit in his office and watch *Breakfast at Tiffany's*. He's out of our way, at least."

"*Breakfast at Tiffany's*?"

"Any of *her* movies," Ginger said. "Except *Wait Until Dark*. He can't stand *Wait Until Dark*. It makes him froth."

"Why?"

"Because Allan Arkin's tryin' to *kill* Audrey Hepburn all the way through it. He's chasin' her with a knife and all. Fish gets upset."

"But—it's only a movie. Won't he even want lunch?"

"No," Ginger said with impatience. "He has a little microwave. He'll make himself popcorn. Eat popcorn and watch movies all afternoon. Like he was a kid at a matinee."

Susannah gave her a dubious look.

"Hey," Ginger said, shaking her head, "he's strange—haven't you caught on? In my personal opinion, he's just gonna go completely wacko one of these days. I kiss this great salary goodbye, and they cart him off to the rubber room. In the meantime, live and let live, I say."

Suddenly Ginger's fountains wilted and died, and the piped-in music ceased. "There he goes," she said. "Can't run his weirdo fountains when his precious movie's on."

"Ginger?" Susannah said hesitantly.

"What?"

"You gave that envelope to Nora Geddes yesterday, didn't you?"

"Of *course*, I did. That's why he sent me, wasn't it?"

"Did you know what was in it?"

"Stuff. Her stuff was in it. From her desk."

"Did she open it while you were there?"

"No. And again, what business is it of yours?"

"None," Susannah said defensively. "It's just—I found…some lipstick in the back of a drawer. It must be hers. And Fish was sitting at my desk today when I came in. Does he go through our desks, do you think?"

"Hey," Ginger said, opening a book of crossword puzzles, "you got something you don't want him to see? Keep it out of his way. It's that simple, okay?"

"I'm asking you—does he go through the desks?"

Ginger sighed. "I don't know. He liked to sit at Nora's, that's all. Before she came in in the morning."

"Why?"

Ginger made a gesture of exasperation. "Because he's *Fish* is why. It's something he started about six months ago. I thinks he gets a buzz out of sitting there. Who knows what it all means?"

*Indeed,* Susannah thought ominously. *Who knows what it all means?*

Lem Colter was dead, Nora Geddes was missing, hundreds of thousands of dollars were being laundered, and Fish had hardly batted an eyelash. Now he was stunned by a letter of two or three sentences. What could make such a cold man register such shock?

She left Ginger and went back to her own office. The scent of popcorn seeped in from around Fish's door.

Her fountains and their music had died. But from Fish's office she could hear the faint strains of "Moon River."

*He's crazy,* she thought to herself. *He really is. He's a psychopath. He's dangerous, and he's coming undone.*

For the first time since she had begun her charade, she was truly frightened.

FEAR OF ANOTHER SORT gripped her as she ran up the rickety stairs to the motel suite. She had much to tell Gus, but she was more worried about emotions than reports. How would Gus greet her? Would things turn awkward between them again? Had he changed his mind?

But before she could unlock the door, he flung it open, drew her inside, wrapped her in his arms and kissed her with such passion it drove away all thought.

He crushed her to his chest as his tongue delved between her lips, tasting her as if she were wine. His hands ran over her body with a kind of desperate hunger.

Her mind exploded pleasantly into a cascade of stars. The rest of the world was darkness. Gus was the shower of stars, burning her and filling her with light.

She dropped her purse, she dropped the computer book she carried. His lips on hers were so *right* that all fear fled, all doubt vanished, and she wound her arms around his neck.

He pulled her closer, so she could feel all his taut leanness. She tasted the hot silkiness of his mouth, inhaled the clean, subtle scent of his after-shave. He drew her up so that her feet no longer touched the floor. Slowly he whirled her around once, then twice.

She hung on tightly, her mouth clinging to his, feeling gloriously dizzied. He kissed her harder and more deeply, then collapsed onto the couch, still holding her, still kissing her. She had the sensation of falling a long way, even though she lay safely beside him, her heart beating wildly against his.

"I thought of you all day," he said, his mouth against hers. He was pulling the pins from her hair, making it spill free. "I thought of this."

"I thought of you, too." If she kissed him any more, she thought, she would faint or die or evaporate.

She laid her cheek against his chest and closed her eyes, embracing him as passionately as he did her. She felt so fiercely in love with him that she couldn't speak. She kept eyes shut, the better to savor his touch.

He had loosened her hair. He ran his hand through it, kissing it and murmuring something in Spanish. "Beloved," she thought he said, and, "My heart of hearts."

He tried to raise her face to his, to find her lips again. Dazed, she forced herself to resist. She shook her head but couldn't bring herself to pull away from him.

*We're going to make love again,* she thought, hardly believing it. *I walked in the door, he was here, and sixty seconds later, we're on the edge of making love.*

But she couldn't deny him. Her chest ached with loving and wanting him. This time when he sought her lips, she gave them to him. His arms tightened around her. He took one of her hands and laid it on his chest so that she could feel the strong, rapid beat of his heart.

"Oh, *tormento mío,*" he breathed. "I meant to tell you that I really love you. To tell you right."

"Actions," Susannah said against his lips, "speak louder than words."

He kissed her forehead, her closed eyelids. His hand gripped hers more possessively. "Women like words. They need words. Sweet words. But you've undone me. All my words have left."

"Love me without words," she whispered against his warm throat.

He kissed her lips again. His tongue played with hers, intoxicating her. Then he stood, drawing her up beside him. He looked into her eyes, his own, hot and desirous.

Her knees shook slightly. She tried to smile, but even her smile was shaky. His face was intent, the line of his mouth straight with control.

*How does he do this to me?* she marveled. *How can he make me feel this way?* She was powerless to look away from him. She wanted him with every atom of her being. His face said he wanted her in the same way, and the knowledge shook her through and through.

Saying nothing, he took off her suit jacket and hung it on the back of a chair. She had, she realized, lost both her shoes somewhere between the door and the couch.

He turned her so that her back was to him. Wordlessly, he unbuttoned her blouse and drew it from her. He folded it and lay it over the jacket.

Then his lean fingers were unbuttoning her skirt, pulling down the zipper. Slowly he drew it down over her hips, and she stepped out of it.

Carefully he draped the skirt over another chair. She stood before him barefoot, in her lacy bra and half-slip. He looked at her, his gaze running down, then up her body, finally meeting hers. He smiled at last, with a knowing quirk at one corner of his mouth. He nodded in satisfaction. He placed his hands on her bare shoulders.

He bent and kissed her over her heart, his lips hot and hungry. Susannah felt faint again. She wondered if her knees would tremble so hard that they wouldn't hold her.

She needn't have worried. Gus lifted her, kissed her throat, then undid her bra. He dropped it to the floor and bent his head to taste and tantalize her breasts. He did so until she gasped. Then he carried her into his crowded bedroom.

He stripped away what remained of her lingerie, his eyes devouring her as he did so. Then he stood and undressed himself.

Lowering himself beside her, he kissed his way down her body until his mouth was pressed, hot and questing, against the inside of her thigh. His hands curved themselves around her hips.

He pleasured her until she thought that she was dying. At last, both of them quivering with need, they locked their bodies together. She twined her legs around him as he filled her with his heat and power.

They moved, thrusting in rhythm with the spiraling force of their need. He held himself back until ecstasy flooded through her in mind-shattering waves, and she couldn't help uttering a little cry.

Then he drove himself more deeply and, shuddering, climaxed. He gathered her more tightly in his arms and buried his face against her throat. Susannah clung to him, possessed and ravished by rapture.

GUS STARED AT THE waning sunlight that filtered through the bedroom curtains. He was not a happy man.

But he was a man ferociously in love, and for this he cursed himself. He had broken all the rules for her, and she had asked him to keep doing so. Now he couldn't seem to help himself. Together they had fallen into sweet madness, a craziness as real as Fish's.

He held her fast, and he worried. He was the professional, the one who was supposed to keep his head. Instead, he'd lost it the moment he'd heard her step on the stairs.

He and Susannah had both been half drunk on danger from the beginning. Now they were completely drunk on desire, which was even more intoxicating than the danger. If he wasn't careful, they could both reel out of control.

Hell, he thought, gritting his teeth, they *were* out of control. Duty, safety, right, wrong—he would have ignored all in her arms. He'd been possessed.

Susannah, naked, stirred sleepily against him. He kissed her tumbled hair and drew the sheet up higher around her.

"Gus," she said against his throat, "that was crazy, wasn't it?" But she sounded content.

He kissed her hair again. "Yeah. It was crazy."

She laughed with an air of shy embarrassment that made him yet a little more insane about her.

"Nobody," she said wonderingly, "who knows Miss Finlay, the very proper computer-science teacher, would believe it."

"*I* wouldn't have believed it," he murmured, holding her closer. "You kept it hidden. I looked at you for over two years and—maybe—never saw you. Until this week."

She made a small sound of pleasure. "*Maybe* you never saw me?"

"I don't know. I think maybe part of me knew this would happen. That's why I asked you here. To see if it would— happen, that is. *Jesucristo*, I can't explain."

He hugged her more tightly, more possessively. She was his and his alone.

She sighed and nestled against him. "We shouldn't have done this, should we? But it was wonderful."

"We shouldn't have done it. It was wonderful."

"But I have so much to tell. And I know you must, too. Everything's happening so fast—"

"Yes. We have to talk."

"And you were right. It's scary."

"Yeah." He raised himself on an elbow and stared down at her face, framed by the auburn richness of her hair. "I could stay in this bed for a week with you."

She smiled, but he touched her lips, stroking the curve back to a serious line.

"We have to be careful," he warned her. He knew he was warning himself, as well. "I think too much about you. So maybe I'm not thinking clearly about anything else. Take a shower and get dressed, Chiquita. With you naked, I can't think at all."

With a harsh sigh, he released her. He sat and reached to the floor for his jeans. He stood and slipped into them. He zipped them as he stared down at her.

"I do love you," he said solemnly. "I don't even know how it happened, but I do. You believe that, don't you?"

She rose on her elbow. She stretched her other hand to him. "If you love me, don't go yet. Come back."

"Susannah," he said in confusion. His mind told him one thing. His soul, his yearning heart, told him another. So did his body, aroused again, in spite of his resolve.

Her beautiful eyes blinded him to reason, and her mouth called to him without speaking, and love and need drove through him like twin knives.

Knowing it was madness, he sank back to the bed and took her in his arms to make love to her yet again.

# 12

GUS BENT OVER HIS cornflakes, frowning. Susannah sat across from him, not eating, her chin in her hands, watching him.

"We've got to stop carrying on like this," he said, not looking up at her. "Every time I think of you, I want to—ki-yi-yi— Never mind what I want. I've got to *stop*."

She smiled, but her smile was troubled.

"Frankly," he muttered, "I've never felt like this before. I didn't know it was possible to feel like this. But we've got a serious situation on our hands here. I've got to *think*."

She had told him that the money Fish had sent to Nora Geddes was mysteriously back again. She'd kept one of the twenties with the recorded serial number, trading it for a bill in her purse. Now it lay between them on the table like an evil omen.

From listening to the bug, Gus had known of the registered letter and something about Fish's reaction. Susannah had told him about the black book, the disk and the safe. He seemed particularly interested in the disk.

She also told him what Ginger had said about Fish's registered letters to Maude Ann Hawkins.

"I don't like it," Gus growled. "It's too strange. And I can't get Olivier to believe me. 'Sit tight,' he says. 'Don't jump to conclusions,' he says."

He picked up the twenty-dollar bill. "This ices it. We got trouble here. Big trouble." He set it down again, as if he didn't like touching it.

"Gus, I think I can get to that disk. We already know the first number of the combination. Once we have the disk, you have your case. A few more days—sooner, with luck—I can do it, copy it. I know I can."

He gave her an oddly somber look, but he nodded. "Yeah," he said. "Let's hope so."

"What about you?" she asked worriedly. "What did you find out?" So far he'd made her do most of the talking.

He shook his head. "Nora Geddes didn't reach Denver. But her baggage did. Nobody claimed it."

"Has anybody opened it?"

He gritted his teeth. "No. It's like pulling teeth. The Bureau just isn't interested—yet. *Damn* Olivier. Local authorities haven't got the clout to get it done. For one thing, she's not officially missing yet. Not for forty-eight hours."

"Even if she's skipped bail?"

"There's no proof yet that she's *not* coming back."

"But the one-way ticket—who actually bought that ticket for her?"

Gus shook his head with displeasure. "Somebody so nondescript that he might as well have been The Invisible Man. He paid cash, left no trail. My guess would be Randolph. He's like a snake, he blends into the background."

"What about her house?" Susannah asked. "Has anybody looked in her house?"

"Chelsea's trying to get a warrant, but it's hard. Nora's main offense was minor. Nobody except me thinks she was in danger."

"What about the blackmail threat?"

"That was Colter, not Nora. We have no idea if he was bluffing. Maybe they had nothing on Fish."

"But if they did?"

"Fish had more than two days since Colter died to find out. My bet is he had somebody over at Nora's very fast—before Colter was even cold—either to shake the truth out of her or to search the place—or both."

Nervously, Susannah ran her fingers through her hair. "But if she had nothing, or if Fish got it back, why did he send her away?"

Gus gave a tense shrug. "Maybe she still knew too much. Maybe she knew that Colter was murdered, that it wasn't any accident."

"How *could* she know?" Susannah asked, perplexed.

"Hell, she could have guessed. Or somebody could have told her," Gus said. "Fish's strong-arm man or whoever he sent. To scare her. To make her turn over anything incriminating she had."

Her forehead wrinkled as she imagined the scene. "Then they told her to go away and keep quiet? That they'd leave her alone?"

"Right. Only they *didn't* leave her alone. Somebody stopped her in St. Louis."

She made a helpless gesture. "But you can't prove it."

He picked up the twenty again. His face grew grimmer. "No. I can't."

"And you can't prove Colter's death was murder."

He threw the bill down. "No. But it stinks to high heaven. This Dunwoody character, this repentant drunk, is *already* out on bail. He's got a high-priced lawyer coming down from St. Louis to defend him."

"St. Louis keeps turning up."

"Yeah. Like a bad penny. I'll tell you what happens next. High-priced lawyer tells Dunwoody to plead guilty to involuntary manslaughter. Dunwoody gets off with a stiff fine and a suspended sentence. In short, he walks. I'm not saying this might happen—it *will* happen."

Susannah shook her head dubiously. "It's an awfully dangerous way to kill somebody, Gus. I mean, I know it looks suspicious, Colter getting killed so soon—"

"Don't go logical on me, Chiquita. You sound like Olivier. It's *not* a dangerous way to kill somebody. It's a damn safe way. Because nobody ever imagines it's murder."

"But Dunwoody?" she asked. "Why would he do such a thing?"

"For money. Then he goes someplace else, changes his name, kills somebody else a different way."

She frowned. "You mean he's a hit man?"

"I mean he's an organization man. He can make a hit if he's told to. He's here to make exactly such a hit—if it's called for."

"Why here? In Branson?"

"Why not here? There's movers and shakers in this town. There's big money changing hands. There's mob business— Fish proves that."

Susannah felt slightly sick. "You mean Dunwoody was just sitting around . . . waiting? That Fish might lure somebody down here, or the organization could arrange it—and Dunwoody would *kill* him? And make it seem like an accident?"

"That's what I'm saying."

"Gus, that's so—cold-blooded."

"These guys aren't exactly Santa's helpers."

"It's complicated. And the way Nora Geddes disappeared—if Fish caused it, that's sophisticated, too."

"Look," Gus said earnestly, "that's my point. We got three people in Missouri, all connected with Fish or his organization. One dies and two disappear in the space of a week. Somebody knows how to make these things happen. Somebody is *expert* at it."

The sick feeling in her stomach intensified. "Gus? Do you think Nora Geddes is . . . dead?"

He looked away from her. "Yeah. I think maybe she is."

"But—but what would they *do* with her?"

"The same thing they did to Marty the Mouse. Brought her here."

"Back here?" She was horrified. "But why? Why go to all that trouble to have her leave, then bring her back?"

"Because it's the last place anybody'd look for her."

"But what? And how . . . and where . . . ?"

He pushed aside his cereal bowl. He put his hand over hers, gripping it tightly. "I'll tell you where. I can't get it out of my head—what you said about that cave."

"The cave," she echoed with surprise. "You laughed when I talked about the cave."

"I stopped laughing. You're right. Why does Fish have it? It makes no special money. So what's it good for?"

She stiffened in horror. "You think he used the cave to hide—hide their bodies?"

"Yeah. And God only knows how many people might be in it."

"How *many?*" she asked, recoiling. "Gus? What are you saying?"

He released her and reached for a road atlas that sat on the table. He opened it to the map of the United States. He looked across it at her, his dark eyes holding hers.

"Olivier wouldn't give me the information I wanted fast enough. He plods. I went around him. You get an operation like Fish's, people get hurt. Sometimes people get killed. Sometimes they just . . . disappear. Since Fish came to Branson, we know of at least six that did just that—disappeared."

She watched him fearfully. He was speaking of the stuff of which nightmares were made.

He picked up a pen and enclosed Branson in a square of black. "Three years ago a certain Alvin Jefferson of Kansas City tried to move in on turf that Fish's organization claimed. One day, he was gone. Just . . . gone."

Gus drew a black star next to Kansas City. "A few months later, a pair of brothers, the Abduls, tried to take a piece of the organization in Memphis. The Abdul brothers disappeared one night. The only thing they left behind were a lot of questions. They vanished. No trace."

He inked two black stars beside Memphis.

"One month later, a kingpin of a rival organization was on his way from Chicago to Vegas. He was supposed to switch planes in St. Louis. He got on the plane in Chicago. But he never made it to Vegas. He disappeared. It had to be in St. Louis."

Another black star appeared beside St. Louis.

"Just like Nora Geddes," Susannah breathed. She put her hand on her midsection, because her stomach had knotted.

His gaze locked with hers again. "Exactly like Nora Geddes. And there's more." He tapped the map at Tulsa, Oklahoma. "Fish's organization has some liquor stores in Oklahoma. Some were at the edge of tribal lands. The Cherokees didn't like it. One, Walter Manyknives, made a lot of noise, was bringing down pressure, publicity. Walter Manyknives disappeared. He's never been found."

He inked still another star beside Tulsa.

"My God," Susannah breathed.

"All right," Gus said, setting his jaw. "Late that year there was trouble in Fish's organization, the St. Louis branch."

"St. Louis again."

"Right. There was a guy in the organization named Renaldo. He wasn't happy. He didn't feel safe from his own people. He made noises to the Bureau that he might like to roll over to our side for protection. The mob sent him to do business in Hot Springs, Arkansas. He never arrived. The last place anybody saw him was Springfield, Missouri."

He made the sixth star beside Springfield.

"Oh, Gus." She bit her lip and shook her head.

The line of his mouth was bitter. He drew a circle around the starred cities. "Now, what do you see?"

"Branson's in the middle," she said weakly. "Less than a day's drive from any of them. But they couldn't be driving dead bodies around. What if they got stopped by the police? Had a flat? An accident?"

"Maybe they didn't drive dead bodies. You stick a needle in a guy, suddenly you're just driving a friend who's asleep. Or drunk. They don't have to be dead—yet."

"You mean they're killed *here?*"

"It'd be safer."

She rose and went to the stove, needing a cup of coffee. Even though it was summer, she was chilled to the bone.

She could feel him watching her. She filled the cup, willing her hand not to shake. It didn't. She sat again, steeling herself and waiting for Gus to go on.

"Now," he said solemnly, "in the space of a week, we've got three more gone. Marty the Mouse. Colter. Nora."

He drew two more black stars beside St. Louis, one next to Branson.

She was appalled. "Gus, that's *nine people.*"

"Yeah," he said tonelessly.

"I know."

"You think they're all in that cave—except for Colter?"

"Right."

"But *where* in the cave?"

"Hey—it's being 'developed.' Who knows what's down there? Plus, you got the deepest underground lake in the region. How deep? I checked. Eighty feet. That's one deep dark lake, Chiquita."

She ran her hand over her forehead. "Have you told all this to Olivier?"

"I tried."

"He won't believe you?"

Gus sneered. "He says I've got no proof. He says it's not my assignment. He'll take it 'under advisement.'"

She pushed the coffee away, untasted. "Under advisement?" she repeated with a hollow laugh. "And in the meantime?"

"In the meantime, I think I know why Fish got so upset today. I think I know what that letter said."

His expression was more serious than she had ever seen it. It made her heart stutter in her chest. "What?"

"I think they ordered him to kill somebody else. Somebody here."

"Gus—no!"

"Yeah, baby. I heard him on the phone after that letter. I saw the messages flying back and forth on CommuCate. He doesn't want to do it—yet. He thinks it's too soon. He's scared. And he thinks he screwed up by killing Colter. I think Dunwoody was sent down here to kill somebody else. Then Fish jumped the gun."

Her eyes widened in apprehension.

But Gus seemed strangely calm. "Yeah," he said almost dreamily. "But it's got to be done. Oh, yeah. Somebody in this town . . . is about to die."

"Who?" she asked. "And why?"

"That's what worries me. You gotta help me. I want you to drive to Springfield. Tonight. While I'm at work."

Surprised, she sat farther back in her chair, staring at him. She hadn't been prepared for this.

"I want you to deliver a message to an operative up there. You met him once—Fritz. He's the guy who gave you the car."

She looked at him questioningly. "A message?"

He nodded, his face masklike. "Yeah. And copies of tapes, printouts from CommuCate. He worked on the Springfield disappearance. He'll understand what we've got here. I've got to go around Olivier. Fritz can move faster. He'll know what's at stake."

"Why do you want me to deliver it?" she asked suspiciously. "You could send it by overnight express. He could have it by morning."

"The express office in this burg closes at five. The sooner he gets this, the better. Can you do it?"

"Of course, I can do it," she said hesitantly. "But—"

"We can't even waste one night, baby," he said, taking her hand again. "I've already called him. He's available. He can meet you at the pizza place near the airport. It's on the highway. It's called Ferelli's. You'll recognize him, won't you?"

She had an excellent memory for faces. "Yes." But something in his manner, in the suddenness of his request, disturbed her.

"Good," he said, and looked relieved. "The sooner you go, the better. If you start now, you can make it by eight. He'll be waiting for you."

"He . . . expects me?"

"I told him I'd call when you leave. Can you handle it, Chiquita? I don't like your being on the road at night, but there's no choice."

"I can handle it. It's no problem."

He paused. "Take your glasses, okay? I get worried, you wearing those contacts so much. They might start bothering you. That's not good. Driving at night and all."

"Sure," she said, but thought it an odd suggestion. She was growing used to the new contacts. And he'd always made such fun of her glasses. . . .

His hand tightened on hers. The look in his eyes became tender, yet somehow pained. "I kinda miss seeing you in those glasses. You know? You still got the fuzzy pink bathrobe at home? The funny bedroom slippers?"

She laced her fingers through his. "Yes."

"I want to see you in them again, soon. When I'd think of you—before all this—that's always how I remembered you. The bathrobe. The crazy slippers. Your hair down."

She smiled, but inside felt an strange sadness mixed with apprehension. "Gus?"

He glanced at his watch. "I gotta go or I'll be late for work. Can you start now, baby? So I can call Fritz?"

*This is happening too fast. We've learned so much so fast, and now everything's speeding up like some crazy piece of film.*

"Sure," she said with more confidence than she felt. "I can go. Have you got the tapes and things ready?"

"It'll only take a minute." He squeezed her hand, then released it. He stood and went into his room, closing the door between them.

She stared after him, more troubled than before. Then she, too, rose. She went into her bathroom and looked into the mirror. Her face was pale, but her cheeks were still flushed from their lovemaking. Mechanically, she took up her brush and brushed her hair. She started to pin it back, then decided not to. Gus liked it loose. She would wear it loose.

She remembered his advice about the contact lenses and took them out, put them in their case. She settled her glasses on her nose. Did he really like her in them?

She wore jeans, running shoes, and a blue T-shirt. Well, she supposed, she didn't need to dress formally to make an information drop to an FBI agent. She went back into the main room. Gus was still in his room, the door closed.

*People have been killed in this town*, she thought, a frisson rippling down her spine. *And now Fish is supposed to kill somebody else. We've got to stop him.*

Gus's door opened. He came out carrying an envelope like the one Ginger had taken to Nora Geddes. He'd taped it shut with several strips of heavy electrical tape.

His expression was almost cheerful again. "Hey. Your glasses," he said. He smiled slightly. "Good," he said.

He handed her the envelope. It was heavy and she could feel the edges of the tapes inside.

"What—what exactly did Fish say on the phone this afternoon?" she asked, fingering the envelope uneasily. "And on CommuCate?"

His smile died. "The same old double-talk. Garden this and bug-spray that. But the message was clear. He's supposed to move again, but he used up his 'best spray' without authorization. That's gotta be Dunwoody."

His brows knit in a worried frown. "Now he's supposed to hit again. But he can't use the 'best spray.' He's being pushed to do something that 'doesn't conflict with nature.' I take that to mean something that won't look suspicious."

"What do you think he'll do?"

"I don't know, Chiquita. He's very tricky. And nervous. I don't know what he might do."

She squared her shoulders. "I was startled by what you said—about the disappearances. It gave me a turn for a minute. But I'm not scared. Really."

His smile returned, a bit strained. "I know. But from here on out, we take every precaution. Be careful. I don't want anything happening to you. I love you, you know?"

She smiled shyly. "I love you, too. Springfield's not that far. I'll be back before you're home from work. I'll wait up for you."

"Yeah. Good." He took her by the shoulders, bent and kissed her. It was a disappointingly brief kiss, but she knew they did not dare anything else. They would be in each other's arms again.

When he drew back, she knew the message her eyes sent him: *I love you too much.*

She was happily shaken to see the same message in his.

"Go," he said, his voice low and almost harsh. "I'll be home as soon as I can. I'll be thinking of you every minute. Be careful—okay? See you around midnight."

She nodded. With obvious reluctance, he let his hands fall away.

"Around midnight," she said softly.

Then she turned from him and left, wondering why she felt such a strong sense of foreboding.

*Something's happening,* her instincts kept saying. *There's something he's not telling me.*

As she started the car and headed out of the parking lot and into Branson's knotted traffic, a clearer, more frightening thought assailed her.

He had been lying to her about something—she knew it.

He was keeping something secret. He was excellent at both things, lying and keeping secrets. But what was he keeping from her? And why?

# 13

GUS SET DOWN THE PHONE receiver. His chest hurt, his heart hurt, and his pulses beat double time.

What he was about to do was dangerous in the extreme. But he had to take Fish down any way he could, and he had to work fast.

And Susannah, thank God, would be gone, would be safe. He'd lied to her, but only to protect her. He'd lied to Fritz, too, which would get him in major trouble, but to hell with that. He'd deal with it later.

Soon Susannah would be on the night's last flight out of Springfield, and by midnight she should be safe in Arkansas again. He'd given Fritz the order to see it was done, even if it meant putting her under protective custody.

She'd be mad as hell. He couldn't help it. She'd signed on for a simple operation to expose money laundering—not to get caught in the middle of a hit operation.

Her safety—that counted most.

Shutting down Fish, that was next in importance.

If he himself got into danger or trouble, that was the breaks. At this point he didn't give a damn.

The first thing he did was call in sick to the Dusty Lester Show. He'd come down with the flu, he lied. He was sick as a dog. He wouldn't be coming in tonight.

The next thing he did was sweep through the apartment, snatching up anything that could be traced to Susannah. If he failed tonight, he wouldn't let Fish find anything that could lead to her.

He cut the labels out of the clothes she'd left behind. He took the airline tags off her suitcases and burned them.

She'd brought a stack of books with her, her name and address neatly written on the flyleaf of each. He tore out the pages and burned them as he had the tags.

He took the label from the case that held her contacts. He burned that, too. She had a beat-up purse in her closet, the one she'd brought to Branson. It contained her old wallet, her real identification.

He cut up a grocery sack, wrapped the purse in the paper, taped the package shut. He wrote her home address on it, but no return address.

He tucked it inconspicuously under his arm and walked to the corner grocery store. From its stamp machine, he bought five dollars' worth of stamps, stuck them on, then stuffed the package into the mailbox in the parking lot. He walked back to the motel quickly but casually.

He searched the rooms one last time, satisfying himself that there was nothing, not so much as a scrap of paper, left there to identify her.

He'd thought all day he should send her back. Maybe that was why he'd grabbed her so desperately when she'd come home. He wanted her in his arms. He wanted her to stay.

But afterward, as soon as he'd heard the first of her story and seen the twenty-dollar bill, he knew she had to leave. That's what had done it: her telling him the twenty thousand Fish had given Nora was now back in his possession.

All his fears had become cold certainty when she'd told him that. The minute she'd said it, he was sure Nora Geddes was dead. Whoever had put the money back in Fish's hands had brought Nora back, as well. Gus knew it with the gut instinct that had never played him wrong.

If Fish had gotten Nora, he'd gotten Colter. If Colter, then why not Marty the Mouse? And all the others? It was more than possible; it was probable.

Gus had been with the law a long time. He knew one of the hardest things to hide successfully was a human body. Corpses had a perverse way of being discovered.

But Fish's cave, with its unexplored depths, its deep lake, was a huge, natural tomb. It could hold a hundred bodies in its secrecy and blackness and stillness.

Killing was going on all over the Midwest, and Fish, like the king of the dead, presided over it. Fish's empire was no place for a lady, most particularly no place for the lady Gus loved. He never wanted her to encounter Fish again.

In the meantime, unwittingly, she'd given him the means to get the information on the money laundering—without using her. He didn't need to drag her into it; she would be completely safe—if he moved boldly enough.

The figures were on the disk, the disk was in the safe, the safe was guarded by an electonic security system. No problem.

He'd broken through more than one security system in his day, cracked more than one safe. He'd just never before done it without authorization.

Gus changed to his darkest jeans, a black T-shirt, and black engineer boots. He put on a tool belt of worn black leather, filling it with wire cutters, precision pliers, screwdrivers, a coil of copper wire, a roll of electrical tape.

He took a flashlight from his toolbox and thrust it into his belt. He slid a box of lock picks into his back pocket. He put on a long-sleeved black cotton shirt and buttoned it halfway up, leaving it out to cover the belt.

He checked the the clip in his .38, put it into its holster and fastened the holster under the right leg of his jeans. Then he called Bobby Chelsea. Chelsea was at home and displeased at being disturbed.

Gus didn't waste time sugarcoating anything. "I got orders to go into Fish's place," he lied. "I'm going alone. I think

I can knock out the alarm system. If it does send a signal, keep back. It's only me."

Chelsea swore. "I'm in the middle of the 'movie of the week,' for God's sake. This is the first night I've had with my family since—"

"I didn't ask for your life story," Gus snapped. "The alarm system's Protronic. Call 'em and tell 'em I'm authorized to go in. If I set something off, I want no cars sent. None."

"You don't want backup from us?" Chelsea asked, suspicion in his voice.

"I don't want anybody in my way," Gus said. He would have loved a backup, but didn't dare ask for it. He was smashing enough rules without dragging the Branson police into an unauthorized break-in.

"So what else do I do?" Chelsea asked sarcastically.

"Nothing. Until you hear from me."

"What if I *don't* hear from you?" Chelsea challenged. "What if somebody walks in, takes you for a burglar, and blows your brains out?"

Gus forced himself to ignore the idea. "If you haven't heard from me by midnight, get worried."

"And then what?"

Gus had his first moment of hesitation. "Call Washington. Get a guy named Olivier. Tell him to contact Fritz in Springfield."

"Hold on, hold on," Chelsea grumbled. "Lemme write this down." He rechecked and grumbled again. "You got any other messages you want sent? In case you don't come back?"

"Yeah," Gus said from between his teeth. "Tell Olivier I said, 'I told you so.'"

This seemed to amuse Chelsea. "If you get killed, you told him so, huh? You must not like this assignment, eh?"

"I like it fine," Gus said, his lip curling. He hung up. His pulse drummed double time again. Then he thought of Susannah. He was doing what he had to do. Because it couldn't hurt, he crossed himself.

He put on a pair of black gloves. He left the rooms, descended the stairs, and set off through the night, toward Fish's building.

SUSANNAH DROVE THROUGH the darkness, worrying.

She had reached the small town of Ozark when worry turned into full-fledged paranoia.

Gus was up to something, she was sure of it. He might very well be up to something dangerous. Had he sent her to Springfield to keep her out of his way for the night? Why?

Their entire evening together now seemed like a surreal dream. They had made love beautifully, but with desperate passion. Why had there been such an undercurrent of frenzy in his kisses?

*He was like a man saying goodbye,* she realized numbly. *Yes—that was it—goodbye.*

Panic fluttered wildly in her stomach, spreading through her. She clutched the steering wheel more tightly and tried to think.

When they'd talked, he'd insisted she give her information first. Then, when he'd told her what he'd learned, he'd been intense, as if concentrating entirely on what he said.

But she *knew* Gus; his mind could be working on three levels at once. He could say one thing with apparent absorption, yet be planning another and plotting a third.

Was he sending her out of town so that he could do something he didn't want her to know? Or was he tricking her in some even more profound way? Did he plan to be gone when she came back?

Or was he planning that she not come back at all?

She clenched her teeth, her heart beating violently. What if he'd told Fritz to *detain* her? Not to *let* her come back? Oh, Lord, she thought, Gus always harped about her safety—always. Was he conniving to send her away? She'd thought it strange that he'd ask her so suddenly to go to Springfield.

He'd said the express company in Branson closed at five. *Did an express service even exist in Branson? And if so, did it really close as early as five?*

She looked for a service station. She saw one a block ahead and sped up to reach it. She braked the car so sharply when she stopped that the tires shrieked. A sleepy-looking attendant snapped into alertness and stared at her strangely.

She almost ran inside. She paged madly through the regional telephone book until she found the number of the express service. It was an 800 number, which meant long-distance but toll-free. With shaking fingers she fed her coins into the phone and punched the number.

"Nationwide Express," said the answering operator. "How may I help you? About what city would you like information?"

"Branson," Susannah said in a choked voice. "I need to know how late the office is open in Branson, Missouri."

"One moment, please."

Susannah put her hand over her heart to slow its painful gallop.

"I'm sorry," the operator said crisply. "There is no office in Branson. The closest is Springfield. That office is open until six-thirty."

Susannah stepped backward as if struck by a blow. *There is no office in Branson.* She had been right; he'd lied.

She hung up and stared, unseeing, at the phone. The service-station attendant walked in, wiping his hands on a rag. He cast her a concerned look.

"You all right, lady?"

"I'm . . . fine," she lied. "I just need a minute."

He cocked his head, looked at her more closely. "Something wrong?"

*Think!* she commanded herself. *Think!*

"There's a—an illness in the family. I've just had bad news."

"Sorry to hear it."

"I . . . have to gather my thoughts."

"Sure, lady. You want a cup of coffee or something?"

She shook her head and mumbled no, thanks. She pushed her glasses up on her nose. Her glasses, she thought, more bewildered than before. He'd wanted her to have her glasses. Because he didn't intend for her to come back.

Fritz, the Springfield agent, had been instructed not to let her come back. But what of the papers, the tapes? Were they only a ploy? Or did he really need them delivered to Fritz? If he did, she couldn't fail him . . . but she no longer knew what was true and what was not.

She looked at the attendant. Tears stung her eyes and she let them. She wanted the man to know she was upset. "I—I was supposed to go to Springfield," she said in a shaky voice. "For my boss. It's important. But now I don't know. Maybe I should turn around and go home."

He nodded solemnly, to show he understood.

"I . . . think I'll just sit in my car a minute," she said. "Try to sort out what I should do."

He nodded again.

She made her way back to the Ford, her knees weak. She sat in the driver's seat and reached for the envelope. The amount of tape on it suddenly struck her as sinister. It was a sign he hadn't wanted her to open it.

She took a deep breath, then slit open the envelope. Three audiotape cassettes tumbled out, and inside was a small stack of computer printouts clipped together, with a note fastened to the top page. It read, "Fritz—This is it. Get in touch with somebody who'll listen. G.J.R."

There was also a long white envelope that bore a single name—her own—in Gus's spiky handwriting.

Her hands shaking harder than before, she opened it and read.

"Baby, I love you and I'm sorry to do this to you. But I can't get you into this any deeper. Do exactly what Fritz says. It's important.

You're good, but you scare me. You take chances. That bit with your stocking today. I was listening. You scared the hell out of me. Let *me* take the chances. It's my job.

I've got a feeling things are about to break—fast. When it's done, I'll come for you. I promise. Forgive me, Chiquita. I wouldn't do this if I didn't love you.

I'm sorry, and I love you, and I don't know what else to say.

> I'm yours
> Gus

P.S. I'm really sorry. And I really love you.

Tears returned, blurring her vision.

From Gus, who was always so glib, so eloquent, this letter was touching in its awkwardness. It was as if, for once, all but the simplest words had deserted him.

But he was sending her away.

Leaving him made her heart feel as heavy and dead as stone. She couldn't do it.

She glanced at her watch. The preshow traffic had been heavy in Branson. She was running late. She'd made herself later by stopping here.

Springfield was only a short drive from Ozark. Fritz might already be at the pizza place waiting for her. In fifteen minutes, he certainly would be.

She put her face in her hands, trying to think.

Gus had assured her that Fish's case was about to break. But nobody except Gus, so far, thought Fish was involved in anything more serious than money laundering.

Gus believed someone else was going to be killed. If he was the only one who believed it, he was the only one who could stop it.

She bit her lip to keep it from trembling and looked through the computer printouts. Gus had been right about them. On their surface, they were exchanges about ridding the garden of a mole. Underneath, they were clearly about murder, at least to her eye.

"Before the end of the week," the woman named Hawkins had insisted. Susannah remembered the one phrase she had seen in Fish's registered letter— *Before the end of the week*...

Panic surged anew. The week's end was near. If Fish followed orders, he would kill within the next few days.

But Olivier wouldn't listen. And Fritz, if he believed Gus, would have to fight the same bureaucracy. How long would that take?

Gus wouldn't wait. He would act alone if he had to—and soon. She couldn't leave, knowing that. She wouldn't leave. A desperate plan formed in her mind.

Another car had pulled into the service station, its driver an elderly woman. The attendant talked to her as he washed her windshield.

Susannah put the tapes and printouts into the envelope, picked up her purse, and hurried back inside the station. She opened the phonebook again and found the number for Ferelli's Pizza Restaurant. She punched the number, watching the attendant carefully as she did so.

She stood near his littered desk. A roll of cellophane tape sat on its corner. As the phone rang, she carefully tore off a strip of tape and patched the slit envelope.

A man answered. "Ferelli's."

"Yes," Susannah said in her most businesslike voice. "I'm supposed to meet someone there. A tall man. About thirty-five. Curly dark hair. A pitted face. Light blue eyes. His name is Fritz. Does he happen to be there yet?"

"Could be." He sounded bored. She heard him call to someone. "Hey—your name Fritz?"

She held her breath.

"Yeah. It's him. You wanna talk to him?"

"Yes." She twisted the phone cord nervously. "Yes, please."

A maddeningly long pause. Then a clipped Midwestern voice was on the wire. "This is Fritz. Who's this?"

"Susannah," she said. "Gus's Susannah. I have your tapes, your printouts."

"Right. Where are you?"

"In Ozark. Something's come up."

"What?"

"Just . . . something. I . . . can't make it to Springfield."

"Wait a minute. Do you need me to get you? Where specifically are you?"

She glanced at the station's large outside sign. "A place called Herb's 76 Station. But I won't be here. What you need, I'm leaving here."

"No. You can't do that."

"I'm doing it," she said firmly. "I'll leave the envelope with the attendant."

Fritz's voice turned hard. "You can't. You can't trust a stranger to—"

"I trust this stranger," she said from between her teeth. "I've got no choice. You'll get your information."

"Where are you going?" Fritz demanded. "You can't do this. You're to hand this stuff to me personally. This is *procedure*."

"This is goodbye," she said and hung up. For the first time since Tim had been in the hospital, she prayed. She prayed for Gus's safety and that she was doing the right thing.

She left the envelope on the edge of the grimy desk. The attendant was ambling back inside.

She gave him an imploring look. "I hate to impose on you, but—but my boss's client said he'd pick the package up here if I'd leave it. Would you be so kind? I—I really want to go home. I'd like to go now."

He gave the package a short glance and her a long one. He seemed slightly uneasy at the suggestion, yet he was a kind man, she could tell. He didn't want to refuse her, and he didn't. He nodded in agreement. She could have kissed him.

"He's a tall man with curly hair. His name is Fritz. Mine's Susannah Finlay," she said. "This package—it's just some tapes and papers he needs. It's nothing valuable or anything. Oh, I can't thank you enough. Really, I can't."

He shrugged that it was nothing and refused a ten-dollar bill when she tried to make him take it.

"You get along home, miss," he said solemnly. "And drive careful, hear? You sure you're all right?"

"I'll be fine," she said. Giving him a shaky smile, she went to her car. She pulled onto the highway and headed back toward Branson.

If Gus was going to face danger, she was determined that he wouldn't face it alone. *I'm sorry,* she silently told him. *I can't leave you. I just can't.*


IT HAD TAKEN GUS AN hour to get into Fish's basement. He'd cut and wired deftly to get inside without setting off the alarms.

Once in, he'd made his way carefully, keeping low to stay out of the line of the electronic beams that guarded the space like invisible bars.

He'd found the circuit breakers and knocked off the building's power. It was a risky move, but it threw the alarm system back on its emergency power supply. Then he cut off the emergency power in a way that shouldn't alert the Protronic Security Company.

The method was Gus's own. It involved one slightly tricky loop of wire, a snip here, a snip there, and two foil gumwrappers. All he had to do was keep cool nerves, a steady hand, and not screw up the bit with the gum wrappers—the part that took as much luck as skill. But he did it. He didn't set anything off that he could hear, and didn't think he'd set off anything in Protronic's monitors.

Using the flashlight, he made his way up the stairs to Fish's suite of offices. He picked the locks until he'd reached Fish's inner sanctum.

He wiped his upper lip, which was sweating slightly. Setting the flashlight so its beam was trained on the wall safe, he stripped off his gloves. He wished to hell he had more sensitive fingertips.

But he knew how to crack a safe. He'd been taught by an old ex-con nicknamed the Georgia Cracker. The Cracker could tickle a safe as if it were a delicate act of foreplay and the thing would sigh open to him in surrender.

Ten right, Susannah has said— *God*, she was observant, he thought with a surge of fondness. He put his ear to the safe and listened to the tumblers fall into place.

Then he tried left and got lucky fast: The tumblers clicked clearly at two. The next movement was harder, and the fourth the hardest of all. Then he paused for a second to wipe the sweat from his lip again.

But at last he had it. The tumblers fell into place again, and with a sound like a tiny, metallic hiccup, the door unlocked.

He picked up the flashlight and opened the safe. Inside was a small pile of cash—about two thousand dollars, by Gus's estimate. The black book was there, and he opened it. It contained only the receipts for this month. Preceding records had been torn out—Fish obviously didn't like leaving a paper trail. Gus replaced the book.

There was also a stack of computer disks—twelve, at least. They were the small ones, three and a half inches square. He picked them up and fanned through them. The cryptic labels on them told him little, but they were dated. He picked last year's disks and left the others.

He swore under his breath as he stuffed the disks into his pockets. He'd steal them, dammit. He'd lose his badge, but to hell with it.

He'd tell the Bureau these were copies, secretly made in Fish's office. That it was a lie didn't matter. What mattered was getting Fish into custody before he killed again.

Lawyers could fight over Gus's methods later. He'd lost count how many laws he was breaking tonight, how many rules of procedure he was flaunting.

Olivier would have a massive coronary. Olivier would throw the book at him. He'd want to prosecute. To hell with that, too.

He closed the safe. He'd take the disks back to the motel, call Olivier. He'd say he'd lucked into the evidence and to close in on Fish, arrest him.

Between the time they busted Fish and they got wise to Gus's handiwork, they could get a warrant and get the rest of the disks legally.

And in the meantime, he hoped Fritz and the homicide experts could nail Fish on murder and conspiracy to murder, and aiding and abetting murder, and anything else lethal he'd done.

Somebody had to be helping Fish with those bodies, and somebody would rat if it would buy him leniency in court. It always happened. Loyalties died fast when a guy's skin was at stake.

He set his jaw and put his gloves back on. He wiped his prints from the safe, took up his flashlight, and started back to the basement. He'd turn on the circuit breakers, remove the gum wrappers and wire from the backup connection, and patch what he'd cut.

Then he'd get the hell out, back to the motel and the phone. Olivier would set the wheels into motion, and with luck, Fish would be slammed into jail by morning. Gus could almost taste the sweetness of it.

And when the dust cleared and the red tape was wound up, he'd go for Susannah. Susannah, who was safe and winging her way home. *I'll be coming for you, baby. And I'll never let you go again.*

He eased open the door of Fish's office and slipped into the next room.

Unexpectedly, a voice spoke, making his heart damn near stop.

"Hold it," a voice said. "Make a move and I'll blow your brains out your ear."

A gun barrel ground against his temple. A light flashed into his eyes, temporarily blinding him.

His heart slammed against his ribs. He gritted his teeth and swore—it wasn't just one man, it was two.

One held the gun to his head. The other shone the light in his face, and Gus thought he had a gun, too.

"Well, well," said the man with the light. "Look who's here. The beaner. The spick."

Gus muttered something savage, and the gun barrel struck him across the cheekbone. He winced, set his teeth, and held his head at a higher, more rebellious angle. He felt the warm dribble of blood on his face. He felt sick.

He was trapped. And in all likelihood, he would soon be dead.

# 14

HE RECOGNIZED HIS captors. They were Epperson and Randolph, two of Fish's flunkies from the Dusty Lester Show. He ignored his pain, fighting to stay focused.

Randolph, the taller man, held the gun to his head. Epperson, the burlier of the two, commandeered Gus's flashlight; he set both lights on Susannah's desk so Gus was caught in their beams.

Epperson came up on Gus, his giant shadow dancing, and struck him in the side of the jaw with his fist. Then, shoving his own gun into his belt, he fastened Gus's wrists behind him with the electrical tape. He patted Gus down and took the .38 out of its holster.

*Not good,* Gus thought with strange objectivity. *Not good at all.*

"Fish isn't going to like this, home boy," Epperson said with satisfaction. He took the clip out of Gus's gun and pocketed the ammunition. "Not a bit. I told him the lights were off. He wanted me to check. He knew something was up. He's smart, Fish is."

Epperson took up his own gun again. Keeping it trained on Gus, he sat on the corner of the desk. By the glow of the flashlights he punched out a number on the phone.

His voice clipped, he asked for Fish, then told him what had happened. He set down the receiver, picked up one of the flashlights and shone it into Gus's eyes. "You're in very big trouble, home boy," he said with the same self-satisfaction.

Fish was in the office within minutes, brimming with cold fury. He stalked over to Gus and stared at him. "Traitor," he snarled, backhanding Gus's face.

"Judas," he added, and backhanded him again. "Snake. Pig." He hit Gus twice more.

Gus didn't flinch, even though Fish's heavy gold ring struck his teeth, chipping one. Gus tasted blood and was tempted to spit it in Fish's face.

"What are you doing here?" Fish demanded.

"Name, rank, and serial number," Gus said out of the side of his mouth.

Fish stepped to the desk. He picked up a flashlight. He shone it into Gus's eyes. "What are you doing here?"

"Taking a poll. What's your favorite color? Who was your favorite Beatle?"

Fish drew back the flashlight and struck Gus hard across the collarbone, then swung again, hitting him in the same spot. Gus gave a wheeze of pain. Savagely, Fish smashed his weapon over Gus's shoulder so hard that the flashlight broke.

"I can beat you to death, you fool," he said, seizing Gus by the shirtfront. "I've beaten men to death before. Answer me: What did you want here?"

Gus said nothing. He stared contemptuously down at the man's shadowy face.

"He took computer disks," said Epperson. "I don't know what's on them."

Fish cursed and stepped to Epperson's side. Epperson nodded at the disks on the edge of the desk. Fish picked them up. He turned to Gus.

"You got into my *safe*," he hissed. "You got through my *security system*. You stole my *records*."

He moved to Gus again, glaring. "You're no ordinary thief. You're law, aren't you? *Aren't you?*"

Gus said nothing.

"I'll pull your teeth out with pliers, one by one," Fish gritted, seizing Gus by the jaw. "You're law, aren't you?"

Gus said nothing.

"Oh, yes." Fish nodded wisely. "You are. What about *her?* My beautiful Miss Fingal. My sweet Miss Fingal. She's in on it, too, *isn't she?*" He wrenched Gus's jaw.

Gus swallowed blood. "She doesn't know anything."

"She spied on me, didn't she? That's how you knew where the disks were, isn't it?"

Gus shrugged. "I figured it out. It didn't take genius."

Fish began to scream. "She spied! She spied! She spied!" He dug his fingers into Gus's jaw. "You brought her in here, and she deceived me!"

"She did nothing," Gus ground out. "She knows nothing." He resisted the desire to knee Fish in the groin because he knew it would make the man more sadistic.

Fish's voice lowered, trembling with anger. "Where is she? Waiting for you in that rattrap? I've driven past it, you know. To see the street where she lives. I thought she deserved better. I wanted her to have better." Then he screamed again: "I would have helped her! I would have helped you!"

He drew back, then drove his fist into Gus's stomach so hard that Gus staggered, hitting the wall.

"Where is she?" Fish demanded, his voice more nearly normal. "In that motel?"

"She's gone." He couldn't keep the triumph out of his voice.

Fish swore. He pointed. "I'm going to kill you."

Gus shrugged. "I figured as much."

"I'll kill her, too," Fish promised, so angry that his pointing finger shook. "I'll kill her first, so you can watch. Do you know what else I'll do to her?"

Gus tossed his head. "She's gone, Fish. You can't find her."

"We'll *see*." He nodded to Epperson and Randolph. "Take him to his place. We'll get her. We'll kill them there."

He stepped closer to Gus. "I'd kill you here, but I want to take my time. And I don't want blood on my carpet." He stood, breathing hard. "Take him out the back way," he said to Epperson and Randolph.

He straightened his suit jacket and stabbed his finger at Gus again. "I'll do it. I'll make you watch her die," he said with cruel satisfaction.

"You can't," Gus told him, his lip curling. "She's gone, Fish. She's safe."

Gus knew he would probably die—die nastily—and resigned himself to the possibility. But Susannah was safe. That thought burned like a white light, giving him strength.

AT THE MOTEL, WHEN Fish saw Gus's recording equipment, the earphones, the wiretaps, the printouts from Commu-Cate, he paled.

"You *are* federal, aren't you?" he said, his eyes glittering. "You're big time, aren't you? FBI? That must be it. FBI."

Epperson's square face looked troubled. "The feds? Killing him means trouble."

Fish glared. "Not killing him's trouble, you fool. Do you think we can let him live?"

"Look," Epperson said, his face taut. "Let's do it and get out. We'll have to split. You used to talk about going to Argentina if things got hot. They're hot, Fish."

But Fish seemed to be slipping beyond reason. He was angry that Susannah wasn't in the apartment. When Gus refused to say where she was, Fish had Epperson try to beat the truth out of him.

Gus was forced to sink to his knees. But he didn't talk.

"You *will* talk," Fish promised, standing above him. "You *will* tell me. I've never met a man I couldn't break."

For a few merciful moments, though, he let Gus alone, letting him recover enough to be beaten again.

Gus knelt, panting and wondering if his ribs were broken. Meanwhile Fish made Randolph scour the apartment, looking for some clue to Susannah's whereabouts.

But Randolph, whose expression never changed, found nothing. And when Fish learned that even the labels had been cut from Susannah's clothes, he seemed dangerously near going berserk again. Epperson warned him to keep his voice down.

"Look," Epperson pleaded. "Let's not do it here. You'll want him to make noise. It's too dangerous here. Let's take him to the cave, like usual."

Gus heard it— *Let's take him to the cave, like usual.* He lifted his head and stared groggily at Fish.

Fish glowered down at him with scorn. "I have a little cave, Augusto. It's full of secrets. I have another lake in it—much deeper than the one I advertise."

"Congratulations," Gus said raggedly. He knew it was unwise to provoke Fish, but he hoped to make him talk. Gus would like to know if he'd been right. But death, he thought bitterly, was a damned high price to pay for being right.

"It's an interesting lake," Fish said, gloating. "It has cave fish. You know—albinos. Blind, because they've lived so long in darkness. They have no eyes at all. But they have mouths. And a taste for human flesh."

Gus pretended to shudder. It didn't take a great deal of acting. "I don't like caves," he said, hoping to lead Fish on.

"Unfortunate."

"I don't want to be down alone in a cave."

"You won't be alone, Augusto. If that's your name. There are the eyeless fish. And other people. Dead people, just like you'll be."

Gus stared up at him, trying to look pitiable. "You got dead people in that cave? You put dead people in that cave?"

"Oh, yes. Two within the last week. You see, I'm really *not* afraid to kill you. I can do it quickly, I can do it slowly. The choice is yours."

Gus shook his head in disbelief. "Two? Last week? That's not human, Fish."

Fish smiled. Behind him, Epperson looked intense, and Randolph seemed almost bored. "Murder's very human," Fish said. "It's simply not humane. Two in one week? It's nothing to me." But his face clouded. "The first one was a man who troubled my friends in St. Louis—he told tales about them. We don't like that. He died the long way. It was quite terrible for him, really."

Gus dropped his gaze. "Does everybody die the long way? Does it have to be the long way?"

"No, indeed," Fish replied, almost gently. "The other one— I was tender with. She never felt a thing. But she'd betrayed me—out of weakness. I had no choice."

Gus shook his head, his shoulders slumping. "Nobody kills three people in a week. Not without getting caught."

"*Au contraire,*" Fish said with a smirk. "I've done it. And you're fourth, not third. There was another gentleman, who had—a little accident. That was over quickly, too. He was dead by the time the ambulance came, they say."

"I don't understand," Gus said humbly, pretending confusion. "You put him in a cave, but an ambulance came.... You're lying to me, you're trying to mix me up."

"You're punchy," Fish said with contempt. "The accident was in the street. These things can be arranged. I make a simple phone call, I set forces in motion. I know many ways to kill people. It's up to you to decide how it'll be with you— fast or slow."

"You already said it'd be slow," Gus said, still not looking at him. "I don't want it to be slow."

"Then it's simple," Fish said seductively. "Tell me where the girl is. And who she is. Oh, I liked her, I did. I liked the idea of the two of you, even. But neither of you has left me a choice. So tell me where she is."

Gus raised his head. There was no longer humility in his face, only defiance. "When hell freezes over," he said.

Fish's face went cold. "Have you ever heard of The Death of a Thousand Cuts? It's Chinese in origin. It can be done in your own bathtub while Randolph and Epperson hold you down—"

Epperson shook his head. "No, no, not here. There's too much screaming. I don't think—"

A car door slammed in the parking lot. Epperson went tensely silent. Footsteps sounded on the outside stairs. All four men looked toward the door. The footsteps drew nearer, then stopped just outside.

A sick expression crossed Gus's face, a look of horrified desolation.

But Fish smiled with a madman's serene satisfaction. He nodded to Epperson, who crossed the room and positioned himself beside the door, flattening himself against the wall.

A key rattled in the lock.

Gus gathered himself to yell—to yell for her to run, to yell so that somebody, somewhere, would call the police, to yell to distract the men, to give her a chance.

But before he could open his mouth, Randolph struck him across the throat, knocking him backward so hard that he fell, sprawling against the wall.

He tried to cry out, but no sound came. He could only watch numbly, as Susannah pushed the door open. Her expression was distracted, and she looked young and innocent behind her big glasses.

"Gus," she started to call, "I—" Then Epperson was on her, one arm seizing her body, his other hand clamping over her mouth.

Gus watched terror flare in her eyes and felt as if he were dying. Tears stung his eyes.

Fish stepped to the door and shut it, then went to Susannah's side. He pinched her cheek, hard, and did not let go. "Miss Fingal," he hissed. "My dear, duplicitous Miss Fingal."

For an instant she stared at Fish in fear and incomprehension. But then she looked across the room and saw Gus. Tears welled in her eyes, and she sobbed against Epperson's hand.

Gus shut his eyes against the pain in her face. *You were supposed to be gone,* he thought hopelessly. *You were supposed to be safe. What happened?*

For the first time since he was thirteen years old he prayed.

THE AUDIENCES OF THE country-and-western shows were getting out. Traffic crawled. Fish snarled and swore. He sat in the back seat. Gus was pinned between him and Randolph, Randolph's gun pushed against his ribs.

Susannah, her wrists bound before her, sat in the front seat, her head bowed. They rode in Fish's white Cadillac with its one-way tinted windows. No one could see into the car.

"One wrong move," Fish had told her, "and I'll have your boyfriend blown away. One false move, and he's dead. Then I'll tie you to his body and throw you both in the lake. He'll sink you. His dead body will drag you down, and you'll drown in the dark."

Epperson drove—or tried to drive—in the snarled traffic. He, too, kept swearing under his breath.

"We should have waited," he kept grumbling. "We should have waited until after midnight." The car moved at barely a crawl. It was approaching the World-Famous Waltzing Fountains, where an outside fountain rose into the night air, dancing and changing colors.

Fish kicked the back of the seat viciously, making Epperson grunt.

"He's right," Gus said out of the side of his mouth. "You've made better decisions, Fish. The big hit man's stuck in small-town traffic. Cute."

Susannah heard the sound of flesh striking flesh and winced, biting her lip. Fish had already beaten Gus badly. Why did Gus provoke him, asking for more?

"Watch it," Gus warned. "You don't want me bleeding on your upholstery. When I turn up missing, the police will look for details like that. Blood all over your car. Sit back and enjoy the traffic jam."

There was the sound of another blow, and Gus's muffled gasp. Susannah hung her head lower, fighting back tears.

"Careful, Fishy," Gus taunted, although his voice was tight with pain. "Police frown on people pounding officers of the law. They're gonna throw the book at you, you know?"

"Shut up," Fish growled, "or I'll have Randolph start breaking your fingers."

*Gus,* Susannah pleaded silently, *be quiet. Stop. You're making it worse.*

"Do your friends know what happens to cop killers? They'll track you to the ends of the earth. They'll give you the chair. Or do they have the chair in Missouri? Is it lethal injection—what? How do they kill killers? Fry them or give them the needle?"

"Break a finger," Fish ordered. "Start with the little one."

"Sure," Randolph said, as calmly as if he'd been asked for a match.

Susannah heard a cracking sound and Gus's sharp intake of breath. His breathing turned to ragged panting. She felt sick and hopelessly angry.

"You annoy me," Fish said to Gus.

"I *mean* it," Gus said. Pain didn't keep the contempt out of his voice. "You do this, and they'll find you. They're already on to you. It's over for you, Fish. And you're getting your friends in deeper and deeper. You might as well shoot us on Main Street in front of everybody."

"Break another finger," Fish said without emotion.

*Gus! Stop! Why are you doing this to yourself?* She shuddered at another sickening crack, another gasp of pain.

"If that doesn't shut you up," Fish murmured, "I'll start on the girl. You want to watch the same thing happen to her?"

Gus swore. His voice was ragged but scornful. "You've screwed up big, Fish."

"Break his thumbs, both of them," Fish commanded. "I mean it. I'll start on the girl."

Gus swore again. There was a scuffling sound, as if he struggled.

*Gus! You're too smart to do this,* her mind screamed.

But suddenly, as if struck by lightning, she understood. Gus *was* smart. Fish *had* screwed up. He had made a simple tactical error, a bad one. Gus had been telling her to take advantage of it—fast.

She knew, then—with startling clarity—what he would do in her place. And she did it.

As quickly as a striking snake, she brought her foot down on Epperson's with all the force she had, driving the accelerator to the floor.

Epperson tried to backhand her, but he was too late. The Cadillac shot forward wildly, crashing into the Chevrolet sedan in front. Both cars were knocked askew and she was thrown against the steering wheel.

But she ground her foot into Epperson's even harder. Using her body and her bound hands, she forced the wheel to the right.

Epperson grabbed her roughly, trying to hurl her away, but the car tore a great gouge of metal out of the rear of the Chevrolet and sheared off a back wheel. The Cadillac jumped the curb and the low wall around the dancing fountain.

With a jolting smash, it struck the fountain's base, then quivered to a halt. Susannah, her body pinned now by Epperson's, gazed up in shock. Rose-colored water gushed in a flood over the windshield, water drummed on the car's hood.

Fish shrieked with rage. "Kill them! Kill them!"

Epperson fought his way free and yanked Susannah to a sitting position. He stared at her in sheer terror.

A siren sounded in the distance, muted by the cascading water. Epperson's expression grew wilder, more desperate.

He thrust Susannah away as if her touch poisoned him. He fumbled to open the door of the Cadillac, scrambled out, and ran, disappearing through the falling water.

"Kill them! Kill them!" Fish shrieked.

But Randolph, too, was struggling to open his door. Susannah turned, watching him in numbed horror. Randolph's face was no longer bland and bored—he was terrified.

Fish reached across Gus, trying to wrench the gun from Randolph. But Gus, with a vicious grunt, kneed Fish in the chest. Randolph, panic on his face, the gun still gripped in his hand, wrestled open the door and, like Epperson, blindly fled. The fountain rained into the car's interior.

Gus kneed Fish a second time. He rolled backward and kicked him, catching him in the shoulder and knocking him against the car door. Gus gritted his teeth and gathered himself for another, harder kick.

Fish's face went blank and white. He looked at Gus in panic, then flung the car door open. He fell, backward, out of the car.

Fish scrambled to his feet and stood for an instant in the fountain's driving downpour. Then he turned and ran. Gus swore, struggled out the open door and took after him, his hands still taped behind him.

Instinctively, Susannah, too, sprang from the car. The Cadillac had broken a pipe in the fountain. A deluge of water engulfed her, and she struggled, sputtering through it.

Fish ran down the sidewalk, his feet pounding, his suit drenched, his thin hair pasted to his skull.

Gus caught up with him and, using his shoulder, drove into Fish, knocking him to the pavement. Gus staggered but caught himself. Fish, on the sidewalk, flailed at him, struggling to rise. Gus regained his balance and kicked Fish so hard that Fish curled into a knot, clutching himself.

Gus's face turned into a snarl, and he kicked Fish again. Susannah ran toward the two of them. People were staring at them, shocked, transfixed, unbelieving.

"Gus!" she cried. "Gus!"

He stared at her wildly for a moment, then gave Fish a look of purest hatred. "And this," he said from between his teeth, "is for my girl."

He kicked Fish a third time. Fish's body stiffened, then went limp.

Susannah reached Gus's side. She couldn't put her arms around him, nor he her. But she pressed against him, laying her cheek against his chest. They were both sodden. His heart was beating so hard she could feel it. She pressed against him harder, assuring herself he was there, that he was alive.

The sirens had grown deafening.

"I'm Augusto Jesus Raphael," Gus panted, glowering at the gaping crowd. "Federal Bureau of Investigation. This man is my prisoner. Will somebody, for God's sake, cut me loose?"

The onlookers, still stunned, were silent for a moment, then a murmur swept through them. A police car shrieked to a halt across the street. Gus stood straight, waiting for reinforcements. Susannah, too, straightened, but she couldn't take her eyes off Gus.

A man with white hair stepped forward. He said nothing. He took a Swiss army knife from his pocket and cut Gus's hands free.

"Her, too," Gus said, nodding at Susannah.

The man cut the tape from her wrists. Immediately she put her arms around Gus's neck and once more hid her face against his wet chest. Gingerly, because of his broken fingers, he put his arms around her and held her tight.

A policeman strode up to them, his hand on his holstered gun. He looked down at Fish in disbelief, then at Gus's bruised and cut face.

"You rear-end that car back there?" he demanded. "You plow into that fountain? What's this? What'd you do to this guy?"

"Augusto Jesus Raphael," Gus said, drawing Susannah closer. "Federal Bureau of Investigation." And slowly, carefully, with remarkable precision, he began to explain what had happened.

WHEN THE POLICE finally let Gus and Susannah go, they drove them back to the motel and left them there.

"I don't want to stay here," Susannah said, remembering. Blood, still damp, spotted the carpet, from Epperson beating Gus.

"Me, either," he said. He remembered her expression when Epperson had grabbed her.

Almost wordlessly they packed a few things and changed clothes. Gus put on a silk shirt and sighed with satisfaction. He kicked off the engineer boots and put on his Italian loafers. Then they drove then to another motel—a luxurious one, on the other side of town.

Gus hobbled. Fish and Epperson had hurt him worse than he admitted. The emergency-room doctor wanted him to stay overnight, but Gus would have none of it. He wasn't leaving Susannah alone, he said. He'd been hurt worse and lived. He was staying with her.

Susannah was glad. She kept having fits of the shakes. She had another one as soon as they were safely in their new room. Gus took her in his arms again.

"Take a shower," he said gruffly. "Change your clothes. You'll feel better."

"No," she said, holding him tightly. "You first. You need it most."

He drew away with a slightly bitter laugh, releasing her. "I'm gonna have to figure out how. I'm not supposed to get *these* wet."

He glanced with rueful displeasure at his left hands. Two fingers were splinted and taped together. He looked as if he wore an awkward white finger puppet.

"Go on," he urged. "You first. We looked like drowned rats."

"I know." But she didn't want to be apart from him yet, even for an instant. She put her arms around him again, and he embraced her. It felt so good, so right, she didn't ever want to move away. She nuzzled his chest. His silky shirt cooled and soothed her cheek. "I didn't mean to hit the fountain," she said.

"You did fine. Besides, I've always hated those stinking fountains."

She kissed the spot over his heart. "I hated *myself*, for not catching on sooner. Fish had really trapped himself, getting us caught in the traffic."

He bent his head and kissed her hair. "Hey—you were great. You caught on fast."

"Not before he broke two of your fingers."

"We had plenty of time. I've got ten."

"At least he didn't break your thumbs."

"Thanks to you. You got a mean stomp, baby. And a cool mind, a fast mouth, and gorgeous eyes. What more could an FBI man ask for?"

She drew back, staring up at him solemnly. "I almost died when I walked into the room and saw you there like that." She touched his bruised face. "Oh, Gus, I never felt so sick."

He shook his head and laid his finger against her lips. "I was sicker when I saw you. I wanted you *safe*, dammit. Why'd you come back? It nearly killed me when you came back."

"I couldn't leave you. I just . . . couldn't."

He ran his hand over her tangled hair, smoothing it. "If they'd hurt you, I'd have come back from the dead to get them. I swear that. But I'd give anything for you not to have gone through this. You should have been spared this."

"Gus, if I hadn't come back—they might have murdered you. It was three against one. I think Fish would have beaten you to death."

Gus tried to give a lackadaisical shrug but his collarbone made him wince. "Ah," he said nonchalantly, "I'd have gotten out of it somehow. I'm like a cat, baby. I've got nine lives."

She didn't smile. "You'd have gotten *out* of it? How?"

He tried the shrug again, and this time it almost worked. "I'm tricky. You know that. Besides, as soon as I saw that traffic, I knew there was a chance."

"You're crazy," she said sternly. "And I'll bet *nothing you* did tonight was authorized—was it? You wanted to stop Fish before he killed somebody else, so you just went off on your own. And nearly got murdered yourself."

His expression remained nonchalant. She'd been with him when he explained to the police about the money laundering, the expected hits, how he'd broken into Fish's office but been caught. He'd been amazingly cool.

"You're not saying anything," Susannah said, lowering an eyebrow. "I'm right. You tried to do everything solo. A one-man guerilla force. You weren't supposed to send me away, were you? You lied to Fritz."

He cocked his head meditatively. "A little."

Fritz had shown up shortly after the police did. He'd smelled trouble and come looking for Susannah. He'd remained remarkably closemouthed with the police, but in the main, he corroborated Gus's story.

"When the police called Washington," Susannah said suspiciously, "and you went into that room and talked for so long—it was because you're in trouble, isn't it? With Olivier?"

"Olivier," he admitted. "And a few others."

"How few?"

"Well," Gus muttered, "Olivier implied that J. Edgar Hoover might rise from the grave to be help skin me."

She put her hands on his shoulders and stared at him in concern. "Oh, Gus. You *love* this job. How much trouble are you in?"

"Some, that's all. I'll get out of it."

"How?"

"I'll talk my way out of it. As usual. Repentance usually helps. Hey, a little fast talk, a little sackcloth, a few ashes, I'll be fine. Besides, we got our man, didn't we? For more than sudsing out some money. Maybe nine murders solved? That's gotta count for something."

"How many rules *did* you break tonight?"

"I don't know. I lost count."

"How many? I want to know."

Gus tried to look unconcerned. "I lied to Fritz, gave him false orders. I broke into Fish's office, an unauthorized search. I took evidence, also unauthorized, so it's tainted. I lied to the police—was going to lie some more, but didn't get around to that. And I left plenty of evidence that isn't tainted."

"Oh, Gus," she said hopelessly.

"Baby, I'm a *survivor*," he said. "Don't worry. They'll give me some grief, and then they'll probably give me a medal. They should give it to you. They not only got Fish, they got Epperson and Randoph. Randolph's already ratting his head off—he's naming names here *and* in St. Louis. We'll get whoever took Nora Geddes at the airport—I promise you. We're gonna sweep a lot of bad guys off the street."

She nodded and fought off another attack of the shivers. Randolph, running drenched through the streets and clutching his gun, had been apprehended almost immediately. Epperson had managed to make it to his car and out of Branson, but the highway patrol had stopped him within two hours.

She tightened her hold on his shoulders. "Gus—do you know who Fish was going to kill?"

He nodded. "I'm pretty sure. Dusty Lester's manager. He was coming to town tomorrow."

"Dusty's manager? But why?"

"He's been our inside man. He just took on Lester last year. He knew immediately something was going on with the money. He asked for a cut and got it—a small one. He didn't like it, didn't like Fish. He started snooping—and talking. To us."

"Fish was going to kill him?"

"They suspected a mole in the organization. They suspected it was him. But he's a high-profile guy, an up-and-comer. That's my guess as to why Dunwoody was sent. To wait confirmation about the guy, then make a hit look like an accident. But Fish panicked. He wasted that hit on Colter."

Susannah couldn't help it. She shuddered again. "Poor Nora. Poor, poor Nora."

"Look," he said, suddenly solemn, "I think I know what went wrong between Fish and Nora. It's another reason I wanted you *outta* here."

"You mean whatever happened about a year ago? What started at that party?"

"Yes. Think. About what Ginger said. About what Fish said. Especially about me."

"He was awfully interested in you. It was strange."

"Fish was strange, baby," Gus said, running his hands up and down her arms. "He was stranger than any of us suspected. He was so obsessed with Nora, it put him over the edge. He was losing her and couldn't stand it."

"But what happened?"

Gus put his hands on her waist and stared into her eyes. "We always knew he was a looker, not a toucher. I think he wanted to see *more*. I think he wanted to pay Nora and Colter to watch them together."

Susannah paled. "Watch them? You mean—"

"Yeah. That's exactly what I mean. And it's sick. What's sicker is I think Colter was willing. Nora wasn't. But Colter was greedy."

Susannah leaned against his chest and shut her eyes. "That's awful. No wonder she came apart. That's what Ginger meant when she said Colter wouldn't stand up for Nora." She shivered again.

Gus held her, resting his chin against her hair. "He would have asked us the same thing. Soon. I wanted to kill him when I figured that out. Break his filthy neck. I didn't want him near you. I couldn't *let* him near you. Not knowing that."

"It's terrible."

"Nora would finally have been free—if Colter hadn't tried the blackmail stunt. Fish went out of control. He started killing on impulse. I think maybe he killed Nora out of disappointment and revenge—no other reason. He wasn't rational any longer."

She tried to speak, but couldn't, only held Gus more tightly.

"Don't think about it," he said gently. "It's over now. He can't hurt her anymore. You asked me once if I still prayed. I did tonight. For you." She nodded. "I prayed for you, too." She raised her face to his. "Oh, Gus. I'd stopped believing in prayers until tonight. Until you."

"You're a hell of a girl," he said, touching her hair. His expression was loving but solemn. "And I was a hell of a fool to get you mixed up in something like this. If anything had happened to you—my God."

She shook her head. "If you hadn't mixed me up in it, maybe we'd never have gotten together. And I couldn't have stood that."

He half smiled and settled his good hand on the nape of her neck. "You always knew we belonged together, didn't you? You just had to wait for me to catch on. You always were the smart one."

"No. I was just the one who loved you to distraction."

"That's how I love you now. To distraction. Will you come back east with me? What am I gonna do with you Chiquita? Send you to the FBI Academy? You don't seem the stay-at-home type to me.... How'll we spend the rest of our lives? Just tell me. And we'll make it happen."

"We'll take one step at a time," she said, her eyes shining. "And we'll get it right. I know we will—no matter what we do."

"We start getting it right," he said emphatically, "by getting married. I want you all mine, by the laws of man, the laws of God—any laws that exist. The sooner the better. Or do you have to have bridesmaids and stuff?"

"I'm the cool, rational type," she said, nuzzling his chin. "I'll leave the sentimental wedding to my sister."

"Sister?" he murmured, nuzzling back. "You got a sister?"

She wound one arm around his neck. "Yes," she whispered. "I do."

"Funny thing," he said, pulling her closer. "I don't remember her very well. Come here. And stay here, sweet Suzy-Q."

He kissed her, then flinched slightly when her hand touched his collarbone.

"Oh—" she drew back "—did he hurt you there, too? I'm sorry."

She unbuttoned his shirt and saw the bruises over his clavicle, the one on his shoulder. She pushed the fabric aside and saw more bruises on his ribs.

"That's awful," she said, pained for him. "What can I do to help?"

His hands rose to her shoulders again, caressing her. "Kiss it and make it well."

So she kissed him over his bruised collarbone, loving having him there, warm and real and whole in her arms. Suddenly tearful with gratitude that he was safe, she lifted her gaze to his.

"No tears," he said softly. "No tears. I've got other places that need kissing."

He pointed to the edge of his jaw. She pressed her lips against it.

"And here," he murmured, indicating a cut near his mouth. She covered his lips with her own.

"Um," he said. "And here." He touched his chin. She kissed him there, as well.

He gave a long, ragged sigh and took off his shirt, letting it drop to the floor. "Honey, I got spots all over my body that need kissing. Keep working on it, okay? Oh, that feels good. That feels very good."

She kissed the heart tattooed on his chest, because it, too, was bruised. He folded her into his arms.

"Oh, my," she said, growing a bit dizzy with love and yearning.

"I'm so glad you're here," he said against her hair. "I'm so glad you're safe. I'm so glad you're mine. You are mine, aren't you?"

"Yes. Yes."

He gave her a rueful smile. "What are people gonna think of this? Of you and me?"

"What do you think they'll think?" she asked, her eyes on his.

"That I'm the luckiest man who ever lived," he said, his smile dying. "I mean that."

He paused, as if he had to search for words. "I—I was such a *fool*," he said with passion. He swore softly. Tenderly, he raised her face to his. "Why did it take me so long to see you, to *realize* about you?"

"Oh, Gus, you were worth waiting for." She gently touched his cut lip.

"No." He shook his head. "But I'll make it up to you. I'll live to make you happy. I'll love you for eternity. I'll make every day of your life—"

"Gus?"

"You taste better than peanut butter," he told her. "You taste better than cornflakes. You taste better than strawberries and champagne, caviar, angel cake—"

"Gus?"

"Better than—"

She put her finger lightly to his lips. "Fewer words? More actions?"

He drew in his breath and brushed her finger aside. The look he gave her made her chest tighten with happiness and her heart warm with desire.

"Here comes action, baby," he said, slowly lowering his face to hers.

He kissed her. And she was right—there was no more need for words.

HARLEQUIN®

# *Temptation*®
## IS TEN!

Join the festivities as Harlequin celebrates
Temptation's tenth anniversary in 1994!

Look for tempting treats from your favorite
Temptation authors all year long. The celebration
begins with Passion's Quest—four exciting sensual
stories featuring the most elemental passions....

The temptation continues with Lost Loves, a sizzling
miniseries about love lost...love found. And watch for
the 500th Temptation in July by bestselling author
Rita Clay Estrada, a seductive story in the vein
of the much-loved tale, THE IVORY KEY.

In May, look for details of an irresistible offer:
three classic Temptation novels by Rita Clay Estrada,
Glenda Sanders and Gina Wilkins in a collector's
hardcover edition—free with proof of purchase!

After ten tempting years, *nobody* can resist

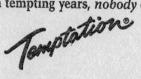

## MILLION DOLLAR SWEEPSTAKES (III)

HARLEQUIN®

*Temptation*

*Lost Loves*

## RIGHT MAN...WRONG TIME

Remember that one man who turned your world upside down? Who made you experience all the ecstatic highs of passion and lows of loss and regret. What if you met him again?

You dared to lose your heart once and had it broken. Dare you love again?

JoAnn Ross, Glenda Sanders, Rita Clay Estrada, Gina Wilkins and Carin Rafferty. Find their stories in *Lost Loves*, Temptation's newest miniseries, running May to September 1994.

Experience *The Return of Caine O'Halloran* by JoAnn Ross. Ten years ago, Caine O'Halloran and Nora Anderson married because she was pregnant. Although it wasn't easy, they had just begun to love and trust one another when their son's death tore apart the fragile marriage. But now Caine is back...determined to regain Nora's love.

### What if...?

Available in May wherever Harlequin books are sold.

# Harlequin Books requests the pleasure of your company this June in Eternity, Massachusetts, for WEDDINGS, INC.

For generations, couples have been coming to Eternity, Massachusetts, to exchange wedding vows. Legend has it that those married in Eternity's chapel are destined for a lifetime of happiness. And the residents are more than willing to give the legend a hand.

Beginning in June, you can experience the legend of Eternity. Watch for one title per month, across all of the Harlequin series.

## HARLEQUIN BOOKS... NOT THE SAME OLD STORY!

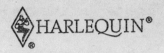

Harlequin proudly presents four stories about
*convenient* but not *conventional* reasons for marriage:

♦ To save your godchildren from a
  "wicked stepmother"

♦ To help out your eccentric aunt—and her sexy
  business partner

♦ To bring an old man happiness by making him
  a grandfather

♦ To escape from a ghostly existence and become a
  real woman

Marriage By Design—four brand-new stories by four
of Harlequin's most popular authors:

**CATHY GILLEN THACKER
JASMINE CRESSWELL
GLENDA SANDERS
MARGARET CHITTENDEN**

Don't miss this exciting collection of stories about
marriages of convenience. Available in April, wherever
Harlequin books are sold.

MBD94

## This June, Harlequin invites you to a wedding of

*Promised Brides*

Celebrate the joy and romance of weddings past with PROMISED BRIDES—a collection of original historical short stories, written by three best-selling historical authors:

> *The Wedding of the Century*—MARY JO PUTNEY
> *Jesse's Wife*—KRISTIN JAMES
> *The Handfast*—JULIE TETEL

Three unforgettable heroines, three award-winning authors! PROMISED BRIDES is available in June wherever Harlequin Books are sold.

HARLEQUIN®

HARLEQUIN®

Don't miss these Harlequin favorites by some of our most
distinguished authors!
And now, you can receive a discount by ordering two or more titles!

| | | | |
|---|---|---|---|
| HT #25551 | THE OTHER WOMAN by Candace Schuler | $2.99 | ☐ |
| HT #25539 | FOOLS RUSH IN by Vicki Lewis Thompson | $2.99 | ☐ |
| HP #11550 | THE GOLDEN GREEK by Sally Wentworth | $2.89 | ☐ |
| HP #11603 | PAST ALL REASON by Kay Thorpe | $2.99 | ☐ |
| HR #03228 | MEANT FOR EACH OTHER by Rebecca Winters | $2.89 | ☐ |
| HR #03268 | THE BAD PENNY by Susan Fox | $2.99 | ☐ |
| HS #70532 | TOUCH THE DAWN by Karen Young | $3.39 | ☐ |
| HS #70540 | FOR THE LOVE OF IVY by Barbara Kaye | $3.39 | ☐ |
| HI #22177 | MINDGAME by Laura Pender | $2.79 | ☐ |
| HI #22214 | TO DIE FOR by M.J. Rodgers | $2.89 | ☐ |
| HAR #16421 | HAPPY NEW YEAR, DARLING by Margaret St. George | $3.29 | ☐ |
| HAR #16507 | THE UNEXPECTED GROOM by Muriel Jensen | $3.50 | ☐ |
| HH #28774 | SPINDRIFT by Miranda Jarrett | $3.99 | ☐ |
| HH #28782 | SWEET SENSATIONS by Julie Tetel | $3.99 | ☐ |

### Harlequin Promotional Titles

| | | | |
|---|---|---|---|
| #83259 | UNTAMED MAVERICK HEARTS | $4.99 | ☐ |
| | (Short-story collection featuring Heather Graham Pozzessere, Patricia Potter, Joan Johnston) | | |

(limited quantities available on certain titles)

| | | |
|---|---|---|
| | AMOUNT | $ |
| DEDUCT: | 10% DISCOUNT FOR 2+ BOOKS | $ |
| | POSTAGE & HANDLING | $ |
| | ($1.00 for one book, 50¢ for each additional) | |
| | APPLICABLE TAXES* | $ _____ |
| | TOTAL PAYABLE | $ _____ |
| | (check or money order—please do not send cash) | |

To order, complete this form and send it, along with a check or money order for the
total above, payable to Harlequin Books, to: **In the U.S.:** 3010 Walden Avenue,
P.O. Box 9047, Buffalo, NY 14269-9047; **In Canada:** P.O. Box 613, Fort Erie, Ontario,
L2A 5X3.

Name: _____

Address: _____ City: _____

State/Prov.: _____ Zip/Postal Code: _____

*New York residents remit applicable sales taxes.
 Canadian residents remit applicable GST and provincial taxes.

HBACK-AJ